'O'Connor's first collection of short stories for twenty years reasserts a mastery of the form… An exhilarating array of sharp dialogue and biting one-liners… A fine compassionate collection'
Irish Independent

'A masterclass in versatility… Atmospheric vignettes bring O'Connor's prose close to poetry… His terrific ear for idiomatic speech makes dialogue sizzle off the page… This outstanding collection exhibits the continuing vitality of the great Irish tradition of richly concise, crisply written stories that Joyce's work began'
Sunday Times

'Full of lovely, delicate perceptive stuff. Joseph O'Connor is in the tradition of masterly Irish writers of short fiction'
Scotsman

'The highlight of these accomplished stories is the superb title story, revealed gradually with beautiful subtlety. Excellent'
The Times

'O'Connor's first collection in more than twenty years is well worth the wait… Individually these stories are quietly unassuming gems; together, a powerful ode to modern Ireland'
Independent

WHERE HAVE YOU BEEN?

Joseph O'Connor was born in Dublin. His novels include *Cowboys and Indians* (Whitbread Prize shortlist), *Star of the Sea* (*Irish Post* Award for Fiction, France's Prix Millepages, Prix Madeleine Zepter for European Novel of the Year), *Redemption Falls*, and *Ghost Light* (Dublin One City One Book Novel, 2011). In 2012 he won the Irish PEN Award for Outstanding Achievement in Literature. His work has been published in thirty-five languages.

JOSEPH O'CONNOR

Where Have You Been?

Stories and a novella

VINTAGE BOOKS
London

Published by Vintage 2013

2 4 6 8 10 9 7 5 3 1

First published in Great Britain in 2012 by
Harvill Secker

Vintage
Random House, 20 Vauxhall Bridge Road,
London SW1V 2SA

www.vintage-books.co.uk

Addresses for companies within The Random House Group Limited
can be found at: www.randomhouse.co.uk/offices.htm

The Random House Group Limited Reg. No. 954009

A CIP catalogue record for this book
is available from the British Library

ISBN 9780099565451

The Random House Group Limited supports the Forest Stewardship
Council® (FSC®), the leading international forest-certification
organisation. Our books carrying the FSC label are printed on FSC®-
certified paper. FSC is the only forest-certification scheme supported
by the leading environmental organisations, including Greenpeace.
Our paper procurement policy can be found at:
www.randomhouse.co.uk/environment

Printed and bound by CPI Group (UK) Ltd, Croydon, CR0 4YY
Typeset in Sabon by Palimpsest Book Production Ltd Falkirk,
Stirlingshire

For Dermot Bolger

CONTENTS

Two Little Clouds

Dublin, 2007

Two decades or more had passed since I'd seen him. But here he was, in the ample flesh, through the glinting window of an estate agency on Fownes Street, a hallucination in shirtsleeves and crumpled suit trousers. Fifty pounds heavier and just about bald, but it was him right enough. I almost wanted to keep walking. Holy Christ – so Ruth had been right that time. Eddie Virago back in Dublin, flogging flats for a living. He grinned and mouthed my name as he clocked me through the window. But he didn't look delighted to see me.

'How's tricks?' I asked, when he came out and shook hands.

'State of you,' he beamed. 'You're gone Victor Mature.'

Eddie was the kind of guy I used to try and latch on to, back in my early days in London. Hip, facetious, indifferent to convention, he'd shape into the Bunch of Grapes in his shabby denim jacket, in his tattered leather jeans and Sid Vicious T-shirt, his brothel-creepers so utterly grubby it was impossible to picture them having once been clean. Saturday nights, the place would be heaving with yuppie Irish – I suppose it was a home away from home. Posters of Killarney cottages and Michael Collins and Joyce. Agricultural tackle hanging on the walls. A regiment of southside Dublin émigrés storming the bar. One glance from Eddie and his pint would be put up. Not even a glance. The raising of an eyebrow.

There was gossip in my crowd that he managed a band, that they'd signed to one of the majors and were about to record an album. I don't know if it was true, but he never dampened the talk. He'd just smile this unassuming grin – think Bill Clinton only with cheekbones, you're not far off – and say he couldn't go into the details. 'For contractual reasons, man. You know how it is.'

I don't know that I ever talked to Eddie for longer than a few minutes. He was always just *around*, chewing it with some wannabe model; slumped against the brickwork like he was propping it up. To be honest, I thought myself too uncool for him to like me. You're twenty-one in London, you want everyone to like you.

I'd spent two years after the Leaving Cert studying to be a Jesuit, and even after I'd jacked it in I still felt people saw me as a priest. They'd make a point of watching their language – infuriating behaviour like that. They'd tell me their sins when they had a few jars on them: their sexual misdemeanours, their secret admiration for Mrs Thatcher. Eddie never confessed, and that was inspirational. He'd take you on your terms. He didn't judge.

You'd see him at gigs: parties; clubs. He'd even pitch up at the odd poetry reading, but he rarely stayed to the end. I was kicking around with this girl who did the London publicity for U2 and one time she got us tickets for a Dylan gig at the Hammersmith Odeon. At the backstage party afterwards, there was old Eddie – in the roped-off area for VIPs, one arm around The Edge, the other around Tom Paulin, flicking his fag ash into a champagne flute held by a one-time member of Bananarama. A face like a Michelangelo, someone once said of Eddie. And a neck like a jockey's bollocks.

It was rumoured around the pubs that he had an on–off girlfriend who was from small-town Donegal and not much of a rock-chick. But that didn't seem likely, and I certainly didn't ask him. He was one of those Irish males you don't question: the type with an ectoplasm of elusiveness around him. Often, if you were jarred, you'd have the impression of him looking *out* at you from inside his head, through this swirling fog of ambiguity. Eddie Virago, the high king of cagey, wearing his Mohican like a crown.

Now the Mohican was gone but his eyes were still bright. We stood there on Fownes Street and he pumped my hand. He hadn't heard I was back in the old home town; if he had, he would have belled me about hooking up for a scoop. Nah, he didn't see much of the old crew any more. Too busy with the job, man. Working his langer to the bone.

'Skinny bastard,' he chuckled, jabbing me lightly in the gut. 'What's your secret? The old liposuction, is it? Course I wouldn't mind gettin' it all sucked out myself. Dependin' on who was doin' the suckin', says you. And where they put the fuckin' incision.'

It was after five by now and Eddie was about to knock off work. So he invited me down to the Clarence Hotel for a bev. I said I was pressed for time – we'd do it some other time. I'd promised to be home by six to give the baby her bath, but for some reason I didn't tell him that. 'Come on for the one anyway,' he said, and he grinned. 'Let's chew the old fat. Plenty to chew, right?'

He'd always been self-assured, but there was brashness in his talk now. Oh yeah, the auld property biz was treating him grand. Dublin was *lousy* with heads wanting to get on the ladder. It was gone completely mad. It was *losing the plot*. Like London back in the eighties, but even more of a head-wreck. Guy with a line in bullshit could rake in a few sovs. 'And you know me,' he said. 'I speak fluent bullshit.'

We turned down towards the quays, to where his car was parked, because he wanted to feed the meter. 'Wankers, these wardens. They'd clamp the fuckin' popemobile.' No doubt he also wanted me to see the car. It was a new BMW, metallic black and grey, with a Bob the Builder sun-guard on the back left-hand window. Yeah, he was a dad now, he laughed quietly. A boy and a child. 'Kurt and Courtney.'

He took out his wallet and showed me a picture of the kids. They were happy-looking toddlers, strong and pink. Lucas and Emma were their actual names. A beautiful dark-eyed woman was dandling them on her lap. She was smooth and cool, wearing sunglasses and sipping a Perrier. I knew her to see. Audrey Harrington. She'd worked back in London doing something for the GLC. The picture had been taken in Glendalough; you could see the round tower and the ancient gravestones.

He started showing me various gadgets on the car, but I was thinking about his children – the strangeness of that. Eddie Virago was somebody's *father*. It was like being told the Queen Mother was secretly a trannie. I said I hadn't even heard he was married. 'I'm not right now, to be honest,' he said. 'Didn't work out. We're still good buds.' He shrugged and glanced away. 'I don't talk about it much. Shit happens, that's all. It's probably for the best.' He stuffed the coins in the meter and pucked me a little too hard on the shoulder. 'So it's you and me tonight, Homeboy. Just like London times. Young, free and single and out on the razz.' He locked the car and we hiked off in the direction of the Clarence.

'So anyways,' he goes. 'How's tricks with yourself? Ever see that mott – what's her name? Ruth O'Donnell? She was one of your posse, wasn't she? Awful-looking minger. And mad as a snake. Bit of a slapper, they always said.'

'Actually, Eddie–'

'Went through more hands than a *Razzle* on a building site. Gave her the rub of the relic myself once or twice – when the beer goggles were on.'

'I'm actually – married to Ruth,' I said.

He chuckled at the idea. 'Bloody sure you are. You'd need a licence to keep that troll in the house.'

'It's true,' I said. 'We're married eight years now.'

He stopped walking. 'Fuck off,' he said.

'Nearly nine,' I said.

'Fuck *off*, you fuckin' bollocks. Before I bate you through that wall.'

He was blushing so deeply, I was almost going to take it back. But you can't really lie about the person you're married to. It might bring down bad karma, or some medieval Celtic curse. So I confirmed it again – I was married to Ruth – and by now he had the grace to look perplexed. He started humming and hawing about some other Ruth. 'Ruth *Murphy*, I meant. Used to hang around the 100 Club. You know the one. Pierced clit and a crucifix.'

Some event was going on in the hotel lobby. There were press photographers and cameramen wandering through the crowd. Chinese waiters in white jackets were handing out glasses of wine. Bono and Seamus Heaney were standing near the reception desk, chatting quietly with the Minister for Health, Mary Harney. 'How's the men?' smiled Eddie as we made for the bar. 'Fine, thank you,' Mary Harney said. Her two companions looked confused.

The bar was jammed with beautiful people. Eddie ordered two double Bushmills without asking me what I wanted, drained his glass in one long swig and ordered another. 'So what are you at, yourself?' he asked me; and when I told him journalism he rolled his eyes and laughed. 'Still at that crack. Will you never get sense? You want to make a few sponds, man, and bleedin' quick. You might hatch out a sprog one of these days, you know.'

'We already have three,' I said.

He nodded. 'My point exactly. Reproduction costs big-time. You'd want to suit up for it. Or have a vasectomy.'

I thought he might at least manage to ask me about the kids, maybe enquire as to their ages or names. But instead he started into a sermon on the massive costs of parenthood, which a columnist in the *Irish Times*, so Eddie informed me, had recently calculated was half a million euro per child. 'You're not gonna rake in half a mill churnin' out ballsology for the papers. That's just fuckin' negligent. Surprised at you, dog.'

'I suppose you're right,' I said. For the sake of a quiet life.

'You want to get into the property racket. Money's obscene. Seriously, man – you're wastin' your life. Brave new frontier just waitin' on you, pal. All it takes is a pair of goolies and a mobile, you're blinging.'

Houses in southside Dublin were going for a couple of million yo-yos. Two per cent commission on every sale. Selling a place in Dalkey could buy the estate agent a yacht. Even a halfway decent apartment, you were talking four hundred grand. 'Course, we all make our choices.' He tapped his abundant belly. 'I could have bought fuckin' Graceland with what I spent gettin' that.'

He ordered more drinks, again without asking me. He was downing the stuff fast; way too fast for my taste. I hadn't eaten since breakfast and I was feeling edgy anyway. Being back in Dublin always makes me edgy. Another round was ordered, then another, and two more. Soon we were on pints. Things started getting woozy. High jinks were remembered, old acquaintances disparaged, albums and bands nostalgically recalled. He rarely went to a gig any more, he said. All that sweat on the walls, piss and lager on the floor. And he found standing up for three hours too much of an effort. 'Adorin' some muppet, like Nazis at Nuremberg.'

He was sorry if he'd been shifty on the subject of his marriage: he just found it difficult to talk about it now. I said there was no problem, I hadn't meant to be nosy. 'I just find it better to let the shit go,' he explained. 'You talk and talk, it only brings it back up.'

'Let's leave the subject,' I said. 'I completely understand.'

'Everyone says that, but they don't,' he sighed. I was getting the ominous feeling that a confession-session loomed. 'You don't understand till it bites you in the hole. You're yackin' and bellyachin', but where does it get you? It happened. It's over. Get used to it, yeah?'

I nodded.

'Exactly,' he went. 'See, that's my point. You don't want to be carryin' it around for the rest of your natural. It isn't like it's the end of the fuckin' world.' He gave a bare laugh and peered into his glass. 'Mind you – the way I felt when she walked out taking the kids, even the end of the world wouldn't have been the end of the world.'

A silence descended over the table. It was as though some uninvited bore had sat down between us. By now the drink had begun to get hold of him. Not that he was slurring – his eyes just looked damp. He loosened his tie, unbuttoned his collar. It only occurred to me now that I had never seen him wear either.

'You look mighty,' he said. 'I'd ride you meself. So what do you reckon to the old town? Dear auld durty Dubbalin, wha'?'

I said I was surprised by how it had changed. Too right, Eddie said. He leaned in close and began to speak furtively, checking over his shoulder to make sure nobody was earwigging. Not that he was a racist or anything. No bleedin' way. Hadn't he picketed the South African embassy in the bad old days? The only problem with the ANC was they weren't socialist *enough* for Eddie. It was just – you know – these immigrant fellahs. They were *different* somehow. Not like us bog-gallopers. Their *culture* was different; their music; their food. Nothing *wrong* with it, of course. All very colourful. But these Nigerians, for example – what could you say?

'How do you mean, Eddie?'

'Well – hackin' off each other's mickies for havin' a ride outside of marriage? That's just not on, man; in all fairness.'

'I don't think they actually . . .'

'I've heard stories,' he said. 'You don't want that crack catchin' on over here, pal. Rastas in Leitrim. Stuff like that.'

'Maybe Leitrim needs Rastas,' I said.

'So does my hole,' he answered bleakly.

A girl wandered in wearing a DROP THE DEBT sweatshirt. She was talking into a mobile and looking at her watch. I was beginning to regret going for a drink with him at all. Really, I was wishing I was anywhere else. You don't see someone for twenty years, there's usually a good reason.

'So where you living these days?' he asked, and he quaffed his drink.

'Chiswick,' I told him. 'It's not far from the airport.'

He looked at me, confused. 'I thought you were after moving back?'

'No, we're only over for a break. Ruth's mother isn't the Mae West. Since the da died last year.'

He nodded blearily and sparked up a Bensons, hiding it in his hand because smoking in public was now illegal. 'Well, you're welcome to London. Armpit of a place anyway. Best thing I ever did was take the old boat home.'

'London's home for us now,' I found myself saying. 'It's been good to us both. The kids feel at home there.'

'I dunno how you stick the kip. Fair balls to you, man.'

'Ruth likes the theatre. I like the football.'

He said nothing.

'It's been good to us work-wise. She's lecturing now. She's a book coming out next year. On Boucicault.'

He gave a jaded smirk. 'Whatever you're havin' yourself, I suppose.'

'We're gone fierce boring now. Real suburbanites, I guess. Mowing the lawn and giving out about the neighbours.'

'And buyin' the Sunday papers on a Saturday night, man.'

I laughed. 'That happens, yeah.'

'Wouldn't suit *me*, pal, tell you that for real. Been there, done that; have a nice life, good luck. Out of it like a hot snot from a headbanger's nose. Once bitten, twice bite – that's young Edward's motto now. I've more of the range to ride before I jam the old nads in the mincer again.'

'You never get lonely?'

'I do in me gicker. I'm out every night.'

Matter of fact, he was heading to a party later. At Eddie Irvine's new gaff, out in Killiney. Several Corrs would be there; so would 'Good Oul Van'. Of course he knew the Corrs – he'd sold Jim a house. He'd sold a lot of houses to Irish celebrities – his company specialised in the quality end of the market – but Jim Corr was probably the soundest he'd met. Deadly guy, Jim. Unsung hero, in many ways. He'd be dandering along to Irv-the-Swerve's later. Elvis Costello'd be spinning the discs. Samantha Mumba was flying in from the Apple. Yer man out of Boyzone. Maybe Colin Farrell. Good Oul Van might bring his harmonica. I said it sounded like a night to remember. He gave a sly wink. 'You peeled the right banana there.'

More drinks were ordered before I could stop him. I couldn't even get away to the jacks, never mind tell him I was upping to go home. My head was reeling. I was suddenly famished. The place felt lurid – I don't know: like a nightclub in a dream. I was busting for a leak but he was off at full tilt – talking *at* me like I was interviewing him at some public event. It was the one thing he missed about London, he said; the diversity of social life in the big city. 'Man, that's a party town. I'll give you that much. London's grand for a rasher and a ride. But Christ, I couldn't stick livin' there.'

It was at one such London party that he had hooked up with Audrey – a reception in Soho for the launch of some documentary about urban deprivation. On their first night together, they'd had sex five times. He'd been in entire relationships where that didn't happen.

'We really don't have to talk about it, Eddie,' I said.

He was up shit creek when she'd met him first. Broke, despondent, with nowhere to live, several failed careers and an urgent need for new fillings. Evicted, dejected, fucking *rejected*, his beaten-up car had been repossessed 'by the devil'. His overdraft was gargantuan, his self-esteem subterranean. Some people had baggage. 'Me, I had cargo.'

'This must be hard for you to talk about,' I said.

'Call that waitress over, man. I feel a tequila slammer coming on.'

They had moved back to Dublin, rented a duplex in town. It was only a short hop from Temple Bar 'twinned with Sarajevo' but the Cultural Quarter was not all it was cracked up to be, 'crack being the operative word, man'. They used to stroll there sometimes, if 'stroll' was the word – rather skidded or slithered or, late at night, ran. The baby came along; another a year later. But Temple Bar was not the kind of place you would take a baby for a stroll, not unless you had a bulletproof pram. There had been talk back in London – booze-fuelled, brave talk – of the civilised evenings they would share in Temple Bar: a tranquil cappuccino, a play at the Project, a saunter round an exhibition of abstract photography. But this glittered Hooligania seemed to him a symbol of why they should never have come home. London was a kip, but an admirably large one, the kind where true happiness was not possible, but a higher quality of misery was. Dublin was turning into Disneyland with superpubs, a Purgatory open till six in the morning.

I tried to laugh, but it came out sounding dutiful. We were drifting, I felt, into the realm of the morose. Like I said, I'd often endured drunken fessing. But this was new. This was strange. It was as though he was talking about himself in the *third person*: spinning me lines he had learned by heart.

Eddie Virago and Audrey Harrington. It had started as the relationship he had always yearned for. It had ended as the emotional equivalent of a groin strain. Monday nights, they watched the soaps like a couple of zombies. Just like on Tuesdays and Wednesdays and Saturdays and Sundays. On Thursdays she went to a yoga class, run by a feminist nun in a former seminary on the northside – 'Unleashing the Goddess Within: Beginners' Level' – leaving Eddie to scrub out her ashtrays and empty the nappy bin. The nappy bin terrified him. He had nightmares about it. How could such a tiny being produce this Croagh Patrick of shit? By the time he was finished, she was usually back home – all Goddessed up like a pagan in leggings, and ready to get into the bath with a bottle of organic Beaujolais. He was invited to share neither bath nor bojo. Some nights they did a crossword. Most nights they didn't. Every Saturday morning they sat down together to buy the weekly groceries on the Tesco's website. He always forgot to remind her to buy razors, 'for her legs'. And every time he forgot, she spread his balls on toast.

That was the type of girl she was: the kind who could screw your head right *off* and hop it around your duplex like a basketball. Fabulous mother, in fairness – but talk about volatile? It was like being married to Roy Keane in a frock. He sometimes wondered if they'd called the feeling between them 'love' in order to save a lot of trouble. 'But as I say, I don't like to talk about it much. Trying my best to get closure. Put it behind me. I hope I'm not boring you.'

'I have to go to the jacks,' I said.

In the Gents, I looked at the clock on the wall. It was *ten past eight*. And I'd promised Ruth I'd be home by six. I dunked my head in the sink a few times. There was a roaring noise in my ears; like a plane taking off.

When I got back to the bar, he was flirting with some girl who was describing his shirt as 'pure knackeragua'. I grabbed my coat and my bag of books.

'What's the crack, Horse?' he said. 'I thought we were gonna have a drink?'

'I'm really late.'

'Jaysus, these bigshot London bollixes,' he said to the girl. 'Going for a drink means going for *a* drink. Afraid of their holes they might have a good time.'

He walked me out to the lobby and embraced me warmly, as though the bar of the Clarence was his country retreat and I was a beloved, slightly deformed cousin about to emigrate to a war zone.

'Well – keep the old faith now. And say a rosary for me, Father.'

'I will.'

'You know how it is, man – if arseholes could fly, Dublin would be an airport.'

'Yeah.'

'You look terrific,' he said. 'It's great you're so thin. I'd happily fuck your brains out. But I see somebody's beaten me to it.'

He clutched at my arse and started humping my leg. Mary Harney, passing by, gave us a perturbed look.

'You should come home,' he said. 'It's a great town these days.' He gestured around himself with a magnanimous wave. 'Just think, man – we could be doing this every night of the week.'

I said I'd think it over, but now I had to go.

'Pram in the hall, huh?'

'That's it.'

'Smug bollocks. Still, we wouldn't want to keep the bosslady waiting. Keep in touch, you skinny fuckin' pussy-whipped Chiswick-dwelling prick.'

I left by the back door and staggered over the cobble-stones, up into Dame Street and past the Olympia. It was still quite bright, the evening was hot. My temples were pounding. I was thirsty; dry-mouthed; in need of a cool shower. That bloody awful feeling of being drunk by sunlight.

Down towards Trinity. No taxis on the rank. Up into Grafton Street, my shirt damp with sweat. A fire-eater was performing by the Molly Malone statue, spitting out globes of fat orange flame. Nearby, two refugee women were begging with babies.

And that was when I bumped into her.

Almost literally.

She was looking magnificent, smartly dressed and elegant, in a stylish black jacket and a dark green dress. Jesus Christ. It was *Audrey Harrington*. But to see her like this, so soon after talking about her – it was an aspect of Dublin life I had almost forgotten, and one I didn't miss: at least not very often.

She asked about Ruth, various old friends in London; a Sean Scully exhibition she'd been meaning to get over and see. She missed London now; with the kids it was harder to get away. Her mother said children were little rays of sunlight, but there were times it seemed to Audrey that they were little clouds too. She made a point of never missing my stuff in the *Guardian*, she said. It was fantastic that I was doing so well, it really was. Eddie was a keen reader of all my stuff, too. He loved finding a spelling mistake or a factual error. It made his Saturday. He'd be happy as a baby. He'd email all our old mates to tell them what an ignoramus I was.

'Sorry to hear the bad news,' I said.

'What news?'

'Well, y'know – about you and himself.'

She looked at me quizzically.

'Your divorce or whatever,' I said. 'That's terrible.'

Her face did something strange. 'Divorce, my arse. I'm on my way in to meet him now.'

'You're – ?'

She laughed a little uneasily. 'Yeah. We're going to a pregnancy class. For couples. He didn't tell you? I'm having bambino number three in November.'

A busker started into an old Rory Gallagher song. An

elderly Garda who was watching him began to tap his foot. The roar in my head grew louder; deeper. I had an image of Eddie cackling like a bastard – him and Van Morrison, howling with glee.

'Oh, that,' I managed. 'Yeah, of course he told me. I must have – got confused about the other thing. Sorry.'

'Jesus H. Christ? That's a hell of a confusion.'

'I'm just – not used to drinking any more. We don't, over in London. Not so much, I mean. With the kids. I–'

'Are you – *okay*? You look a bit weird. Do you want to get a glass of, like, water or something?'

'I'm grand,' I told her. 'But really, I have to head.'

'Well – give us a bell when you're over again,' she said, uncertainly. 'We're in the book: Virago in Ranelagh. Come for dinner or whatever. Meet the kids. Eddie's just great with them, you wouldn't believe it. Course, the size his tits are after going, he could breastfeed the new one.'

My mobile started to ring as I hurried away, but I didn't want to answer, so I switched it off.

The taxi driver said the traffic was only fucking wojus. Rush hour got longer and meaner every day. Longer in the mornings, longer in the night. What kind of country could stand for traffic like this? They were laughing at us in England. They were *breaking their holes* laughing. You wouldn't see it in *Africa*, traffic like this. Going over the northside was torture now. As for the southside at rush hour – don't be talking.

One of these days it would be rush hour all the time. And they said we were a civilised country.

Orchard Street, Dawn

New York, 1869

On the landings of the tenement house the women
had gathered to pray. They stood in the candle-
light, in small, shadowed groups, murmuring
litanies to the Holy Virgin and then to St Jude, the patron
saint of lost causes. It was an hour before dawn. When their
candle burned out, they prayed in the quarter-light for Agnes.

Vater unser im Himmel,
Geheiligt werde Dein Name . . .

Bridget Moore could hear their supplications as she wept
by the little one's cradle, wiping the infant's forehead,
clasping her emaciated hands. They were praying in their
German dialects, and, as other women came to join them,
in the Latin adjurations that united all those of their faith: in
the *Aves* Bridget had learned in her girlhood in Ireland, in the
glorias and *credos* and muttered *Pater Nosters*. It was spring-
time in New York; only three weeks after Easter. The trees
were leafed out. Her child was dying.

Her husband had fetched an ice block from a *Bierkeller*
on Ludlow, had hammered it down to chunks which he

wrapped in a fold of old muslin, so the child could be cooled and her fever assuaged, for he had convinced himself there would be hope in coolness. His hammerings had awakened Kate and little Jennie, the former aged four, her sister two and a half. He had bawled at fretful Kate to get out, *get out*. Bridget Moore had beseeched him to go easy.

It was April 21st, 1869. Bridget Moore was in her twenty-fourth year. All night she had kept watch in the tiny, cramped kitchen, with its acrid redolence of sickness arising from the cradle, and the odour of scorched chimney-soot from the empty black grate, and its print of the Sacred Heart.

Joseph had watched along with her almost until dawn, exhausted by the effort of walking the city for hours, searching for any doctor who would come to a tenement. They had no money left to pay.

Dr Topping had appeared weary; he was doctor to the poor. He wore a yellowed nightgown beneath his heavy frieze raincloak; of late, the city's nights had been cold. He had barely looked at the child before pronouncing the case hopeless. The patent cure they had purchased would not heal her, he said. Nothing would heal her. It was scrofula, and 'wasting'. 'Marasmus' was the medical term. There was nothing he could do. She was simply too feeble to live.

They could dose her with alcohol, if they had any, for the pain. She would be dead by morning, he told them. In his two decades of practice he had uttered many such verdicts; they had never grown easy to say. Joseph Moore had answered tremulously that perhaps the doctor was incorrect; surely something could be attempted, even now. She was only five months old. She could not be permitted to die. Bridget Moore said nothing, as though she already knew it was too late. She seemed to the doctor like a woman who was wondering why he had been summoned at all.

The sun rose slowly on the ghettos and mansions, reddening, then silvering the rivers of Manhattan, and reddening, then silvering the windows of the slums, and coaxing loamy smells from the earth. The birds in their nests gave small, bright shrieks. Tugboats stirred on the Hudson. At dawn Bridget Moore could hear the rasping croak of a rooster and the quarrelling of a Bavarian couple from somewhere downstairs, and from lower in the house the slam of the heavy door as the plumber who lived there hurried out to his work. Joseph nodded unconscious on a backless chair by the stove, with Jennie face down and asleep across his knees, and Kate, thumb in mouth, clutching a poppet he'd once made for her, asleep in the crook of his arm. Water was puddling on the floorboards where the ice had melted. His clothing was soaked. He was barefoot. Bridget Moore woke her husband to say he was wanted now. It was important to be brave; she needed him.

He watched, weeping silently, as though ashamed to be weeping, while Agnes Mary Moore, the youngest of his three children, died in her mother's embrace.

Through the flimsy walls of their home, in which they had lived only a few months, the couple heard the muffle of the Lord's Prayer. It rose in volume and sharpened in pitch, as though the women on the landings knew the terrible thing that had happened. The Irish couple inside had lost their tiny daughter. The little ones had lost their sister.

Dein Reich komme,
Dein Wille geschehe,
wie im Himmel, so auf Erden . . .

In the years to come Bridget Moore will remember this moment, picturing it from the vantage of her child's departing spirit, as it gazes down sadly on the rooftops of Kleindeutschland, on the steeples and palaces and meadowlands of Manhattan, on the synagogues and sweatshops, on the grid of the streets, which diminish in size, blurring into one another, as she nears the homeland of Heaven. But that is a picture for the years to come. This morning there are no such pictures.

Then the women on the landings heard the pierce of Kate's weeping, for at four she was old enough to understand what was told her by her parents: that the baby had gone away to Paradise now, where Lord Jesus would mind her in his love. She would suffer no more. She would cry no more. A priest from the cathedral arrived.

The priest from the cathedral was young, still shockable. He begged forgiveness for having come to them so late. He, like Bridget Moore, had been awake many hours, for six others of his parishioners had been close to death that night, and there were not sufficient priests to see all of them. He had never been to this house, its rooms crammed with immigrants, its single creaking water pump for the use of twenty families. There were worse tenements, he knew, in the Five Points, and elsewhere: slums of abject misery where everything you touched stank of death. This place was at least newly built: a step up for its tenants. But this room he would never forget.

He believed in the God who walked with the poor, preaching the holiness of hunger, the sanctity of the forgotten. He prayed by the body of Agnes Mary Moore: that ruined and deserted house.

Neighbour-women came and took Kate and Jennie to their apartments, to mind them an hour and to feed them and hold them; to share what little they had. Then two others came in, quiet as a rumour, an older woman and her sister, born a long way overseas, to wash the child's body and prepare her for burial, for Bridget Moore, they felt, could not be asked to do such a thing. She was too young to be asked.

A ribbon of black crape was pinned to the door, with a card bearing the name and age of the dead child, which a neighbour, a printer's apprentice, had written in lines of black ink, for he felt it was the only solidarity he could offer. He was born in rural Ireland, had seen many die in the Famine: buried in pit-graves, unremembered, dumped; he would not see a child disrespected. The women washed Agnes Moore, and placed candles by her body, which they dressed in the linen robe in which she and her sisters had been baptised. The undertaker, Mr Hart, brought a coffin so small that he could carry it unassisted up the staircases of the tenement. It was white, as was the custom when the deceased was a child. Joseph Moore could not watch such an object entering his home. The priest helped Mr Hart with his work.

James Kennedy, a mason who lived downstairs, knocked quietly and came in to condole. One of the few Irish neighbours in this dwelling-house of immigrants, he was a decent man; quiet, sober in his habits. It was said he had a wife someplace but nobody knew where, nor even if the stories of his marriage were true, for often they contradicted one another. He spoke to Joseph and Bridget with his brown eyes lowered, as though afraid to confront their grief, as though looking at them would burn him. They were barely able to reply.

A coffin for my child. A casket small and white. How can such a conversation be happening? You do not bury your child. Your child buries you. As though all of it was a fever-dream from which Bridget Moore might awake, to the street sounds and rhythms of another day in New York, and the cry of a baby for the mouthful of milk that the rich might give to a cat.

There are moments, late at night, when she remembers her life in Ireland. The stillness of the lanes. The smell of wet turf. The faces of the old people as they talked of the past, of pieties and weather and local events; and the sounds of spoken Gaelic. A cartwheel on the wall of a blacksmith's forge. Her uncles footing turf on the bog. A long time has passed since she last stood in a field in Ireland or walked the familiar thoroughfares of an Irish town. Dead wasps in the windows of the sleepy little stores. Soldiers in red coats. Beggars. Ploughboys. The sea air apple-crisp, as though you could take a bite out of it. A ruined, ivied monastery where only foxes live.

Onward she walks, through the cacophony of Orchard Street, past pitchmen and stallholders, through clusters of hawkers, past the windows of Schubert's butcher shop, past the little German beer hall where carters are unloading clanking crates. Memories blur like the spokes of a wheel.

It was another life, a lost one: her seventeen years in Ireland. A girlhood that seems far away.

Embrittled, scooped-out, she walks as in a dream, her eyes grown sore from tears. Strange languages swirl around her like fluttering streamers: the tongues of Saxony, Bavaria, Prussia; of other lands across the sea. Faraway places and wandering peoples. The smells of strange food. Spices she cannot name. From the embrasure of a window comes the sound of rabbinical singing, for a boy who loves Jehovah lives in that room. And there, on the corner of Stanton and Essex, stands the little Florentine pedlar, with his ribbons and combs. This city with its hundreds of thousands of immigrants, its parlances, its musics, its impenetrable slangs, its countless deities, its ghettos and rookeries, has nothing to say to her grief. A black woman is selling strawberries: people say she was once a slave. Everyone in this neighbourhood has a story behind them.

So does Bridget Moore, whose infant daughter died this morning, who prayed and hoped, to the last. She walks slowly, heavily, through the windblown dust, traversing the busy, dung-smirched streets, for there is a funeral to be arranged and Joseph is too broken to do it. This time yesterday morning his daughter was alive. Sick, yes; but life means hope. He will not go to the chapel, says he cannot face the priests, for he would be afraid of the things he might say to them. He wants nothing of God. *There is no God now*. It is Bridget who goes to the chapel.

Her husband does not like her to talk about Ireland. That is all in the past, Joseph says. It's the Irishman's trouble in the United States. The Irishman won't forget. He'll keep holding on. If only he'd assimilate, he'd be running America today, instead of being trodden on by these Yank sons of bitches. 'But the past is an anchor,' Bridget Moore tells her husband. A proverb of her mother's from home in Ireland. 'Anchors weigh you low,' Joseph answers dismissively. What is done is done: his creed.

She has memories of the ship, but it disconcerts him when she voices them. He asks her not to speak of it in front of the children. It would only upset them, Joseph insists. There is no need to go talking of such distressing matters. Let the past be the past, he says. She knows nothing of his own voyage, except that it started in Dublin. Asked once by little Kate how he had come to New York, Joseph had winked at his curious questioner. 'I swam it,' he said. 'Then I flew like a seagull. Your papa got all sorts of queer trickeries, so he does. Your papa got wings you can't see, girl.'

'Mama says she came in a boat. And the people was hungry. And the half of them died on the way.'

'That's only a story. She don't mean it. Eat your porridge.'

Bridget walks on. The ship tilts in her mind. The mind is an ocean, fathomless, turbulent, with eyeless creatures in its depths. She had watched the coastal mountains of Ireland recede, wondering to herself were there mountains in New York. The flap of the mainsail: fricative, like wings. The creaking and groaning of age-old timbers. She will never forget the crawling terrors of that passage. Long ago the ship had been used to transport stolen slaves: it was said among the passengers that the lower deck was haunted, that a cry could be heard near the fo'c'sle at night and that if you heard that eerie and terrible shriek, your death by morning was certain. You would be buried at sea, without stone or cross to mark you. Sharks roamed the chasms of the Atlantic.

A night in a storm when the billows struck so hard that the ship was almost beam-ended and every glass on board was smashed. Three weeks of seasickness, but, worse, the lack of privacy. Even the women without the slightest privacy. Then the blessed smell of the land: the green fields of Brooklyn. The sight of a farmer in his pasture near Red Hook, waving his hat in greeting as the ship drifted coastward. Around him, his milk-cows; their udders fat and heavy. He seemed to Bridget Meehan an angel of America. The passengers were singing a hymn.

> *Agnes beatae virginis*
> *natalis est, quo spiritum*
> *caelo refudit debitum*
> *pio sacrata sanguine . . .*

Bridget enters the church. It is cool and dark. Candles burning low beneath the statues of the martyrs. The odour of beeswax and incense. The rich, heavy wood of the serried lines of benches, and the purple of a confessional curtain. And high in the rafters, the carved faces of men and women, cut there by the boatwrights who fashioned the timberwork on the corbels. The images of their people back in Ireland, it is said. And one of those graven, imperturbable faces has always reminded Bridget Moore of an uncle back in Ireland, who went away one autumn to pick the harvest in Shropshire and never came back to the townland. She looks up at the rafters through the mote-filled beam of light. Her grief is like a swallowing of ice.

It was here in this church on a bright winter Sunday that she first saw Joseph Moore. He had been kneeling beside another man; she watched them going up to receive Holy Communion. His eyes met hers as he returned to the pew. There was a brazenness about him, an assuredness that struck her. He was not like the weakling boys back in Ireland. The next Sunday morning he approached and introduced himself in the porch. He had a flower in his hand and he gave it to her.

If your people were around you at a time like this. Your mother and father. All those you grew up with. If your mother were here, it would help you.

Saint Agnes. 'The lamb' in the language of her faith. And *Agnus Dei*: the lamb of God, who died and was resurrected to the life eternal, who conquered death by love.

A wreath of withering lilies on a plinth before a plaque for the Irish boys who died in the war. The fighting Irish. Heroes of Gettysburg. Joseph has no time for 'all that auld talk'. They want the Irish to build their roads for them, fight their wars, kill their Indians, whose land was robbed off them for nothing, he says. Then get soused and die quiet in some gin shop, he says. And that's the Yanks' plan for the Irish. The way the Americans talk, you'd swear no Irishman ever did anything bar shooting some innocent soul and spouting the rosary. He likes being mischievous. It's one of the reasons she loves him. He sees the world differently. His own man.

America was at war when she came to New York. Recruiting officers were gathered on the dock. She had watched some of the boys sign up to fight, as though joining some brotherhood of revellers on a spree. Barely a minute in America, still staggering with sea legs, pucking one another on the shoulders, saucer-eyed with excitement. A boy she had fancied, Michael English from Ennis, had led two of his cousins to the tent in Castle Gardens and demanded of the Yankee sergeant a uniform and a gun, for he was ready to prove himself in the country of liberty. *'Tis a tiger you're looking at here, boss. I'll kill ten rebels before breakfast.* It had seemed strange to Bridget Meehan — to come all this way in the hope of a new life, only to fight in another man's war.

She did not understand the war, its causes, its purposes. Joseph had tried to explain it to her, but she suspected he did not fully understand it either. The whites of the South wanted to be free of the North. They wanted to own slaves, he said.

'But they don't truly own them, the way you'd own a cow or a beast.'

'To be sure they do, girl. That's the way of the South. They auction the Negro on the block like a beast.'

'But all men are free in America,' she said.

'Not the Negro,' he said. 'He ain't free.'

'Ain't,' said Joseph Moore, and she thought he said it proudly, as though displaying his allegiance to his adopted city like a medal made out of its slang. His eyes were sea-green, and they glittered like new coins. He loved New York. He would make himself a home here. His hope was to make that home in a German neighbourhood, for Germans were industrious; good strong Americans, serious, optimistic, who didn't keep singing of the old country, who never looked back. His children would be Americans. It was the greatest country on earth. Sometimes he spoke in contradictions.

She drifts up the shadowy aisle and asks dazedly to see the priest. She is Mrs Moore, she tells the aged nun who is dressing the altar. Mrs Joseph Moore of Orchard Street; mother of Agnes. Yes, little Agnes Moore, who died this morning. The funeral. Yes. The nun nods.

There is a wedding in progress in the chapel near the transept. The party is small, no more than half a dozen guests, but the bride and groom, who look nervous and excited, are an affecting sight to those watching. Two elderly women observe them, taken by the spectacle. '*Go hálain*', one of them says. The Gaelic words for 'beautiful'. A memory of her own wedding arises in Bridget's mind while she waits for the priest to come to her.

Joseph had looked princely as he waited on the steps of the church, with his cousin smoking furiously, as though he was the one getting married. It is not the ceremony itself she tends to remember; not the words of the priest, nor the prayers, nor even the vows, but the way Joseph had looked at her from outside the chapel that morning. An expression of such kindness, of hopefulness and courage. It was the moment they had married, so it seemed to Bridget Moore, the instant when she knew he would always care for her, that God might be a witness to the promises of marriage but that the sacrament had already happened. 'I thought you wouldn't show up,' Joseph had joked to his bride. 'I nearly didn't,' she said. And he laughed.

He was always laughing. Always with a joke. 'When I first met my Bridget,' he used to tell everyone, 'there was straightaway an attraction. A powerful attraction.' He would pause a moment or two before adding, archly, 'And before too long, I felt the same way.' His gaiety was a currency, a passport.

'I am sorry for your trouble, Bridget,' Father Hanahoe

murmurs. He is an old man, born in Sligo; Bridget Meehan has washed his clothes. She takes in the priests' laundry; it earns a little extra for the family. She keeps some of the money back to send to her mother in Ireland. She suspects Joseph is wise to her, but he silently permits it. Her parents at home need help, he knows. You cannot forget where you came from.

Now she weeps, wiping her sore, tired eyes with her thumbs. Father Hanahoe will say the requiem for Agnes. An old man, courtly, who has seen many mothers weep, and she tries to swallow her tears, but she can't. And if only Father Hanahoe would take her in his arms, but he cannot, for a priest would not be permitted to do that; and so he must watch the rawness of her pain as it spills. The bride and the groom, alerted by her quietly echoed sobbing, turn from the side altar and stare a little resentfully.

'Courage,' whispers the priest. 'Be strong. Your children need you. Be certain that you have an angel in Paradise this morning. We are promised that, Bridget. Have not the smallest doubt. It is hard for you now. You are sharing the cross. But Agnes is sharing the Resurrection.'

The child needed milk, she wants to tell the priest. *Perhaps I didn't give her enough. We had so little to spare. I don't know what to think. I don't know what to do. Do you think it is my fault? Was there something I could have done? The money I sent to Ireland? Should I not have sent money? My mother and father have nothing to eat. Should I not have sent the money to Ireland?*

Some days she walks over to Mott Street, where she and Joseph lived as newlyweds. Mary-Kate was born there. They had been happy times. The neighbourhood was rowdy, full of toughs and low gin shops, and at night you could hear raucous singing from the den across the street, and once – Joseph denied it, told her she had too much of an imagination – the *pok pok* of gunshots from an alley near the shambles. But there was love in that cell of a room she had shared with her husband. It had seemed a consolation, a protective shell. The fictions we believe when we are young.

A married woman. She would silently repeat the phrase to herself, as she walked the astonishing streets of the Five Points. Through the grits and the cinders and the turmoiling flies, by the rancid open sewers and wild-eyed dogs. Past the watching eyes of corner-boys and hardscrabble gangmen. By the gaze of penniless women, burnished hard and cold by hunger, who had crossed half a world to find plenty and peace but had found only newer kinds of want.

Nothing can touch me. I am married now. She had believed it like an article of faith.

Joseph, a Dubliner, was warm-hearted, handsome. When he entered any room, girls looked at him. He worked as a waiter in hotels near the park; he would also do saloon work. He worked hard. He knew all the Irish ward bosses; they liked him, assisted him, though in truth he had little interest in politics. All he wanted, he told her, was work; a chance. 'I'll kiss their arses, the bloody fools, if it puts food on the table. I'll be Irish as long as it pays me.'

He had a Dubliner's sense of himself; his endless possibilities. He disliked the maudlin ballads the drinkers in the barrooms would sing, of old Irish places, half-forgotten love affairs. *Fare thee well to Claregalway, fare thee well for a while . . . Adieu, my dark Sarah, to new lands I go . . . 'Tis far from home this morn I roam, in lonesome Brooklyn town.* He'd chuckle about the singers, say they were looking back over their shoulders. It was 'rawmashe' they were singing, a Gaelic word for trash-talk. 'What use was Ireland to me or mine?' he'd scoff. 'It's well out of it we are. I'd rain bombs on it if I could. The Queen of England can keep it. Ireland don't matter a damn to me, girl, for Ireland don't grease no pan.'

That shabby room in Mott Street. Their palace, he used to laugh. In the tenements of Dublin, they'd have had to share it with another family. He had seen pitiful sights in Dublin nobody would believe. Children in prostitution. Old people abandoned to beg. The poor were as nothing in the teeming, filthy hovels. But that was in the past. Before America.

Sometimes they bickered about her feelings for Ireland. He was not an angry man but he could be impatient, truculent, his edginess fuelled, so Bridget often felt, by the sense he had of time being an enemy to the poor. What irked him most was when she said, as she sometimes did, that she hoped one day to see Ireland again, that it would be a blessing for the children and for her family back at home. 'It's me and them girls is your family now,' he would say. 'Wish to Christ you'd quit your dreaming, for it only leads to sadness. You'd want to wake yourself up, girl, and look at where you are. Ireland's only a stain on a map.'

Joseph took a drink, but he wasn't a drunkard. He'd seen what drink did. You work in a city's barrooms, you see too much of misfortune. The hard luck story and the good man ruined. He'd take a bottle or two of porter of an evening at home, but he didn't touch whiskey for that was bad news in a glass and you go looking for trouble, you'll find it. *I never met me an Irishman didn't have a head full of bastards; a sup or two of the hard stuff and out they march.* And then, when the first of their children was born, he had taken a pledge of total abstinence. His way of thanking God for such a blessing, she knew, though he had always denied it, saying her head was in the clouds. Sometimes he missed Mass. He seldom went to Confession. Religion was for old women and foolish boys, he said. The priests lived as princes. *I seen queer sights in the world but never a skinny bishop. Them's the fellahs can eat all day, girl. Come over to me now and sit here on my knee and I'll soon have you saying your prayers the way you said them last night.*

—*Joseph, for decency! The children are listening.*

—*You're not always so pious, my little holy wildcat. Look at the blush of you. It'll scorch me in a minute. Do you think I don't see your smile over there and you trying to hide it?*

—*For heaven's sake, quit such talk, you rogue and a half, or I'll march you down to the priest this minute.*

—*Sure he fancies you himself, the dry auld baboon. I could tell him tales of you now that would straighten his hair for him; come here and give us a kiss like a darling.*

He always made a great show of mock-quarrelling with her about the dues for the church. Why would they give any of his hard-earned dollars to the priests who'd only spend it on dancing girls and gin? It drove her demented. The children would laugh. But one night she had found him on his knees by Mary Kate's cradle, praying in a whisper; it had shocked her to hear his words. *I beseech thee, Christ in Heaven, hold my child in thy heart. Blessed Jesus, have mercy and build thy strength in these arms. Mary, my mother, intercede for her blessing, and assist me in her fatherly protection.*

My child will be buried in New York City, and I will never see my mother again. Far in the future, in decades, in centuries, the body of my child will be part of New York City. And I, myself, will always be here now. I will never see my mother again.

The funeral is to be held tomorrow, for in cases such as these, a longer period of mourning is unwise, says Mr Hart. He speaks with the scrupulous diplomacy of all his profession, in euphemisms, sidelong looks, in silences. Flowers would be useful to have in the room. Lilies, if possible, for their smell is sweet and heavy. Better for the casket to be closed, Mrs Moore. When the deceased was so young, and also so very thin. And he falls silent, as though bearing a guilt.

Even though there is so little time, she consents that there should be a wake. For some reason, it seems important to Joseph. She watches as he drapes the mirror in the parlour, the way the people back in Ireland prepare for a waking. The few dollars he has managed to raise at the pawnshop on Grand Street are spent on food and drink for the mourners. There must also be tobacco, Joseph insists. A wake must be done with propriety.

Is he trying to help her? Does he think it is what she wants? Or somehow does he want it himself? He borrows chairs from the Germans, places them carefully about the room, neatly, efficiently, like a waiter preparing a function, never once looking at the terrible object in the corner. His face is slickened with sweat.

They file in to the parlour quietly, as though trespassing on a privacy, the women clutching rosary beads, the men with hats in hand. It is as though they are waiting for something to happen: a revelation produced by their solidarity, their sitting together in a room. Some of the callers are neighbours: others she does not know. Men from the bar where Joseph works, she assumes, for they seem to know him, greet him quietly by name. Dockers, stevedores, navvies: all Irish, and a man who is an organiser for the Democratic Party, and another, from the Ancient Order of Hibernians, which has offered a little money towards the funeral. And others who insist on addressing her in Gaelic, as though the sound of the old language could heal. And the German women come in, speaking quietly in their own language, which she does not understand, so replying is impossible, or in broken phrases of English, or saying nothing at all, but sadly shaking their heads and touching her hand. But it hurts to be pitied, for there is nothing to answer, no matter the language or the kindness lying behind it. She wishes they would all go away.

They sit together in the room, the women around the coffin, the men in a huddle by the doorway. *That is not a body. That is my child. Why are all these people in my home?* Candles burn down. The visitors murmur. The child, she is told, has gone to a better place. A place where there is no suffering, where the poor are loved and honoured. It is how her elderly parents used to talk about America. A land of honey. Of milk.

And she recalls the wake held for her on her last night at home. Her father and mother and the gathering of neighbours. A drover singing a ballad in a corner of the cabin and then a fiddler came in, but he wasn't good. 'Get up with me, Bridget,' said her father, late in the night, 'and face me in a step. Will you do that for me, girl? For likely it's the last dance we'll ever have in this world.' And she and her father had danced in the kitchen. In the morning she had left for the port, with a couple of shillings and an address in New York: an agency placing Irish girls as domestic servants in Manhattan's wealthy houses.

Dear Mother. She imagines the letter, as tobacco smoke purples the air. Bridget Moore cannot write, and her mother cannot read, but Joseph sometimes helps his young wife to write a letter, and the schoolmaster back in Ireland helps her mother understand the news. So it will be the voice of the elderly schoolmaster, whose name Bridget Moore cannot now remember, that will pronounce the words of the terrible letter: that Agnes Mary Moore, who lived only five months, has lost her life in New York.

My child is dead. Why can't you understand? There is nothing you can say to me now.

Honor Frawley, an old Connemara woman who lives on Elizabeth Street, comes into the apartment clad in a ragged black shawl. Leather-faced, black-eyed, something Spanish about her. She bends to kiss the tiny coffin and immediately begins a keening: a soft ululation, wordless at first, but soon settling into the *ochóns* and *bróns* of Gaelic. The German women stare at her. Some look frightened. From outside in the street come the cries of the vendors, then a bawled obscenity, and the rattle of a cart. Rain spatters the windows. The room is too full. The children are restless on the floor.

But the letter cannot be written by Joseph, she

understands now, because that would be to ask him to live again what has happened. She will have to seek the help of somebody else. A neighbour-woman, maybe. One of the priests at the cathedral. She does not realise that what has happened will be recollected every day, for the remainder of her life, for the remainder of Joseph's, that mourning is not what happens on the day of a funeral, but in the months and the years to come. Grief unfurls in instants, in memories and desires, long after the mourners have departed the room. It is carried in the senses, in the body itself, which each of us inhabits alone. Around the corpse of a child stand a multitude of ghosts: the child herself, the child's own children, the lovers unmet, the friends unmade, the dreams undreamed, the hopes annulled, and the ghosts of the parents, now living in a world where the sacred rules have been aborted. They will see an infant in the street, or hear a baby's squalling cry, or smell the miraculous aroma of a newborn's precious head, and be speared, in that moment, by all that might have been. They will know the amputation of such a grief as this. There will be nights when they dream they are orphans.

He stands by the doorway, in a suit that does not fit him, one he borrowed from Mr Solomons, the tailor on Delancey. The shirt collar is too tight; its pressure is reddening his face. He looks hollow-eyed, close to tears, but he will not weep. He would never weep in public; he thinks it unmanly, and she is glad, for she could not bear to see it.

He moves among the mourners, offering drinks and plates of food as though attending the plentiful tables at the hotel where he works. There are murmurs among the German women that the landlord should come to pay his respects, or at least send his wife, as if any of that would matter, but someone keeps translating the murmurs to Bridget, and she glances across the parlour at her husband. It is only when the rosary begins that his shoulders start to quiver, and quietly he departs the room. But she cannot leave the room. The children need her presence. A woman has no other choice than to stay.

Once, in the summer of her first year in New York, when she was working as a housemaid for a family on Washington Square, she had paused while shining the silverware in their parlour to look at the magazines on the card table. She could not read English well but she recognised the word IRISH under a cartoon of a leering, apelike man with a cudgel in one paw and a bottle in the other, and two filthy decrepit crones by his side. Was that how the family thought of her? The ape-woman of Ireland?

And another time, when she was walking home from evening Mass, a soldier had approached in the street making drunken propositions. He would pay her a dollar. Two, if she pleased him well.

'I'm an honest girl,' she said. 'You'll not talk to me so.'

Recognising her accent, the soldier gave a scoff. 'You're a nigger blanched white and an Irish bitch. That's all you'll ever be here.'

Joseph told her not to speak of it. America was a good country. There were oafs and thundering louts in every land on God's earth. We'd be better not to mind them or to give them any credence.

It was shortly before they were married.

* * *

My dear mother,

I write with hard news and do not know how to say it. Our little daughter Agnes died on Wednesday the twentyfirst, and was buried in Calvary Cemetery. Our hearts are broken. There is nothing for me in the world. The priest says I am to say my prayers to the Holy Virgin, and I do say my prayers – but they do not help me.

My husband would not let go of the coffin when the time came for to bury her, only standing by the graveside and destroyed with his tears. The good of his life is gone, and I am afraid for him now. Mamma, say a prayer for us. How I long to be at home. I would give anything to see you, anything in the world.

I wish you could have seen her for she was a beautiful looking child and every time I looked on her I thought of you and Daddo.

I enclose four dollars and hope it might be of use to you.

Pray for us. Your loving
Bridget

Spring turns to summer. Neighbours leave the house, and others, newer immigrants, come to live there. In the basement of the tenement there is a busy German tavern, and at night the crowds of drinkers spill out into the street. She can hear them as she scrubs at the priests' old clothes; laundering, mangling, folding, pressing. Washing until her hands grow wrinkled and sore. Cassocks draped around the room like strange weeds.

He gets the moods of an evening. He works too hard. There are times he comes home from his work after midnight, jaded by the exhaustion of having to be cheerful all night, for a bartender has to stay cheerful, no matter how he feels, no matter his private thoughts or the troubles of his home. Men don't want sullenness in a barkeep, ever. And Joseph doesn't want it in his wife.

He hates his shifts in the saloon but that's all the work he can get since he was dismissed from his job at the hotel. A drunken diner insulted him. Called him a dirty Irish leech. Told him to get home to the cesspit he hailed from. There was an angry scene; he was ordered by the boss to apologise to his abuser. He would be dismissed if he refused to. He quit.

He sits silently by the window, staring down into Orchard Street, listening to the drinkers, their shouts and catcalls, about girls, or politics, or nothing. You can't approach him any more. Lately he can be bitter. This man, that man: all of them are untrustworthy. The German neighbours don't like us. They hate the Irish. Call us Tammany thieves. Bogtrotters. Monsters. These Lutherans around here: they stick to themselves. That Schneider, who manages the *Bierhaus* in the basement below – he'd no more employ an Irish than a black man or a Chinese. She tries to point out that the Irish are the same, they will only support their own, but he won't listen. *What chance has a man in a town such as this?* Coming here to New York was the worst mistake he ever made: this is what he says when the blue mood descends on him. Hostilities he doesn't mean. Intolerances he doesn't feel. Opinions he would ridicule if uttered by others. As though his body is emitting a colour, she often thinks. He has changed since Agnes died.

Can't you keep them children quiet? . . . Can't you let me alone? . . . Can't you get yourself some work? . . . I am weary, I told you . . . Can't you make the money last? . . . No, I don't want to talk . . . I'm after talking all night . . . I've a pain in my face from talking . . . Will you let me alone! . . . Can't a man sit in his goddamned house? . . . Is it out to walk the streets I have to get for some peace?

The city now eludes him, like a friend he'd like to make but he doesn't know the words of introduction. Stories of other men's success in America seem to savage him. A Sligoman who made a fortune out beyond in San Francisco. A Dubliner who owns a silver mine in the new state of Montana, yielding tens of thousands of dollars a month. A Galwegian born in destitution on a famine ship in the harbour, who now employs hundreds of Irish navvies, and who is building a mansion so opulent and gracious that even the Yanks are envious. She has dreams of Joseph wandering a hall of many doors, opening them, one by one, but finding nothing behind. *It's here*, he mutters. *Someplace it's here.* As though the thing he seeks so frantically he already owned, but he lost it, or it was stolen by a burglar.

Once, in the August after Agnes's death, she saw him on the corner of Rivington and Allen, staring at a poster in a dirty window: A THOUSAND MEN WANTED FOR NORTHERN CALIFORNIA. OPPORTUNITIES FOR ALL. DO NOT DELAY APPLICATION. GREAT FORTUNES TO BE MADE BY THE MAN WHO WILL WORK. There was gold in California. Nuggets the size of your head. For a week or two, he had talked about moving out west. Scrape up a few dollars. Wipe the dirt of New York from their feet. *Think of it, Bridget. We'd live like royalty, so we would! Get out of this kip and never look back. It's a new start we need, I can see that now. I'd been praying for a guidance and here it is.* Although terrified by the prospect, she had agreed it was a good idea. For she knew all he wanted was someone to agree with him. He has a man's need to be valued, to be listened to, admired. New York does not provide him with that any more. Not since Agnes died.

He borrowed a map. There were pamphlets, gazetteers. Land was available to everyone in the west. The terrible wrench of his feverish enthusiasms, as he plotted how they would get to California. But there was never enough money to save for the journey; they were in arrears for the rent; the children needed food. The plan was quietly forgotten, as though it had never been made, and one night, when they were cold, he burned the tattered map for kindling, and he left the apartment abruptly, slamming the heavy door behind him, and did not return until late.

Months turned to seasons. Orchard Street under snow. The mournfully beautiful entreaties and praisings drifting out from the synagogue on Norfolk. Christmastime comes, and he works longer, harder; in hotels and kitchens and barrooms and cafés; he takes every shift he can find. A busy time of year for a waiter in New York; often, he works sixteen straight hours. And Bridget works harder, and the priests' clothes keep coming, and she sends a few dollars home to Ireland every month: money she can scarcely afford. Her hours, her days, are measured in chasubles, in walks to the post office to send money. She buys milk for the children. She will go hungry to buy milk. She beseeches her two daughters to eat.

The fears for health. The terror of another pregnancy.

Her chest is not good. The German women tell her she is grown *totenblass* or *totenbleich*: their words for sickly pale. Lately, climbing the staircases in the house has been harder; she is breathless, swimmy-headed, plagued by strange, ferocious hungers, which never alleviate no matter what she eats. And there are days when neither of them eats.

She and Joseph have talked but such conversations are difficult. They embarrass him, she knows. They embarrass her, too. There are certain times, she says, certain weeks of the month, when a man and wife can lie together without a child being made. A woman in the house has told her; it is a matter of calendars. Joseph consents, for he could not bear her loss. It would kill him if anything were to happen to her, he says. But they are young, with the longings of the young for one another, for the comforts of the body, the escape of that intimacy, and they believe in the God who will protect them from the unbearable cross, and if a new life is willed by that heavenly ordinance, the sin is in wishing things otherwise.

A new year comes in. A child is growing inside her. Joseph promises that they will manage; the better times are ahead. Their luck will change. It must, he believes, for America extends a hand to the man who works hard, who is honest and loyal and who stands by his family, who never asked for charity, who never begged or stole. It might take a little time for the promise to be made good. But it will be. He believes it. There is no other way.

She watches the newer immigrants come to the house. She sees them in the courtyard, clustered around the water pump, waiting to use the single privy the tenement affords, or playing with their children in the smoke-filled air. Some of the men mutter of politics, a revolution that will come, when the poor of the whole world will be brothers together, and nations will be abolished, and all chains will be broken, and the starvelings will arise from their slumber. They seem so young to her; a sign that she is ageing. She feels for them: these people with their bundles and delusions. Has anyone ever told them the truth she now knows? That this country of freedom can be cold to the stranger. That to emigrate might well be to shorten your life. There will be poverty, bigotry, the mistrust of the locals, who will whisper that you are lazy, that you bring disease in your wake, that you never assimilate, that all your kind are strange, that you do not belong, do not *want* to belong, only to come here and scrounge off your betters. And through all of it you will work every hour you are able, and raise children in the hope that their lives will be better than yours. To leave a home and cross the ocean for the sake of a chance. Only a chance. Not even a likelihood. There are moments when she wonders if it is the land of the free. But it is certainly the home of the brave.

Bridget Meehan and Joseph Moore never see California. Nor do they ever leave New York. The merciful immigrant sisters who washed Agnes Moore's body live many long years in Suffolk Street, Manhattan, until their home is demolished and they take to sleeping in the streets, in the doorways and alleys of the Lower East Side, among the whores and ruined creatures on the Corlears Hook waterfront, until they simply disappear from view. Others of the women who assisted that morning will always know hardship in the newfound land, as will many of the men who gathered in that room to stand with their grief-stricken neighbours. Some will die in poverty. Some will eke a way. Several of their children will serve their city with honour: police officers, firefighters, schoolteachers, workers; one will be a public defender; another a criminal; several will be American soldiers. Jennie Moore will marry. Kate Moore will not. In her teens, Kate will work as a hair weaver, Jennie as a maker of paper flowers. James Kennedy, the stonemason, will share his immigrant surname with a President. Many heroes will move through those small, lightless rooms. Some will never leave them.

Bridget and Joseph Moore move on several times: to Elizabeth Street, a neighbourhood of savage destitution, where many of the residents are Irish, the lowest of the poor, and then to Third Avenue and 28th. Bridget Moore gives birth to five more children. No headstone will ever record their names: Josephine Moore. Elizabeth Moore. Cecilia Moore, who died at seven months. Teresa Moore, who died aged five. And Veronica Moore, who lived only four days, and who rests in Calvary Cemetery with her family. With her mother, who dies at the age of thirty-six, and her father who lives to his seventies. His last move is to 31st Street and Second Avenue, where he resides with his eldest daughter until she dies at the age of forty. His final years are lived alone.

An elderly Irish waiter is sometimes seen in Orchard Street. He stands by the doorway of a dilapidated tenement that looks as though it should be condemned by the authorities. One time, he left a bundle of wild flowers on the steps in the doorway; another, he made the sign of the cross. But mostly he stands for a short time alone, looking up at the windows, unnoticed by passers-by. Nobody knows or cares why he should come here any more. A pale old ghost of a father. He dies in the bitter winter of 1916, the year of the Easter Rising in Ireland. Like his loved ones, Joseph Moore will have no headstone.

Remembered by the air of the immigrant city; by those rooms through which they moved, in which they breathed and bravely lived, thinking of how it might have been, and of how it truly was. Remembered by a building in the city of New York. Empty. Shadowed. Its worn, faded corridors. Where children ran, where life was faced, losses endured, and wild hopes nurtured, while out in the street the world hurried past, never looking up at the windows.

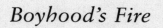

Boyhood's Fire

London, 1988

On the morning of the match, he had a case of the shakes. He swept back his straggling, greasy quiff, leaned over his desk and continued meticulously forging the expenses docket for his training course. The sun roared in through the office window, making him feel sweaty and panicky, but simultaneously not quite alert. He unscrewed the cap of the Tipp-Ex bottle and began to apply the white fluid to the dotted line with the devout delicacy of an ancient Irish monk. One of those chubby little fusspots who did the Book of Kells. He was in a good, bad mood. Life was fine.

The telephone rang, causing him to start and fumble.

'Liam Hynes,' he said.

'It's me,' said his sister.

'Patricia. I'm up to my tits. What do you want? Can it wait?'

'Charming.'

'Sorry. How's Paris?'

'Fine. Yeah. Looking forward to the match?'

'Can't watch it. Have to go to a fucking wedding with Siobhan this afternoon.'

'Ah well. Not to worry. Sure it's only a match.'

'That's what Siobhan said. Several fucking times. Ireland versus England in the European Championships and I have to go to a fucking wedding with her hayseed relations.'

'Liam, have you a minute? I've a bit of news I need to tell you.'

'What's that?' He picked up his coffee. 'You and Phil the loser finally getting engaged?'

'No. It isn't that. Liam, I'm after having this accident.'

'He hasn't managed to somehow impregnate you, has he?'

'No . . . Just . . . look . . . I had this accident the other night, right? I'm in the hospital. Here in Paris. I need you to listen.'

'What kind of accident? Patricia? Are you there?'

'Well . . . don't go spare on me now, but I got run over on Sunday night.'

'You what?'

'Run over. Stop asking me questions. I don't have long, I'm on a payphone.'

'Jesus, that's . . . Are you okay? Did you get his number?'

'It wasn't a car that hit me.'

'What was it?'

'A train.'

'What?'

Her voice started to crack. 'I'm so scared, Liam. I was pissed. I'd been out with Philippe and we had a row on the way home. We were gee-eyed and I fell over on to the train tracks. And a train came along, you see, and it hit me, kind of side on . . .'

'Patricia. For fuck sake. Tell me you're pulling my wire here.'

'Liam,' she said, 'I'm after losing a leg.'

He spluttered a mouthful of hot coffee down his shirt. 'You *what*?'

'I'm after losing a leg, Liam. They had to amputate it. On Sunday.'

The line crackled with static. He felt sweat soak through his forehead.

'Jesus,' he said. 'Jesus. Hold on.'

'I'm so scared, Liam,' she sobbed. 'Can you ring Dad and tell him?'

He heard himself whinny, 'No fucking way.'

'Please, Liam. He'll kill me if I call. He'll make me come home. I couldn't face it. Not at the moment. Go on, Liam, will you please? I need you to promise to tell him and not tell anyone else first. I couldn't stand for him to hear it told back.'

'Patricia, I . . .'

'I have to go now, Liam. The nurse is here with my painkillers. Fuck.'

'Wait . . . Patricia . . . *Wait*!'

The line went dead. He slammed down the receiver, stood up shaking and went to the window. His sister had one leg. It was eleven o'clock in the morning on 12 June 1988. He was on the fourteenth floor of an office block in central London. Ireland were to play England that afternoon in Stuttgart. Bonner, Morris, Hughton, McCarthy, Moran, Whelan, Galvin, Houghton, Aldridge, Stapleton and Paul McGrath. London was below him. Buses were passing. And his sister had just telephoned from Paris to tell him that she only had one leg. He said those devastating words out loud.

'Stapleton and McGrath,' he said. Out loud.

My sister has one fucking leg, he thought, then. I got up this morning and I had salami on toast for breakfast and I read the pre-match reports in the *Guardian* and I listened to the radio, and all that time my sister had only one leg. It suddenly occurred to him that he didn't even know *which one*. Was it the right or the left? He wondered if he could ring the hospital and ask. How in the name of Christ would you say that in French? *Quelle jambe, Monsieur le Docteur? La droite ou la gauche?* Was that it? Jesus. How did you say 'amputation'? Leaving Certificate French didn't cover situations like this.

He stared at the telephone as though looking at it could make it ring. His father would be at home, in the garden in Dublin. Five minutes passed. He thought. He sat. He swigged from his Evian. He peered down into the street. Outside Feisty O'Grady's Irish Bar, people were already milling around and drinking. A huge banner had been hung from an upper balcony window, depicting a squinting malevolent leprechaun about to kick a British Bulldog in the arse, all under the enormous green, white and orange words: GIVE IT A LASH JACK! OLÉ OLÉ OLÉ!

He came back to his desk, lit a cigarette, picked up the telephone and tried his father's line in Dublin. It was engaged. Thank Christ. He noticed his fingers were trembling. He tried again, dialling very slowly this time, hoping this would somehow make a difference. Still busy. Jesus. Who was his father talking to? He never talked to anyone, not for days on end. ('The dog does me for company since your mother passed away.') Maybe it was the hospital. Had they telephoned from Paris? But it didn't seem likely, Patricia was so frightened of him knowing. Words tumbled and churned in grim rehearsal.

'I think you should probably sit down before I tell you this, Dad.'

'What's up with you, son? Nothing wrong, is there?'

'Just take the weight off your feet for a minute, Dad. Okay?'

On second thoughts, maybe he wouldn't put it like that.

Charing Cross Road shimmered with heat. Harsh light poured from the offensively blue sky and smells drifted out from the cafés and burger bars, strong coffee, stewed vegetables, spiced beef and fried onions. A long line of Hare Krishnas shimmied around the corner from Leicester Square, banging their drums and chanting. A tall languid girl in an open white shirt, black bra and flower-patterned flares ran across the street with a portable television in her hands. The newspaper man called out to passers-by 'Standard. Evening Standard. Early Edition!' The billboard at his feet proclaimed in black lettering: ENGLAND SET TO CRUSH JACK CHARLTON'S REP OF IRELAND.

The English newspapers seemed to be incapable of referring to the Irish team without mentioning the manager. It was as though the name of the actual country had been changed by deed poll to 'Jack Charlton's Republic of Ireland'. Maybe it should be, Liam Hynes thought. He wouldn't mind that on his passport.

Suddenly he felt her arms twine around his waist from behind. He turned and kissed her. She kissed him back, hard. She was wearing a knee-length dark green dress he didn't know she had, a black silk jacket, the droplet earrings she'd made him give her for Christmas. He wanted to laugh out loud because she looked so beautiful.

'I wore green for Ireland,' she said, 'with the day that's in it.'

He adored her accent, its soft Ulster inflections and rhythms, the music of her drawn-out vowels.

She glanced at her watch. 'Are you right, so?' she said. 'We're wild late, Liam. My zip burst on me when I was changing. I'm after putting on weight.'

'Yeah. Listen, Siobhan . . .'

'Maybe I'm pregnant,' she grimaced. 'Wouldn't that be great altogether?'

'You're not pregnant,' he said. 'I'd have seen it in a nightmare.'

She stepped away from him and into the street, waving her hand. A taxi pulled up in a chugging miasma of diesel fumes.

'Euston Road Registry Office,' she said.

Heading up Charing Cross Road and on to Tottenham Court Road, the traffic was moving slowly. Telecom workers had dug up a long section outside the Dominion Theatre and there was a parked fire engine outside the entrance to the tube station. The inside of the cab was stiflingly hot. It smelt of leatherette and lemon-scented air freshener.

'Siobhan, listen . . .'

She turned to him, licked her finger and ran it along his eyebrows.

'Mammy rang this morning to say Uncle Peter might be over from home. You'll get a kick out of him, Liam. He's a character.'

'Great. Look, Siobhan, there's something I wanted to say to you.'

'Now Liam, listen a wee minute, try to be sociable today

will you? And stay off the politics with Aisling. She's a bit of a Republican, but a bride is entitled to peace on her wedding day.'

'How do you mean, a Republican? Not another one of your quasi-Provo friends?'

'Her daddy was interned with mine back in the fifties.'

'Your dad was interned?'

'Yeah.'

'You never told me that.'

'Of course I did, Liam. Sure everyone knows that.'

'You didn't, Siobhan. You said your uncles, not your dad.'

She smiled drowsily, grabbed his hand and moved it between her bare knees. His girlfriend had two legs. His sister had one. Averaging it out wasn't wise.

'What's up with you, Liam?'

'Nothing. I'm just thinking.'

'Not still in a sulk about your bloody match, are you?'

'No.'

'I don't know why you'd want to go and get skulled in some pub with a load of your mates and watch some stupid match when you could be with the sexiest woman in London.'

He said nothing.

'And if *she* can't make it, there's always yours truly.'

'Very funny.'

'Wee-boy, come on. Smile and give your face a holiday.'

He decided not to tell her about his sister and her leg. He would save it up for later. That would bloody well show her. Oh, by the way, Siobhan, I know you're having a really fabulous time with your woollybacked refugee-from-*Deliverance* relations here, but my sister had to have her leg off last Sunday night and I just thought you might like to know. It might come in handy if she was enjoying herself too much. He didn't really like it when Siobhan enjoyed herself too much. It always felt uncontrollable to him.

'Seriously.' She poked his thigh. 'Are you all right today, Liam? Is there something on your mind? You don't seem yourself.'

He shook his head firmly. For some reason, that hurt his teeth.

'Football deprivation,' she said. 'Bad for the heart, eh? If you have one of those. You little Dublin misery.'

'You're hilarious, Siobhan. Really. You crack me up.'

'Don't be such a dry shite. If you really don't want to come with me, you can get out right now. You'd be doing me a favour if this is how you're going to be.'

He turned to her, doing his best to appear hurt at her petulance. 'I do want to come. I never said I didn't. That doesn't mean I have to fucking *like* it, does it?'

The cab paused in the traffic. He looked out the window again. Another newspaper billboard caught his glance. ENGLAND SET TO TRIUMPH OVER CHARLTON'S EMERALD ARMY.

'There's times you drive me mental,' she said.

The registrar was a beautiful Pakistani woman who couldn't seem to stop smiling. One of the kids, a boy of about ten, was dressed in a Republic of Ireland strip, with the name STAPLETON emblazoned across his back.

After the brief ceremony was over, everyone clapped, except for the bride's mother, who looked about as cheerful as a person who has recently sat through a documentary about the Great Irish Famine. Siobhan turned to him and whispered: 'Look at the mug on Auntie Betty. She's raging because it's not a church job.'

'Because the fucking groom is English, you mean. Bigoted wagon.'

She shook her head. 'It wouldn't be that. You don't even know her.'

'Who are all these people? They keep *looking* at me, Siobhan.'

'There's a lot of relations over from home. I didn't think so many would be over. I hope Uncle Peter comes. What's the time?'

The boy in the strip wandered over towards them and Siobhan ruffled his hair.

'You're the bonny lad today, Johnny,' she said with a smile.

The kid blushed impossibly and buried his face in her thigh.

'You're my handsome little boyfriend, aren't you? You and me'll have a wee dance later for certain sure. That's if my fellah here allows me. He gets jealous.'

Outside the Camden Irish Centre the cars were double parked. Kids in baggy jeans and baseball caps were desultorily kicking a ball to one other. Loud ragamuffin music boomed from a ghetto-blaster on the footpath. Her relatives were gathered in groups by the staircase.

The John F. Kennedy Memorial Function Room had been decorated with flowers and tinfoil stars, strings of green, white and orange bunting. Plastic tables and chairs had been arranged around the edge of the long wooden dance floor. Women in aprons were moving between the tables, folding napkins into cones.

It was woollyback city in adult portions. When he closed his eyes he could practically hear 'Duelling Banjos'.

He sipped tensely at the day's third pint of lager and looked around at the guests. You could tell which ones were Irish, somehow. A waiter brought in a huge tray of drinks and put it down on a table. The groom's relations were sitting by themselves in the most distant corner, looking restrained and politely uncomfortable in their neat hired suits.

Near the alcove, some of the men were watching a tiny television that was showing previous Irish matches. A black and white Steve Heighway, dribbling a ball past defenders in tight shorts. Liam Brady looking shy and modest and handsome. Johnny Giles with a big bushy perm and magnificent sideburns, like a former member of Lynyrd Skynyrd who left for an ill-advised solo career.

Where was it now, the leg that had been cut off? Had a bit of it just been left *lying there* on the train tracks? Had some manky Parisian perv taken it home as a souvenir? Or had someone thought to pick it up and put it in a bag – a shopping bag, perhaps? – and bring it to the hospital on his fucking *bicyclette*? Would they be able to make her a plastic one? Or maybe a wooden one? Hadn't the guy who invented *The Muppets* or *Spitting Image* developed some shit-hot technique for manufacturing artificial limbs? There'd been a documentary about it on BBC 2, frighteningly late on a Sunday night.

He peered around the function room, wishing he was anywhere else. He didn't know where Siobhan was now, and he felt uneasy, already drunk. Women in pink dresses came wandering in from the bar. Someone put on a record and a few of the younger guests started half-heartedly gibbering to it. Then two old women got up and waltzed with each other, even though the record was a fifties rock and roll song. They waltzed steadily, martially, as though they had learned the steps out of a book. An old man jived with a nun.

He thought about his sister and how she would never be able to dance again. The realisation struck him as appalling.

Lunch was chicken with weirdly fizzy potato salad and slices of greasy ham. When Siobhan asked the waitress where the food had come from she said Tesco's in Neasden or possibly Crouch End. Liam said it tasted like it had walked the whole way. Everyone at the table talked about the match. Siobhan embarrassed him by asking whether Charlton Athletic was named after Jackie or Bobby.

The speeches finally started and went on for too long. The best man said he was looking forward to receiving a framed picture of the happy couple, 'preferably mounted', and everyone laughed as though keeping a promise. The groom stood up in a daze of embarrassment and thanked everybody for their help. When he mentioned the bride's mother as particularly deserving of gratitude, she stared down at her plate and forked meaningfully at her leftovers.

As the after-lunch drinks were being served, Liam noticed an old man on one crutch come shuffling into the room. He had eczema scars on his cheeks and a black patch over his right eye. A couple of the guests jumped up and ran to him as he limped painfully across the floor. He shook hands, kissed some of the women, then nudged one of them, pointed down at Siobhan. He put his finger to his lips as he edged over to the table and tapped her on the back. She turned.

'Uncle Peter,' she cried, jumping up, 'I wasn't sure you'd be over.'

He hugged her hard, kissed her cheek and then slapped his chest, panting slightly.

His high-pitched voice was frail.

'Oh well, Jackie Ryan ran me to Belfast. And I got the British Midland. I was treated in fine style so I was.'

'Liam,' she said, 'this is my uncle, Peter Toner. Peter, this is my passionate lover, Liam Hynes.'

'I'm delighted now to meet you, Liam. We've heard all about you over at home.'

'You have?'

'Liam's a bit of an intellectual, don't you know, Uncle Peter. He was in the university down in Dublin. He has brains to burn so he has.'

The old man inclined his head and weakly smiled. 'S'that, pet?'

'He was in the *university* in *Dublin*.'

'Oh aye, and what's this you were studying, Liam?'

'English.'

'Say again, son?'

'*English literature*.'

'Lovely. Lovely. Novels, is it?'

'Well yeah,' Liam admitted. 'Novels and poetry.'

The old man sighed. 'Queer how they do be calling it English, all the same. When the best practitioners are Irish. Would that be the word, Liam? Practitioners?'

'I suppose so.'

'Aye. When the monks and scholars of Ireland were saving civilisation, weren't the pagan English cantering around the forests in their naked pelts and they barely up to wiping their behinds?' He coughed. 'Still. Not to worry. Eh, son?'

Siobhan took her uncle by the arm, led him to a chair and poured him a glass of wine. In the far corner of the room, surrounded by ministering friends, the bride's mother was crying. A woman was on her knees beside her, holding her hand and offering copious napkins.

'What's the matter with thon mother of sorrows over there?' asked Peter Toner.

'She's upset, Uncle Peter, that Aisling didn't get married in the church.'

He shrugged, slopping wine over his chin. 'That woman's never happy unless she's something to be miserable about,' he said bleakly, and he pulled a tissue from his pocket and wiped his mouth.

A short, stocky old man with a moustache and a ruddy face barrelled over to the table, carrying two pints of Guinness.

'Is it the blaggard Toner?' the man shouted amiably. 'Would you look at the bloody get-up of it. Is that suit paid for yet, citizen?'

'That's Sean Moylan anyhow,' Peter Toner chuckled painfully. 'I'd know that ignorant Cork prattle of him a mile off, in the dark.'

The man plonked the pints down on the table and took Peter Toner in his arms. The two embraced lengthily, clapping each other on the back. 'How's the auld bastard. It's great to see you, *a Pheadar*.'

'Oh sure, I'm still trotting along anyhow, thank God.'

'The man above doesn't want us. He'd be afraid we'd start trouble.'

'You've met my niece Siobhan Kearney and her intended?'

'I've not had that pleasure,' Moylan said, shaking hands with them both. 'She didn't get the looks from your side anyway, Peter.'

'What's that? Speak up?'

'She's a *lovely looking girl*, I'm saying.'

'Oh aye. She is. Tell me, is your Maureen with you at all?'

'She's not been well since the bypass. I had to make her stay at home today.'

'Och, that's a shame now. Tell her I said hello.'

'I will of course, comrade. She'll be raging she missed you. But you're looking fit to beat the band yourself anyhow. You must be running after some woman and hoping she'll slow down?'

'What's that?'

'Is it a wife you're on the hunt for, with the cut of you?'

Peter Toner laughed. 'I'm too old for all that caper. Thank God, says you.'

'Oh, I'm thinking you've a bit of spirit left in your auld still, what?'

'Say again?'

'Siobhan, love,' said Sean Moylan, 'I could tell you stories about this comanche here. From the days gone by.'

The old man turned to him. 'What's that again, Sean? Speak up?'

'I'm saying I could tell them stories, *a Pheadar*. From the old days of struggle. *The yarns I could spin them, eh?*'

'Oh, aye.'

'Yes indeed, yes indeed. A man and a half. The friends we love are by our side and the foeman trembling fore us. Eh?'

'God,' said Peter Toner, in his womanly voice, 'weren't they great days, Sean? I think of them often. And I seen on the paper they buried poor Mike Twomey there last week in the Rosses.'

'Yes,' said Sean Moylan. 'There's few did as much as Mike, Lord have mercy on him. But he wasn't well at all the last few years. You could say it was a merciful release.'

'They're all going now, one by one. Joe Mullan, Shay Connolly, poor Mike gone now. And I seen the family said no to the tricolour being put on the coffin.' He tutted. 'That's the kind of times it's after coming to now. Not like the proud old days. The world's gone upside down entirely. You wouldn't know which end is the sleeves.'

Sean Moylan nodded again. 'But sure, won't there be more good days. Better days than ever were. The Republicans won't always be down.'

'Say again?'

'*Better days coming, Peter.*'

'Oh aye. Please God.'

They stood in silence while Peter Toner looked around the room as though he didn't recognise it.

'Did I ask you, Sean?' he said. 'Is your Maureen here?'

'She's away home in Cork and she busy with the grandchildren.'

'Is she?' Peter Toner squinted. 'That's a queer one, now. I thought I saw her just a minute ago and I coming in from the taxi.'

'There's none of us getting any younger, Peter, the dear knows, isn't that right?'

'That's right, aye.'

'Still, you crafty rogue, I never saw you look better in my life. If my nabs Charlton had you on his team, we'd run the English into the ground, what?'

'Eh?'

'You look *great*, Peter, so you do, in the suit and everything. You're like my nabs, John Travolta. Isn't that the one, Siobhan?'

'Where did you say she was? In Cork, was it, Sean?'

Moylan glanced at Siobhan and winked. 'We'll sit down now, Peter, and have a jar and a natter, what? Let these youngsters head off with themselves while you and I talk a bit of auld treason. Away you go, Liam boy, and give that girl a dance.'

She led him across to the middle of the crowded floor, put her hands on his waist and leaned her forehead on his shoulder. The room was stifling now. She looked up into his eyes and moved closer to him slowly. He could feel the softness of her body through her dress.

'He's a bit gaga today,' she said. 'I'm embarrassed.'

'Don't be.'

She smiled. 'You look beautiful, Liam.'

'So do you.'

They circled in each other's arms, while a slow song played. 'Last night was lovely, wasn't it, Liam?'

'We should have used a condom.'

'I suppose we should. I'm mad about you. God help me.'

He tried to laugh. 'Don't say that.'

'What's on your mind? Are you pissed off with me or something?'

He said nothing.

'Look, they'll have the stupid match on out in the bar. The lads here'll be slipping in to watch. I don't mind if you go with them.'

'It isn't the match.'

'What, then?'

He sighed and looked around the room. There was no easy way to put it.

'My sister had an accident in Paris last week. She swore me not to tell anyone until I spoke to my da. But it's doing my head in. She had to have her leg amputated.'

She stepped back from him, disbelief on her face. 'Fuck off,' she said. 'Patricia?'

'Yeah. I know. She rang me earlier about it.'

'Jesus Christ, Liam. You're not serious, are you?'

'I am.'

Her mouth was open wide and her eyes looked frightened. 'God almighty . . . Jesus, Liam . . . Did you not say you'd go over to her?'

He slid his hands into his pockets, feeling awkward and ashamed. 'I suppose I didn't think. But look, there's something else. Patricia asked me to ring up my father and tell him.'

She looked into his face. 'Oh Jesus, Liam. The poor dote. Fuck.'

'Yeah,' he said. 'Fuck is right.'

The disc jockey put on 'Danny Boy'. Over at the table, Peter Toner and his friend Sean Moylan seemed to be watching them.

In the lobby, his father's number was still engaged. He went into the bar and had a quick vodka by himself. The room was filling up: a semicircle of drinkers had formed around the television set. Eamon Dunphy appeared on the screen, saying that Ireland had only ever beaten England once. While he continued to talk, excitedly and passionately, they cut to a wide-angle shot of the stadium in Stuttgart. A uniformed brass band was marching in formation up and down the beautiful lime-green pitch, but the tune was drowned by the Irish fans singing. 'You'll Never Beat the Irish. You'll Never Beat the Irish'. There were close-up shots of some of their banners. Sallynoggin On Tour. Paul McGrath – The Black Pearl. Davy Keogh Says Hello.

He ordered a double whiskey.

'Irish or Scotch?' the barman asked him.

'Surprise me.'

When he came back into the function room, she was sitting in a corner with Peter Toner and Sean Moylan. All three of them seemed to be tipsy: she was laughing loudly and holding her hand up to her mouth. He had the feeling that the conversation had been terminated because of his presence. She said something in Irish. Moylan guffawed.

The plastic chairs had been arranged in a wide, untidy circle around the tables, which had been cleared of dishes and glasses. A few hairy young men produced guitars and fiddles; one had a bodhrán, another, an accordion. All of them looked like the image of Jesus on the Shroud of Turin. People were arguing about who was to start the singing.

'Any luck with your dad?' Siobhan said, peering up at him.

He shook his head and told her his father's line was still engaged. He sat down and took a sip of her drink.

'Get up there, Martin Thornton and give us a song,' shouted Sean Moylan to the bride's father.

'I will not indeed. I've no voice on me these days. Don't be mocking the afflicted.'

'"Revenge for Skibbereen",' someone cried out.

'"The Boys of the Old Brigade",' another called. But the bride's father shook his head and waved down the requests.

'Let's get the singing over,' a male voice shouted, 'because there's a match on soon that I want to watch!' Everyone laughed.

'Martin Thornton, get up for the love of Christ,' Moylan yelled again. People cheered and rattled their forks against their glasses.

'Jesus, all right, all right,' the bride's father sighed, 'I'll give you a quick few verses. Don't say youse weren't warned.'

He stood up to a chorus of whoops and whistles. The bridesmaid handed him a microphone. He pulled up the sleeve of his jacket and made a great show of looking at his watch.

'Well, Ireland do battle with England in a few minutes,' he said, with a blushing grin. 'God knows, it's not the first time in history that happened.'

'Nor the last,' someone shouted down the back. He smiled grimly and nodded.

'And I suppose, when you think about it, with Aisling and Steve, that's another wee match between Ireland and England.' People laughed and clapped appreciatively at the well-rehearsed joke. 'Ten to one I know who's going to win both of them, too,' he said, to more laughter.

His lined face took on a serious expression. 'I want to

spend a moment today to think of absent friends. Absent comrades, too, I'm not ashamed to say it. Brave men I thought would be here at my only daughter's wedding. But who won't be. No need to dwell on it. I only want to remember. They gave their all for their beliefs and were happy to give it. Sometimes Aisling here, she'll say to me, Daddy, forgive and forget. And the young people now, they think that's the way forward. Maybe they're right and maybe they're wrong. All I know is, I might forgive one day, when there's justice at last in my country. But I don't think I can ever forget.'

People shifted in their seats and looked at the floor. Seeming to sense this, he leaned back on his heels, in an attempt to parody his own seriousness away.

'Anyhow. There. That's enough of all that. I think you can imagine what Betty and myself said when her ladyship here arrived in home one fine May morning and announced she was marrying an English lad she was after meeting in the college in Birmingham.' The listeners laughed. 'Well, of course,' he went on, deadpan, 'we were thrilled skinny, so we were.' The guests chuckled louder. 'Personally,' he smiled, 'I think it's Ireland's revenge for eight hundred years of colonial oppression and I therefore give it my blessing.' There was a great gust of laughter and a round of applause. Even the groom's family were clapping.

'To be serious,' he continued, 'Steve is the finest lad you'd meet in a year's travel. He's no lad, in fact. He's a man. And a fine one. Betty and I have come to know him and respect him for a hard-working decent young man. A credit to his parents, Nigel and Rosemary, who we welcome here today. He'd never tell you a lie. He's good, through and through. I know he loves my daughter. And that's good enough for me. And we welcome him into the family today. I've a new son now. I'm proud of him and Aisling and I wish them every happiness as they set out in life. We'll always be here for them. You all feel the same. As for Steve being English, well, I think of the words of my late noble lord, the Duke of Wellington—'

'Ah shut up and sing, will you,' someone shouted.

'A rebel song,' another yelled.

'I was thinking earlier about what I might sing today,' he said, 'with the match being on, and something occurred to me. And I hope our English friends won't be embarrassed or think me impolite, if I tell you that when those lads in green go out on that field in a short time, there's another field I'll be thinking of, closer to home.'

Silence descended. 'What's this is the way it goes?' he said, staring up at the ceiling. He closed his eyes then, and started to sing very slowly, in a faltering baritone that might once have been powerful.

'When boyhood's fire was in my blood
I read of ancient freemen,
For Greece and Rome who bravely stood,
Three hundred men and three men;
And then I prayed I yet might see
Our fetters rent in twain,
And Ireland, long a province, be.
A nation once again.'

One of the young men strummed his guitar, trying to gauge the key. Others turned to him, scowling and shaking their heads, and he put the instrument back on his knees.

'And from that time, through wildest woe,
That hope has shone a far light,
Nor could love's brightest summer glow
Outshine that solemn starlight.'

'Go on,' shouted some of the guests. 'Good man, Martin.'
'Keep her lit.' Siobhan put her fingers in her mouth and
blearily whistled. The groom's family were looking
uncomfortable.

'It seemed to watch above my head
In forum, field and fane,
Its angel voice sang round my bed,
A nation once again.'

He leaned forward and splayed his fingers on the table,
leaning his weight on it, sucking in a deep breath. A long
moment passed. He appeared to have forgotten the words.
He looked down at his wife. She whispered something to
him, but he didn't seem to hear what she was saying. He
began to sing the next verse, then stopped again. He blushed,
rubbing his lips with the back of his wrist. His wife stood
up slowly and took him by the hand. She looked into his
eyes, smiling, as she started to sing. He nodded as they sang
together now, her voice sweet and clear, and quivering a
little on the grace notes.

'It whisper'd too, that freedom's ark
And service high and holy,
Would be profaned by feelings dark
And passions vain or lowly;

For, freedom comes from God's right hand,
And needs a Godly train;
In brotherhood we pray our land
A nation once again.'

He turned and threw his arms around his wife, kissing her hair, crushing his forehead against her neck. The bride went over, weeping, hugging them. Tears were streaming down her father's face as he resumed his seat. Cheers and applause filled the room. He raised his hands to acknowledge it, shaking with emotion.

'Up the Republic!' someone called, to fierce shouts and whistles.

Liam felt Siobhan's glance on him. 'It's a great old song,' she said. 'Isn't it?'

He felt the drink pulse through his veins, the muscles tighten in his throat. 'It's a load of fucking shite. A nation, my sainted hole.'

Her face purpled suddenly and she tried to smile. 'Don't say that, Liam. People have strong feelings.'

'If they've such strong feelings what are half of them doing living over here?' In the corner of his eye he could see that Sean Moylan was looking at him now.

'It's only a song,' she said. 'What harm is there in a song?'

'It's twenty-four-carat bollocks,' he said.

'Do you hear this terrible West Brit, Uncle Peter?'

The old man turned, his one eye bleary. 'What's he saying, love?'

'Leave it, Siobhan,' Liam sighed.

'He's saying it's all shite, Peter, everything in our history.

That's what they all think down in Dublin, of course. All too busy being cool to give a damn about anything else.'

Peter Toner said nothing. He looked around himself like a man who had just woken up in a strange room.

'Trendy little so-called liberals,' she continued. 'Nelson Mandela on their T-shirts. Blinkers on their eyes. When there's people in their own country were third-class citizens, murdered on the streets of Derry.'

'Want to talk about murder, Siobhan? Let's talk about Darkley.'

She continued, riding over him. 'They'd hand the whole place back to the Brits in the morning. That's what they really want.'

'What they want is peace,' Liam said, bitterly, 'If it's okay with the Islington Branch of the Troops Out Campaign.'

Peter Toner raised a finger and wagged it from side to side. 'Ireland and England should never be in bed together, son. No peace down that road. Nor ever will be.'

'What are you on about? They *are* in bed together.'

'Pardon me?'

'And what good ever came of it, Liam?' Sean Moylan said. 'Can you answer me that? In all fairness. What good?'

'Would you go back to sleep.'

Siobhan stood up, shaking with rage. 'Who do you think you are? Don't you fucking *dare* speak to him like that.'

Moylan laughed as he reached out and took her by the hand. She sat back down, folded her arms and looked away.

'Maybe we'll leave the politics for another day, Liam,' he said. 'We all want a happy occasion.'

'Politics, man? Shooting people in the back of the head?

Smashing their kneecaps with concrete blocks? Send me your manifesto some time, I'm sure it's a great read.'

The smile froze slowly on Moylan's face. 'Hold on now, buck. Nobody's saying mistakes weren't made. That happens in any war situation.'

'Mistakes, man? Enniskillen? You think blowing up old-age pensioners for a united Ireland is a good idea?'

'That should never have happened. I could never defend it. It was an evil thing to do and no true Republican could say otherwise.'

'Listen, blow it out your arse, man. No one's listening any more.'

'That's lovely talk now, from an educated person. The young people today, they haven't a notion, do they, Peter?'

'You think?' Liam said. 'I've bad news for you, pal.'

'What's that?'

'They don't give a flying fuck. Ireland versus England. To me, man, that's a football match, and that's all it is. That's all it ever should be, too.'

'Is it my fault it isn't?'

'It's sure not mine.'

Peter Toner looked up and tried to smile, his old head quivering. 'Maybe that's what people fought for,' he said, 'all those years. So you'd have the right not to care. To live your own lives. To sit you there and watch thon football match without a trouble in the world. Ever think of it that way, son?'

'No, I didn't. But thanks a bunch. It's all clear to me now.'

'You ignorant little Donnybrook smartarse,' Siobhan said. 'Socialist, my hole. Putting posters in the Common

Room. Buying albums by The Clash to play in Mummy's drawing room when she's out at the golf club. You'd have shot James Connolly for a fiver.'

He put his glass down and made for the doorway, bumping into the groom, who was drunk now and staggering around in an embrace with his best man, crying and telling him he loved him. Halfway across the empty dance floor she caught up with him and grabbed his arm.

'If you walk out that door you can fuck away off.'

'Scare me some more. I'm terrified, Siobhan.'

She turned away from him, suddenly sobbing, bowed her head and wiped her eyes. He reached out and touched her face but she slapped his hand away. 'You had to spoil everything,' she wept. 'You just had to. Like always. Everything has to be about *you*.'

'Oh thanks. Fucking thanks a bunch. *What about my sister's leg?* I'm really sorry here, honey, but I've got more on my mind than you and your four green fucking fields, you know what I mean?'

Tears were spilling down her face. 'If it wasn't that, Liam, it'd be something else. You take the good out of everything. I don't know why. Just get out and leave me alone.'

His father's phone was still engaged, so he went into the bar.

The room was packed. The match had just begun. One young man was wearing a green Afro wig. A cloud of purplish cigarette smoke had formed under the fluorescent lights.

The commentator's voice buzzed as he named the players

in a speculative English move. 'Stevens . . . To Sansom . . . To Peter Beardsley . . . To the mighty John Barnes of Liverpool.' People were sitting around the room in groups, some of them wearing green shirts or scarves. 'Beardsley to Wright . . . To Robson . . . England advance . . . But it's a free kick to Ireland . . . Free kick to Ireland in the sixth minute . . . A little . . . debate about it from Stevens. But German referee Herr Kirschen very definite there.'

'How's it going for us?' Liam asked the barman.

'All over us like a fuckin' rash. Runnin' us ragged.' He filled the glass and placed the pint on the counter.

'On the house, bud,' he said. 'You look like you need it.'

A deafening roar exploded. People jumped to their feet, wildly punching the air and screaming. A table overturned, sending glasses and ashtrays spilling. Teenage girls in Ireland shirts hurried in from the corridor. A fat man Liam didn't know grabbed him and kissed him. He pushed his way through the room and towards the television in the corner, dimly aware of the urgent crackle of the commentator's voice, but the noise of cheering in the bar was too loud to make out what it was saying.

The stadium was a riotous mass of fluttering green flags, the camera panning along the whole length of one of the stands before it cut to a scrum of green-shirted players hugging one another. Players were running and diving into the pile of bodies, followed by substitutes still in their tracksuits. A linesman ran on to the pitch and bawled at the players. Peter Shilton picked the ball from the back of his net and swung a boot desultorily at the goalpost. Ray Houghton broke from the scrum and tottered like a man drunk with bliss to the touchline, where he stood with his eyes closed, arms outstretched towards the ecstatic crowd. He jabbed at the air with his fingers. The shot showed the back of his body, the swaying field of green in front of him. They were singing his name. He raised the hem of his shirt to his lips and kissed it. Packie Bonner was down on his hunkers, staring at the grass. He closed his eyes, bowed his head, and made the sign of the cross. Jack Charlton's face looked like it was carved out of granite. There was a long, tight close-up of his haughty profile. Someone in the dugout nudged him. He turned slowly towards the camera, half smiling, and casually shrugged, as though none of it mattered and he'd rather be fishing. People in the bar howled with joy.

'*Goarn, Jack, yeh fuckin' man yeh.*'

A close-up of the scoreboard now filled the screen. REPUBLIC OF IRELAND: 1 ENGLAND: 0

'*Yesssssssssssssssss*'

And then the action replay began. Kevin Moran's free kick drifted down near the touchline. Stevens and Wright were momentarily confused. Sansom sliced at the ball, sending it skywards. It seemed to fall slowly to John Aldridge, who nodded it to Houghton, who headed it powerfully past the flailing keeper and into the net. The crowd in the bar roared again, as though it was the first time they had seen it.

Liam could hear applause and cheering from all over the building now, from below and above, from outside in the street. In a window across the laneway a middle-aged woman was waving a tricolour. The bride's father was standing in the doorway with the young strip-wearing boy from the registry office in his arms.

A heavy man with damp broken-veined eyes grabbed Liam by the lapels and roared into his face. 'That'll fucking teach them. That'll teach them, won't it? *Teach the fuckin' English a lesson for themselves now.*'

Liam had the strange feeling that if he pointed out Jack Charlton was English, the man might actually head-butt him.

It was half an hour later when he finally got through to his father.

'My Jesus, Liam-boy. That's awful news.'

'Look, Dad, do you think you should go over or something? Do Ryanair fly to Paris? Should I book you a ticket?'

'Well . . . I'm a bit busy just now, Liam. Can I talk to you later?'

'Busy?'

'Well, yeah. I'm watching the match. I'll give her a ring in a while.'

'You're what?'

'I'm watching the match here with Uncle Joe and George from the office. Mighty goal, wasn't it? Do you think we can hang on till the end?'

'Christ Almighty, Dad, I'm saying your only daughter has just lost a fucking leg, man.'

'Well I know, but – *oh Jesus – oh fuck! – oh Jesus Christ!*'

'What?'

'Packie's just pulled off this *magnificent* save. I've never seen anything like it in my natural life! Jesus, but this is a game and a half, isn't it, son?'

'There's one or two factors kind of interfering with my enjoyment of it, Dad.'

'Yes, a neutral might feel Lineker's a bit off form. But England's difficulty is Ireland's opportunity, as Pearse used to say. Padraig Pearse, I mean. Not Stuart.'

There was silence for a moment, and then his father gave a snuffle of guilty laughter.

'I'm not seeing the humour of the situation here, Dad.'

'Sure Patricia's as fit as you or me,' he chuckled. 'One leg my arse. Sorry, Liam, son. I was in on the caper all along. The two girls hatched it between them. They wanted to play a bit of a joke on you.'

'A joke?'

'Sure I thought you'd cop it in thirty seconds flat, Liam. Otherwise I'd never have gone along with it at all.'

'What, Dad?'

'Siobhan and Patricia cooked it up between them. I thought you'd see through it straight away. Did you not know they were winding you up, no? It's such a ridiculous story.'

Liam paused, his heart thundering. Somewhere above him he could hear people singing. *'Who Put the Ball in the English Net? Hough-Ton, Hough-Ton.'*

'Well, yeah, Dad. Obviously. I mean, Christ, what do you think I am here?'

'One Packie Bonner. There's only one Packie Bonner.'

'Ooh-ah, Paul McGrath, say ooh-ah Paul McGrath.'

He put the phone down. Siobhan was standing in the lobby.

'You fucking monster,' he said.

'I know,' she said. 'I'm really sorry, Liam.'

'No,' he said. 'The Nazis were sorry. You fucking . . . unbelievable . . .'

'I didn't reckon you'd get so upset. I thought you'd cop that it was only messing.'

He sat slowly down on the stairs and put his fingertips to his boiling face.

'Maybe I'll head back inside,' she said.

He held up his middle finger. 'Swivel on it.'

In the back of the minicab she held his hand. They sped through the empty city, both of them drunk and tired.

Westminster Bridge had been closed off by the police, and a long line of cars and lorries had formed. Plain-clothes officers stood on the pavement with machine guns in their hands, while soldiers searched the cars. The Big Ben clock said it was half-past two.

The driver cursed under his breath, turned out of the lane and sped back down the street.

'Do you think we'll ever get married?' Siobhan said.

'Urgh, God,' he groaned. 'I think I'm going to be sick.'

'Always changing the subject.'

'Patricia's only got one leg,' he giggled.

'She's legless.'

'You're one fucking wagon.'

'I'm not,' she said. 'I'm nice, really.'

He rolled down the window and cool air flooded the car. 'So Uncle Peter's never going to speak to me again,' he said. 'Probably gonna have me kneecapped.'

'He told me he thought you were great.'

'I'm sure he did.'

'He's dying, Liam,' she said, quietly. 'He's riddled with cancer. He'll be gone in a few months.'

The driver started to hum along with the radio.

'Gone by Christmas, they reckon.'

'I'm sorry, Siobhan.'

Outside on the street, a group of dejected-looking English fans trudged along, Union Jacks wrapped around hunched, slumped shoulders.

'So did Aisling enjoy her wedding day?'

'Yeah. I think so.'

As they turned on to Lancaster Place, the blue flashing light of a police car appeared in the rear-view mirror.

'I feel sick, Siobhan,' he said. 'It's all your fault.'

She didn't seem to be listening to him. She was staring ahead, softly gnawing her lip. Then she turned to him and smiled and touched the side of his face. 'I love you so much,' she said. 'I'm sorry, I swear.'

'Yeah. I love you too.'

'Try not to get so excited about it.'

'Sorry. I get scared. It's my nature.'

She put her hand on his thigh. 'We'll be okay,' she said, gently. 'I wouldn't ever hurt you again, Liam. It was a horrible thing to do. I don't know what possessed us. It was one of those stupid ideas that started as a dare. I'm totally ashamed. So's Patricia.'

The police car pulled out into the middle of the road and started to overtake. The officer in the driver's seat stared in through the window with a frown on his thin face as he motioned for the driver to stop.

The night was surprisingly cold. Gulls whirled in the wind. In the middle distance a burglar alarm was wailing. Towards the east, the dome of St Paul's loomed over the city, and the blue lights of the NatWest tower glimmered in the mist.

By the time they had finished searching the car Siobhan was asleep in his arms on the edge of the pavement.

'Sorry about this,' the policeman said. 'We had a bomb scare earlier.'

'Yeah.'

'You watch the match?'

'Not all of it, no. I had to go to a wedding.'

'You heard who won?'

'I heard. One nil.'

'Only a game though, eh?'

'Only a game.'

The sergeant pointed his torch at him. 'Bloody get you next time, though.'

'It's a date. Goodnight.'

Siobhan stirred. He held her tightly and kissed the corner of her mouth. She murmured and twined her fingers through his. And she looked so beautiful now, and so happy too, that for one long moment he didn't want to wake her up and take her home. But the taxi driver said he was in a hurry, and he needed to be somewhere else. And anyway, it was too late for love.

Death of a Civil Servant

Dublin, 2004

His father has descended into fretfulness with age. Untouchable crime lords. Stray dogs roaming the shopping centre. The insolence of teenagers. Sicknesses among the neighbours. Cancer stalks the lawns of his mind at night, pointing *that one* at the lamplit windows. Undependable taxi drivers. Immigrants. Weather. He murmurs of his anxieties with the troubled watchfulness of a child in an unfathomable world.

'I wouldn't mind only there's so many of them. I don't object to a few. But now every dog and divil has one working in his shop.'

Senan Mulvey does not answer. He concentrates on the road. The interior of the car is too hot and he is smoking. Earlier this evening, he wrote four brief notes. They are leaning against the kettle in his kitchen. On the worktop is an envelope containing a copy of his will and a request that there be no prayers at his funeral.

He is aged thirty-seven, a civil servant, a statistician. He has been separated almost two years from his wife, a university teacher. Their only child is dead.

His father's wheezing gentleness, distracted, muted, like

the rambling of a faded soprano who lives alone in a maison-
ette where she gossips to the teacups for company. There
was a day many years ago, in Connemara or Kerry, when
Senan Mulvey saw an old currach that had been dumped
in a bog. Cross-bench crushed and buckled, rotting tiller
wrenched askew, it had sunk to its oarlocks in the oozing,
black peat. Often, of late, when he thinks of his father, the
image has appeared in his thoughts.

'God, we have to pull our weight like, I'm not saying
we don't. I mean plenty of our own had to go away in the
bad times, Lord knows. We'd've been rightly scuppered altogether if America didn't take them. But you'd wonder if
there's any halt to be called to it.'

A quarter-moon behind the obelisk on the summit of
Killiney Hill. The undercarriage scrapes on a speed-bump.
His father clicks his tongue like someone chirking a horse
and the road begins a winding descent. Old houses of new
millionaires set back from the avenue, sombre electric gates,
signboards of silhouetted mastiffs, security floodlights
blazing on as the wind trips their circuits. Twenty miles in
the distance must be the mountains of Wicklow but it is
too dark to see them now. He imagines being on the
Sugarloaf – gorse in mist, the smell of goats. He grinds
through the gears – it has begun to rain – and a susurration
fills the car as the radio signal ebbs. The rain summons
presences as his father talks on. But Senan Mulvey does not
believe in ghosts.

'I don't mean to be racialist. It isn't that I don't like
them.'

'I know.'

'They're grand people, give them their due. Hard-working.

Lovely manners. And they're family people too, they're very good with their children. Did you ever notice that, Senan? They don't be vexed with them crying like we do. And you don't see the Africans begging, not like certain little gutties we have of our own. It's only there's an awful lot of them suddenly. You just feel – I don't know.'

He waits for his father to say what he feels. But his father falls silent and looks ahead of himself at the windscreen. Men of his father's age are uncomfortable saying what they feel. They're unaccustomed to being asked, lack the language to answer. It doesn't mean that they're insensible, only that they're lost, with the inarticulacy of babies wanting to howl because they can do nothing else. If you want to know the fears of an old man like his father you have to raise a subject of seeming unimportance, preferably while not meeting his eyes: politics, or gardening, or the price of things. The radio is playing quietly and the glass has begun to fog. It is almost midnight now. He is driving his father into Wicklow.

His father, a retired Garda sergeant, is treasurer of a walkers' club that undertakes this arduous hike once a year. They start out at Ballinalea at one in the morning, slog overnight into the city, all the way to Dublin Castle, through Greystones, Bray, Killiney, Blackrock, the sleeping villages of the southside coastline. They follow the DART tracks. No compass is needed. Most of the hikers have completed the trek so many times that a map would be collegially laughed at.

You couldn't trust a taxi man to collect you at eleven. Nobody these days would honour a commitment. That was the problem with Ireland now: a fickleness of spirit, people only it in for the buck, everything contingent on a more lucrative door not opening. Senan Mulvey had offered to drive his father to the meeting point. It would be a way of saying goodbye.

Posters for a Sinn Fein meeting on the lamp posts at Ballybrack crossroads. The words *Sweet Home Alabama* spray-painted across a supermarket's shutter with an attempt at a Confederate flag. Young people taking shelter in the forecourt of a petrol station; the attendant gazing out at the trio of pumps from behind the security window.

Rain thrums heavier as they cross the little bridge north of Shankill and soon afterwards enter County Wicklow. The motorway is quiet. He takes the exit for the Sally Gap. In his apartment, in Donnybrook, near the television station and the university, is a coil of scarlet hosepipe he purchased last weekend at a garden centre off the Naas dual carriageway. He left it in its shrink-wrap for a couple of days. Tonight at the apartment, he opened it.

The artificial lake in the grounds of the university campus can be seen from his living room window. The water tower, too, a vast tulip bulb of concrete, and the roof of the students' gymnasium in which he received his degree sixteen years ago. It was a morning that seems part of some other man's life: a bright-hearted, much-befriended, scrawny student radical, a believer in things that don't happen. In winter the view is clearer; the trees outside his window are stark. The leaves dappling in summertime slightly obscure the scene. Wilderweed sprouts in the window box. The birds in the branches – thrushes, a robin – regard him through the double glazing like baffled neighbours. They have witnessed strange occurrences: a man staring at them, crying, pacing naked in the quarter-light of approaching dawns, dressing himself in yesterday's clothes having had no sleep at all and gathering his papers for work. A cat once climbed the cypress – three storeys – impossible – and having failed to snag its quarry watched Senan Mulvey fully half an hour while he wept in a dressing robe that had once belonged to his wife. A London hotel monogram on the ripped breast pocket, the belt-loops frayed asunder by over-laundering.

The car obeys its driver. The engine surges. There is a bottle of powerful sedatives on the draining board in the kitchen. He has had them several years, since fracturing his ankle and fibula. It was Christmastime; they were in Manhattan, Senan Mulvey and his wife, a resolvedly peaceable couple on work secondment to New York, the envy of their less intrepid, more settled friends. She had taken a notion to go skating in Central Park. He had implored her to go easy, not to stray from him. The flit of scudding blades, the frosted tree trunks gleaming, a fatboy in plastic antlers hawking Statue of Liberty key rings, her blasphemies as she skidded and veered. She was seven weeks pregnant; they had told nobody the news. The freeze seemed to come needling through the buttonholes of their padded overcoats, American, like duvets with sleeves. Wintering. Slithering. Ears livid with cold. A concentrate of happiness, of utter acceptance of the fates, such as can spate with giddying suddenness in a city of New York's verticalities.

Festive muzak as they clung to one another, ridiculing, messing. Dublin far away and unconsidered. A sublet to go home to. The phones switched off. A bottle of good Merlot and a fire-log in the grate and the Cuban takeout from the cantina on Prince Street. Nothing to get up for. A Bach CD playing. Glenn Gould humming an arpeggio as they fucked on the couch like ardent lovers in the arousal of their first shared home, not people who had been married five years. Often he has the sensation that this memory has entered him physically, that some secret lobe of his cortex designed to store up protections had downloaded it as a bulwark against all that was to come, for it has visited him in dreams and in sudden irruptions of the day – snow on the fur of her hood, the sky billowing around him, the rime-frosted ice as his forehead slammed into the barrier, the key-ring seller laughing, the eternity before pain bites, and the nauseating, impossible, world-blackening thirst that comes with the shock of a fall. Skaters trying to help him up. A soldier saying *Dude, that shit is fractured*. The gargoyles of marble eagles on the cornices of a skyscraper. A monstrously obese paramedic with confetti on his epaulettes, speaking curtly at first and then with maternal benevolence, addressing his patient as *Fightin' Irish* or *Buddy*. And the knowledge, as intensely present as the agony and the eagles, that the pain did not matter for he was not alone to endure it. Marie-Thérèse would help him and it would one day be a story. *The Christmas I fell skating in New York*. What they charged us for the ambulance. The embarrassment. The crutches. It became one of Marie-Thérèse's quips, a sort of private endearment, to say that if the baby were a boy they should christen him 'Adam', for he was made in the city of the fall.

He has the use of a garage in the car park of the apartment block. He will wait until his neighbours have left for work.

His father is staring at the façade of the radio, which blinks subtly and rhythmically, as though trying to placate something. The midnight news comes on but there is a rustle of static. The mountains interfering with the signal.

'Would they not be better off at home? In a place they *understand*, like. What has them over here, Senan? Is it handouts?'

'I don't know.'

'They must have families over beyond. Would you not think they'd miss them?'

'Yes.'

'A wife, maybe. Or little ones. And they without a father in life. It's sad when you think of it. God love them, all the same. Isn't it terrible unfair, Senan, the way the world is gone so wrong?'

'Yes.'

'I mean plenty of our own had to go, I'm not saying they didn't. In the Famine times and later. Jesus help them, they'd no choice. All around here, too. Wicklow was hit terrible. Whole townlands died in Wicklow. Little weanlings starved. And that bitch Queen Victoria giving five pounds to the relief fund. Same as you'd give a dogs' home. Imagine.'

'I know.'

'Even in my own day. I was all for going myself. I was often sorry I didn't. Boston I'd have liked. They've great lives for themselves over in Boston, I believe. But Mammy never wanted to. And she wouldn't be said. So I suppose we can't be giving out and the boot on the other foot.'

'No.'

'But if only there wasn't *so many*. We'll be sorry before we're finished. They're in the garage, the Tesco — God between us, they're everywhere. Jimmy Dunne has one of them working for him above in the Post Office. Quiet sort, he is. And he giving out the pensions. Does be looking at you queer-like, same as *yourself* is the blow-in. Or you're not *entitled* to the pension when you paid into it forty years. I do often want to say to him "I've a bullet in me yet, lad." I've a bullet in me *yet*, buck. And I *earned* what's mine. And you needn't be giving me anything *isn't* mine, thank you. You can keep it so you can. It's not wanted.'

'I'm trying to concentrate on the road, Dad. I think we're after going wrong.'

'An engineer, the same hero. Back in wherever he hails from. Liberia, I think. Is that in Africa, Senan?'

'Yes.'

'I don't like to say anything. I wouldn't want to offend the man. But I think they're after making a great mistake.'

'Who?'

'The government. The authorities. The way they let so many come in. We'll be sorry before we're finished, you mark my words. I suppose you saw a lot of them in New York. But New York is New York.'

'I suppose that's true,' Senan Mulvey says quietly.

'Exactly,' says his father. 'But who listens?'

It was August when she left. A Bank Holiday weekend. For weeks, he told nobody she had gone. Half believing she would return, he would buy food enough for two on his way home to Seapoint from his work in the city. One night he convinced himself he had heard her latchkey in the front door. But there was nobody outside when he opened it.

If people phoned, which happened rarely, he revealed nothing of her leaving. He bantered, endured jokes; made vague agreements to meet. And then her father called to the cottage one autumnal Sunday morning, saying he wished to collect her books and a few remaining clothes. He looked frightened, close to tears. She would not be returning. He did not know what had happened. Marie-Thérèse was with a friend. He had been asked to give the message that a solicitor would be in touch. He would not reveal her whereabouts. He was very sorry, he said. His loyalty had to be to his daughter.

To be in the cottage without her soon came to be unbearable. After work, he would go alone to a film in the city, or to a performance at the concert hall, or a play. Afterwards he would drift around Grafton Street or the Liffeyside quays, taking his meal in some late night café or burger joint in Temple Bar, only returning to the cottage in the small hours. Before long, even those hours could not be faced there. He took a room in an inexpensive bed-and-breakfast near the coach station on Gardiner Street, a place used by backpackers and recently arrived immigrants, and in the false bravery that can follow trauma continued a night course he had been attending in the city, for little other reason than to occupy an evening. His wife's going had made him a man of timetables, neurotically filled schedules. It was one of the fruits of despair.

Play-writing had been a secret interest at college – he had written skits and little satirical sketches for the student drama society, had once helped a talented classmate translate a Brendan Behan play from Irish – and in the thunderstorms of self-confrontation that had followed the death of his daughter, he had dared to wonder if this might be the truer calling his mother used to say so few people realised they had, and if it was laziness or weakness of character or some phobic dread of fulfilment that had coaxed him so successfully into its avoidance. Strange, the escapes found by speechless grief. Something had restrained him, he came to feel.

Perhaps it had been his marriage. So it seemed to him now. For a season after she left, he continued at the night college, even as his imaginings of self-destruction, obliteration, became the sirens of every awakening. His fellow students were younger; had works-in-progress, passions. They dressed coolly, had seen everything, traded knowledgeable critiques, were fluent in the terminologies of stagecraft. They were hard-working, ambitious, implacably self-believing and saw play-writing as a stepping stone to the movies. Not one of them was like any young Irish person he remembered from his own youth. One girl had interviewed David Mamet for her website. His own rare contributions were tolerated with that particular civility we reserve for difficult children not our own. 'Workshop' was a verb. 'Ask' was a noun. The tutor remarked one evening at the end of the session: 'Senan certainly gave us a big ask with what he workshopped tonight.' He could read it for the dismissal it was.

Rumours came to him in October that his wife had begun a new relationship. He was prescribed Prozac but it made him agitated, easily confused. He began seeing more of his father, mainly because there were so few other options. The invitation was extended to move back into the family home. 'Your bed is still there, Senan. It's a shame to see it wasted.' He declined it repeatedly and his father stopped offering, in the end helping Senan Mulvey, on a Saturday afternoon, to move his suitcases and boxed belongings into a rental apartment in Donnybrook that was small and belligerently new. It reeked of paint and fresh carpet, the cheap kind seen in modern offices. The taps in the kitchen sink still wore polythene sheaths. It was 'grand', remarked his father, an ambiguous adjective when used by any Irish person about a dwelling.

The coastguard-sentry's cottage Senan Mulvey had owned with his wife was sold hurriedly, cheaply, to the first of its bidders. It yielded little when the several mortgages were repaid along with the loans they had taken for renovation. Her solicitor wrote soon afterwards, saying Senan could keep the furniture if he wished – she had accepted a lectureship in Scotland, it would be too expensive to ship. In the end it was given to a charity.

He found it difficult to sleep, despite being permanently tired. He began leaving on the hallway lamps throughout the night. One lunch hour he purchased a night light intended for infants in an expensive store on Nassau Street that sold designer clothes for children. 'They're terrors when they don't sleep,' the assistant remarked. 'But it doesn't last for ever. Thank God.' He returned to cigarettes after seven years without. His blood pressure, he was warned, was in the pre-hypertension range.

Darkness frightened him. He would find himself half-dazed on the balcony at dawn, looking down into the car park, at the trees and new flowerbeds, the office workers in suits leaving early to beat the gridlock, the lorries trundling past from the ferry-port at Dun Laoghaire. He would fantasise about others' lives – those of truck drivers, seamen; people free of domesticities, wanderers. A homeless man tramped the dual carriageway in a grimy tartan blanket, bearing a staff like a prophet's, with a dog on a string. It was rumoured he had once been a Professor of Mathematics at Trinity, had suffered some brutalising loss – failed love was involved. His beard reached his navel – people said he had never cut it. Senan Mulvey would observe him early in the mornings, a Moses rummaging in the skips.

Often he imagined what it would be like to leave the apartment and start walking. South into Wicklow, or westward towards Galway. To throw his key ring and wallet into a drain as he went, or take the daybreak ferry-sailing to Holyhead or Liverpool, with no plan except not to return. Could a life be walked away from? How long would it take them to find him? Perhaps others had such facile, middle-class fantasies. Perhaps everyone had, of every class.

He had inherited his mother's books; tea chests of them filled his spare bedroom, piles of paperbacks in the wardrobes and cupboards. He turned to O'Casey, Kate O'Brien, Mary Lavin, old ballads – anything for distraction, a way of passing the night hours – but often what he read became a projection or a mirroring of the hurts he was attempting to evade. His marriage seemed to loom at him from the cheap lines of spy thrillers, from love poems, Dickensian ghettos, from Orwell, from Joyce. If an aria of parted lovers began playing on the radio, he would switch it off immediately.

A hard Christmas came and went. The season began to turn. He drove often into rural Wicklow, walked the Department of Forestry woodlands, the fishery at Annamoe, the ruined monasteries and graveyards, sensing that something subsisted in the landscape into which his brokenness could be resolved, a reconciliation at least made visible.

Many dawns found him haunting the lakesides, the cold mountain paths. Dusks saw him driving the boreens near Avoca or the Glen of Imaal, often in the wake of the coaches and minibuses that brought tourists on excursions to places seen in successful Irish films. The buses inched heavily through the hedgerow-bounded lanes. The cows in the fields stared at them.

Poets and revolutionaries had haunted these hills. As a boy, he had been touched by their stories. He drifted into a rereading of the old gazetteers of Wicklow that his mother had gone through a phase of collecting. As a teenager he had taken a bookish schoolboy's interest in local history, had occasionally done assignments about it as homework. The curiosity had been coloured by identification, for Senan Mulvey's parents had often visited Glendalough and had scrimped for several years to buy a ramshackle cabin there, a lace-maker's abandoned hut. The plan had been to renovate it as a holiday retreat, but that had never happened, the days of their marriage were numbered. In the end his mother bequeathed him the field in which the cabin had rotted. Since her death, he had never gone to see it.

She loved dark, serious music, novels that had been banned. She was beautiful, damaged and turbulent. One Good Friday she was apprehended for shoplifting in an exclusive department store on Grafton Street. She told the store detective she was a battered wife whose husband had deserted her, and that her son, who was watching her inter-rogation in petrified shame, had recently been diagnosed as autistic. It was a powerful performance. The detective released them. Before her marriage she had been a trainee designer with a jeweller in the city. People said she looked like a film star, and before her drinking years she did. She told lies for no reason her son could see or understand: she had met President Kennedy during his visit to Wexford, had once seen the ghost of a stillborn child; a distant marital aunt of hers, a woman disgraced by a pregnancy, had been a housemaid to Oscar Wilde's widow. She told stories to everyone. No one believed her. Her son had found it heartbreaking, this trait and what it meant: her desire to be at one with the people in books and legends, her powerlessness before her own imagination. It had marked him, he came to feel while he was still quite young. It would always be a part of his inheritance.

He paged through his mother's books now in an enervated pointlessness, unable any more to progress chronologically through a text, but dipping, skipping soliloquies, back-turning, over-advancing, conjecturing distractedly about the lives of people mentioned in editors' acknowledgements ('my wise friend and colleague', 'my beloved wife'), tracing references in indexes, hoping to catch out the indexer in an oversight. Often he would happen upon passages his mother had underlined and he would wonder why she had thought them worthy of emphasis. It was as though the words he had first encountered in adolescence were themselves an eluding landscape in which some holy well of healing might be stumbled upon.

One Sunday evening he found himself driving through a rainstorm to Bray, with the intention of seeing again the district of his childhood. He had slowly driven the 1970s estate, its cul-de-sacs and hedged crescents, as though a ghost he needed to encounter might be glimpsed in the gardens. The sodden lawns were tidy, the GAA field deserted;

lamps glowed in the pebble-dashed houses. The little news-agent's around the block was now an all-night Spar. In the side garden of the semi in which he had lived his first four-teen years, a granny flat had been built, squeezed in. He had fallen asleep in the car at some point, awakened close to dawn, driven slowly to the seafront, past the snooker halls and fortune tellers and shuttered amusement arcades, and parked by the Martello tower. Rain dreeping from the cluster of old sycamores by the gateway. A bend in the drive where the gravel was wearing thin. A trio of wild swans in a leafless oak. From the avenue could be seen the narrow windows through which the soldiers had once kept watch, star-shaped holes in the glass.

Vague night-thoughts of returning to New York cohered violently one morning. As though watching a frenzied char-acter in someone else's story, he realised he had withdrawn the last savings from their joint account and was purchasing a ticket in the Aer Lingus office on Dawson Street. Yes, he wished to go this afternoon, he told the assistant urgently – a family funeral in Manhattan. The cost was of no importance; it was a matter of absolute necessity. A one-way ticket would suffice. Perspiring, trembling, he walked up and down the street afterwards until a one-time college friend of his sister's happened into him and asked if all was well. He folded the ticket into his pocket. It would never be used. He had known this even as he paid for it.

He made a fool of himself with a married colleague – they had been among a group attending a team-building conference in Sligo – and soon afterwards he had slept with a journalist acquaintance he had known since university. She had made it clear that there might be something more between them if they took a little time, got to know each other's lives. In fact, their short affair, drink-fuelled and fraught, had ruined already improbable chances. She had asked him to stop calling. His indecision was too much. He didn't know what he wanted, or even what he didn't want. He was stuck in a moment he couldn't get out of. She advised him to seek professional help.

He missed Marie-Thérèse. Her companionship, her sparkiness; the sound of her walking around in the mornings. He missed having a home with her, a door that could be closed against the world, buying books and CDs with her, being ribbed for his tastes, the small rites and observances that hold a marriage together, even the tacitly agreed evasions, the dishonesties. He missed their talks. The way she entered a room. On nights when she worked at home he would often bring her a coffee or a glass of wine. He missed the sight of her glancing up at him in spectacles from behind the untidy desk – the small endearing vanity as she took them off. There was something about computer light that made most people uglier. Not her. It made her eyes palely glow. When she left him, she did not bother to take her computer – he should have it, she said, she had saved what she needed. There were nights when he found himself trawling its memory for a clue to their sundering, or sitting before it silently, staring at the pulsing console, irradiated by loss, by the screen-burn of her absence and trying to visualise her now. Her fingertips had touched these keys; what had they written? He did a memory search for the words 'I love you.' It yielded nothing.

The way she read a newspaper, quietly commenting on the articles, making hypercritical remarks when she disagreed with what had been written, as though the journalist were present in the room. The aroma of her shampoo, of an Italian moisturiser she used. Her kindliness. Her intelligence. Her tact. The way she would glance at the cottage windows during a sea-storm in winter, as though fearing the force would blow them in. And he missed her physically, which you were not supposed to say. But it was true. He missed her sexually.

They had been so compatible, he had always felt. Other couples sometimes hinted that their ardour had burned away. There were stupid jokes about it in sitcoms. People discussed it on radio shows. He had several times heard them in the car on his way to work or on late-night radio at home. It caused sadness for many couples. It had never happened to him and Marie-Thérèse.

Their bodies had changed, were no longer those of teen-agers; but her jocular flirtatiousness, the fervour of their deep kisses he had found as thrilling as ever. And there was an ingenuousness that had grown in the sexuality of their marriage; they had become able to talk, to say what gave them pleasure, to ask, to offer, to play. Sex had been a part of their comradeship, their amity. At least that was what he had always thought.

Once, not long after their wedding, overnighting on a work visit to Belfast, he had telephoned her to say goodnight. He had had a few pints with the British civil servants; she had drunk a glass of wine after finishing her correcting. Neither had been able to put down the phone. They had talked for more than an hour. She had asked him to describe the bedroom at the hotel, told him teasingly how she wished she were there with him. Would he like it if she were? Was there a nice big shower? What would he do to her? What would he like done to him? His voice, she told him, sounded sexy down the line. It was a turn-on, she said, just hearing it. If he didn't stop talking, she might not be responsible. His voice was an occasion of sin.

Her soft, low laugh. Should she open her shirt? Did he think the British authorities bugged the telephones in Belfast? What would they say if they heard this conversation? Would they be arrested as perverts? Would the tape be played in court? How about if she suggested something very bold indeed? Was he feeling sleepy now or was he game for a dare?

There were flowers on his desk when he arrived back to the office in Dublin. SILVER-TONGUED DEVIL said the card.

Awakening alone. Eating breakfast alone. Coming back to the apartment in the evenings. The whine of the lift gliding up and down through the building, the slam of the fire doors on the landings. Bank Holiday weekends in the apartment alone, knowing the whole block was empty, its silence. He had never thought no longer being married would be so ferocious; so amputating, as it must have been for his parents. He had never considered that. He found himself welling up at stupid movies.

He came to have a foreboding – it often poisoned his awakenings – that he would never again know sexual intimacy. The grief was shocking. Never to touch another. Sex had been part of his life with her, lovingly or for fun, like talking; it was a kind of conversation. He grew to fear his naked reflection, to find flirtations among his colleagues impossible to witness.

He was *jolie laide*, she used to joke, one of her favourite terms in French, though usually it was employed about women. It meant 'beautiful despite imperfections' or because of them, she said. In his case – and in her own – because of them. He had come to think of his whole marriage as *jolie laide*, too. But that hadn't been enough to save it.

'How is the night class coming along for you, Senan?'

'I told you, I gave it up.'

'That's a pity, that's a pity. It's a nice hobby, writing. Mammy was a great one for the books. But you know your mammy, God rest her. Was it a play you were trying to write?'

'No. It was nothing.'

'What was it about?'

'It wasn't about anything.'

'Don't be biting the head off me. I was only asking.'

'It was a love story.'

'People always like love stories.'

After the separation he gained weight. He was uncomfortable in his clothes. A colleague at the Department, one of that year's new intake, had greeted him one morning with a sleepily amiable nod and the well-intentioned words: 'How's the Bigman?' He had never thought of himself as a big man. It seemed a sentence, a verdict. 'Grand,' he had replied uncertainly. It had disturbed him.

Glimpses of his reflection in the windows of shops. Wearing a darker-coloured suit, even on warm Dublin days. Women didn't look at him – not that they ever had, much. But now they had a way of peering straight through him, as though he were street furniture, or weather.

He bought an expensive membership of a gym near his apartment but only attended twice. His was not the usually stated reason for falling away – the ubiquity of beautiful bodies, the imperfections of one's own. It was more that he could not deal with the other men in the locker room. Since the separation, his facility in small talk had gone.

He grew afraid to be among people, was beset by strange panics. Always he had understood that most conversations are about nothing, but are simply an assertion of non-specific goodwill, the willingness to bond, at least temporarily, but it had never been a problem; he had accepted it. He had been one of those men able to construct an exchange around sport, though in fact he had never liked Gaelic games, the parochial allegiances that went with them, and secretly he detested rugby and its guffawing devotees, and soccer with its grandiose pundits. He was uneasy talking politics or civil service gossip, except with a few trusted friends, but most of those had sided with Marie-Thérèse. The telephone in the apartment seldom rang any more and when it did, he stopped returning people's calls. Their sympathy was unbearable. He came to feel that the point of their calling was their own reassurance, not his. His mobile was hardly worth the rental.

The therapist he began attending advised him to keep busy. She had once been a nun, he felt sure. She was careful, spoke placidly. She did not interrupt. Many times he wished that she would. There was a thing in the way she talked, a mid-Atlantic tone, an argot that floated up a fog between them. She was 'not into value judgements'. She was into listening 'and hearing'. He found the usages distancing.

Everyone had 'stuff'. Everyone needed 'to be heard'.

Everyone had 'an inner child', she advised Senan Mulvey; a core personality, a buried version of the childhood self; it was important to 'check in on it' often. She spoke of 'giving ourselves permission', issued handouts about seminars, information on training to become a therapist himself. Several of her clients had progressed to qualifying as therapists – he wondered if the verb 'progressed' was not itself a value judgement – so long as their own issues had been 'closured', of course, so long as their baggage had been unpacked. There was a sticker on her window, reading IT'S OKAY NOT TO BE OKAY. Sometimes he felt okay until he noticed it.

She used the first person plural in every other sentence. *What would we like to look at today?* In ways, seeing a therapist was not unlike making confession, although in those days you got a penance, not a bill. It cost fifty euros to see her. She smiled embarrassedly when he paid, as though the exchange were a compromise, something shameful or corrupting, when to him it was a form of safety. To feel he was a customer of someone only doing her job provided the illusion that he didn't feel invaded by her questions. Had we issues around trust? Had we issues around womanness? Where were we at, sexually? Had we tried reiki or yoga? What was coming up for us? Where were we at? The increase in our weight: what was that about? What was going on for 'Little Senan'? The death of his daughter – his having been a father at all – he never so much as mentioned. He found he couldn't.

Keeping busy demanded effort; it was almost as exhausting as doing nothing. He kept up with contemporary fiction, read the cultural sections of the *Guardian* and the

Irish Times, and periodicals about literature and art. He wrote short reviews of novels and biographies for the in-house newsletter at work; often his assessments were praised by his colleagues. A couple of times he had been asked to contribute briefing notes for the Taoiseach, for gallery openings, conferring ceremonies, the unveiling of a new theatre. He was regarded as the office bookworm, 'a bit of a monk', someone said. People would ask him for assistance with crosswords.

He had an aunt, a National School teacher, who had published short stories in regional newspapers and in a little magazine of nostalgia, *Ireland's Hearth*. She advised him to try his hand at fiction; it was enriching, therapeutic. He bought notebooks, a new computer, but it was still in its box. He was not going to write. It was a ridiculous idea. There was nothing he wanted to say.

He ate lunch, alone, at the National Gallery restaurant. Sometimes, afterwards, he walked the park in Merrion Square, or went into the bookshops on Dawson Street. On those weekends when he couldn't bear to see his father he went to an exhibition or a reading. Always he went alone.

'Senan,' said his supervisor, 'I asked you to come in because there's something I needed to say to you.'

'Okay.'

'Look, an incident was reported to me, Senan. I have to say it disturbed me. There's a regard for you here in the office. I was taken aback.'

'How do you mean, Mary?'

'One of the security staff who's on at night – I don't want to name names – anyway you probably know who I mean – he's an older man – he says he found you in a state of distress some time ago in the filing room. He was badly shaken by what happened. It was three in the morning.'

'I'd been working late on something. I fell asleep.'

'Senan, there are health and safety issues here. I can't have people stressed to that extent.'

'I wasn't stressed at all. I was only working late.'

'Look – you weren't asleep when he found you. He says you threatened and verbally abused him when he tried to help. He was frightened by your behaviour; you were acting irrationally. He was upset by whatever occurred and discussed it with some of his colleagues. It became clear that this wasn't the first time. Similar things have happened before. What's the story, Senan? Do you want to think about it for a minute?'

'I was tired. I lost my temper. I don't deny I went too far. I went to him the next night and apologised. I understood we'd cleared it up.'

'It's not a matter of apologies; the man doesn't bear you any grudge. But there's a feeling going around the office – you may as well know it – that you're not quite yourself of late.'

'So who am I?'

'Do me a favour and ease up with the smart talk, okay?'

'Is this a formal reprimand you're giving me? If it is, I need to speak to the union. I'm entitled to representation if I'm being accused.'

'If you'd prefer to go the official route on it, I don't mind telling you we can. I won't have staff abused and you'd want to get that straight. This is supposed to be a place of governance, in case you'd forgotten, not some venue for people to vent their frustrations.'

'I hadn't forgotten. I'm very sorry. It will never happen again.'

'Then give me something, Senan. What's up? Let me help. Anyone can see from your demeanour lately – people are concerned. I don't mean to be difficult or intrusive – but is it the same issue as before? If it is, and you need help – a break or whatever–'

'There's language used in the office every day of the week–'

'For Christ's sake, Senan, you threatened a sixty-year-old man. This isn't a bit of collegial banter over coffee. We're talking grounds for a formal accusation of bullying and harassment. Do you realise the ice you're on now?'

He said nothing.

'I'll have to ask for your security clearance. I'm amending it, as of today. I don't want you in here after eight at night when the office is empty. Okay?'

'That's when I do my extra work. I've no time during the day.'

'I don't want people overloaded. I've arranged for someone else to take over those duties. I'm sorry, Senan. There's policy on this.'

'I'd like you to reconsider. I'm absolutely fine. With respect, you're overreacting. There's really nothing wrong.'

'Would you go down to your desk and get your clearance-tag for me now? If you want to have a private conversation, I'm here.'

A cold spring came. He found himself noticing the young. The boys had lionly confidence, their clothes cool and expensive. The girls wore those crop-tops, those miniskirts and low-slung jeans. A colleague, a girl from Cork, had had her twenty-fifth birthday party in a nightclub on Nassau Street. He had been dutifully invited, most probably, so he felt, because to leave him uninvited would be so tactless as to make a point. He wondered if they somehow knew about the overdose, the hospitalisation. It was still a gossipy town.

How freely they moved and touched one another as they danced. He was becoming his father, he felt. In work they dressed conservatively; here it was different, the boys in vests and trainers, you could see the girls' nipples through their tank tops. The lyrics of the rap songs were lurid, misogynistic; but none of them seemed to care.

He had sat at the bar with the rest of the oldsters, nursing too-cold pints of Guinness and wishing he could smoke. The younger guests drank vodka cocktails, slammers, shots of Cointreau. For months, he had been afraid to weigh himself.

Very late in the night, they had insisted that he dance with them. They had applauded and cheered him: he had hated it. 'Fair fucks to you, Senan.' 'Go on, you mad thing.' 'Fatboy Slim, how are you?' One of them had taken a photograph of him on her mobile phone and emailed it around the Department as a joke. He had become the Good Sport you can never imagine weeping, that figure most admired in a crippled country: the man who doesn't take himself too seriously.

'Fair balls,' slurred the birthday girl, badly drunk at the end of the night. 'I had you down as a dry shite. But fair balls.'

It had occurred to him to ask if she would consider coming home with him. But he was afraid she might say yes.

* * *

'Everything's all right with you, is it?' his father asks absently, peering at his guidebook, riffling its pages.

'Grand. Yes. Well: how do you mean?'

'You seem a bit quiet.'

'No. Just jacked, I suppose.'

'That month you were off work? When you had that virus or whatever. Did they ever get to the bottom of it?'

'It was only a chest thing.'

'Was it asthma?'

'Yes. Something like that.'

'The fags don't help asthma.'

'I know, Dad. They told me.'

'Would you not give them up again?'

'I will in a while.'

'The fags are the worst lads of all.'

A number of years previously, a senior colleague had taken maternity leave and asked would he cover one of her duties while she was away. It was something she thought might interest him. There would be a little extra money. He would do it very well, she sensed. In the event, she had not returned and so the task had become unofficially his. It was to liaise with the Taoiseach's officials on which works of art might be exhibited at Government Buildings.

The paintings and sculptures were kept in various places around the city – some on display in galleries, others stored by the Office of Public Works. It was an assignment he liked and regarded as important. They changed around the holdings every nine months or so. His suggestions were appreciated, he felt.

He enjoyed drawing up the lists, discussing them with

the Taoiseach's officials. He gave it scrupulous attention; if anything, too much. He would clip essays on Irish artists from scholarly journals, photocopy reviews of exhibitions for the files. In the old days he had discussed the selections with Marie-Thérèse too; her post-doctorate had been an analysis of colonial portraiture. It seemed worthwhile – how ridiculous, he was not sentimental, was uneasy about nationalism, had always voted Labour or Green – yet it had seemed to him not entirely a sham: this image of Ireland as a place where the arts were respected. He had seen it as an idea to which most could give allegiance; in that sense, a sort of presidency. To be in the office alone at night when the building was almost empty, working on his lists and catalogues while the city was sleeping – it brought a quiet, consoling pleasure he came to value.

One afternoon, at work, during a session of the Northern Ireland peace talks, he had gone to a corridor in Government Buildings to retrieve a file of photostats he had left by the water cooler. A member of the British delegation, a junior minister, was in the passageway sipping a coffee and looking at a Louis le Brocquy portrait. His protection officer was at a distance, in the French windows that led to the garden. The Minister's glance met Senan Mulvey's and he nodded towards the picture as though taken by an aura it transmitted.

'Very striking,' said the Minister.

'Isn't it,' said Senan Mulvey.

'Who is it, do you know? Sean O'Casey?'

'It's actually Samuel Beckett.'

'I thought it was O'Casey.'

'Yes, there's a resemblance right enough.'

'My wife is interested in theatre. She'd scold me for not knowing. She loves Beckett, Wilde, all those Irish guys.'

'I see.'

'Forgive me; we haven't met.'

'Senan Mulvey, Minister. You're welcome to Dublin.'

'Interesting Christian name. Senan?'

'He was an Irish saint.'

'Rather a lot of those, aren't there? Some in this building, I guess.'

Senan Mulvey laughed obediently. The Minister laughed too.

'You're with the Taoiseach's Department, are you?'

'No, I'm Economic Development.'

'We're all in favour of that,' the Minister said and smiled.

'I hope you'll forgive me but my father would be disappointed if I didn't tell you what a great admirer of your government he is. He was a policeman; he was shot and wounded by paramilitaries in a post office robbery here in Dublin. The work your colleagues have been doing on the peace process means a lot to him.'

'That's very kind. Please tell him thanks for his support. We appreciate it very much. And thanks for clueing me in about the painting.'

'There'd be a print of it available in some of the gallery bookshops.'

'Must get one of those. I don't know much about Beckett. But I like that picture. Have to say, it grabs the attention.'

'He wrote *Waiting for Godot*,' Senan Mulvey found himself saying.

The Minister looked at him.

'Quite,' he said.

'Marie-Thérèse rang the house,' his father says quietly. 'It was on Monday night. I hope you don't mind.'

'It isn't my business any more who she calls.'

'It was Mam's anniversary. You probably forgot.'

The gears grind dully. One of the wipers is squeaking on the glass.

'I went up to the grave,' his father says. 'I left flowers from you, as well. I like to see it kept right.'

His father in a cemetery with a bundle of garage-bought chrysanthemums and a house-key to scrape off the moss.

'You might get up at the weekend, Senan. It'd be nice if you could. Or if you're passing in the meantime, just run in for a minute.'

'I'll try, Dad.'

'I knew you would. I told her you would.'

'Marie-Thérèse? What the hell business is it of hers?'

'No, your mam, of course. I told her you'd drop by if you were passing.'

He has always been uneasy when his father converses in this way. He does not understand it, finds it vaguely embarrassing. He has never felt connection to that Irish sense of the dead's closeness. His mother is not listening to anything.

Shame flickers up in him, the guilt of the escapee. Soon, he himself will hear nothing. He realises – strange thought – that he is not afraid. If there is pain, which he doubts, he will endure it.

'There was a little thing I wanted to say to you, Senan. About Mam and me.'

His father does not speak for a moment or two, and when finally he does, his voice is apprehensive, as though he has learned what he is about to say by memorising it from a book but is troubled now the moment has come to speak it.

'You didn't talk about certain subjects, not in those days. But I'd want you to know that I loved her. And she loved me, too. When I met her she was the most beautiful girl I'd ever seen; I mean a beautiful-looking person, as well as everything else. It was important to us both. In our marriage, I mean. To find the other person physically attractive. Do you know what I mean? I'm probably not putting it very well.'

'I know what you mean,' Senan Mulvey says.

'The pill was great that way, you know, when it came in. Well, we didn't like to go down that road because the priests would cut the lard out of you; but then we thought, after all, it's our own lookout what we do. I wanted to say that to you. To you and your sister. You were very much loved. You were children of love. And I know things went wrong. But we had our happy times too. And you'd have been very much part of those.'

They do not speak again for several minutes. He can't think of any way in. Lately his father has been talking like this: fixed on the past, on things that can't be changed now. As though some very simple statement needed to be made but could only be advanced in camouflage.

'A woman can lose her confidence in the house all day. It's better for women, now, when you think of how it is for them. No running to a husband for an allowance or that. If she wants a pair of tights, or a hairdo, or whatever. I often think, with your mam, if she'd had a little job, it might have given her an interest. Did you ever think that?'

'About Mam?'

'Yes.'

'I don't know. I suppose I didn't. She seemed happy enough at home.'

'A little job in a shop. She liked being around people.'

'I think she was happy enough at home.'

The lie quietens his father. Senan Mulvey is grateful. He does not want to talk about his mother, or Ireland, or society, or progress, or anything else. Most of all, he does not want to talk about Marie-Thérèse and he senses that his father does.

Not long after the death of their baby they had returned from New York. Some months later, they had attended a dinner party at the house of a colleague. A Dublin literary journalist was holding court at the table, entertaining the company outrageously. It used to be that the Irish were divided between Catholic and Protestant. These days, the critic mocked, the warring categories had changed. Waxing had replaced Confession, cocaine was the new pilgrimage, and a nation still pumping out turgid novels on the Famine could wear its fucking belly as a kilt. It was suburbanite Buddhists in Dalkey versus supertanned chavs, only that wasn't a lucrative theme. Not one of the Brit-garlanded literati was writing about the Ireland of the boom, a country where you couldn't smoke a cigarette in the pub any more but you could buy a condom and a croissant in a garage. Forget Jesus Christ, the holy name was Jo Malone. Ireland's younger authors were grossly over-praised in England, he said. They'd go down on Richard and Judy if it resulted in a bestseller. As for Oprah, they'd chew off her underwear while reciting quotes from Yeats in order to score an appearance on her show. A few of them could barely write 'shite' on a wall. But Irishness was becoming fashionable, a profitable stock, and some of those boyos and girleens were operators too, with agents and advances to match their ambitions and airbrushes to help the effort. A successful author's name was mentioned; the journalist mimed choking. 'Let me get this straight. You actually think she can, like, *write*? I mean words, sentences, paragraphs, et cetera? You're not being deliciously ironic?'

People were laughing; drunk. It was strange to be home. No one in New York conversed so freely and mischievously. It was a thing they had almost come to miss during their year in Manhattan: the social cattiness and smartarsery of Dubliners. You realised it meant nothing; was only a way of passing the time. As soon as you left the room, they'd be knifing you too. And even though he had cared for the work of the author being ridiculed, Senan Mulvey had laughed with the rest. It meant nothing.

It was the night everything changed. They'd been driving home from the party. Many times he would ask himself what would have happened if they had decided not to go; if anything would have played out differently.

She'd been here in the car. In the seat where his father sat now. She'd been wearing a beautiful jacket he'd bought her in one of the designer workshops on Elizabeth Street in Manhattan: dark green with a belt, expensive. She was smoking with the window rolled halfway down, hand trailing out with the cigarette.

There was something on her mind. It had better be said. There wasn't a right time to say it.

'Fuck off,' he laughed, when she told him what it was.

But Marie-Thérèse was not laughing.

She was moving out at the weekend. It was something she had to do. Even before Keelin's death, she had been unhappy. There was a trauma she needed to deal with, a painful event in her past. Since what happened with Keelin, the pain had sharpened. Before being married, she had suffered an experience that wounded her terribly; it had happened during her second year at Oxford. She had thought she was over it, but in fact she was not. She could not move on, and the marriage had become part of the grief, somehow, for there must be a reason why she had never been able to tell him and still could not do so now.

The separation might be temporary; she could not say at the moment. She was sorry for the deception, the lies. She did not know how it had happened, but she didn't love him any more. She could not go on pretending. There was only one life. He was a man of extraordinary decency. He deserved better than she could offer. No, there wasn't any point in counselling.

He realised, through the pulses of drink-fuzzed shock, that he would always remember the words she was saying, and the thought had struck him as intensely strange, for most life-changing moments are only recognisable as such in retrospect, where this one had the scald of present tense.

She was talking about rental agencies for apartments, the closing of their joint bank account, the cancelling of insurance policies, the splitting of the bills. There would be no need for lawyers, at least not initially. The cottage would probably have to be sold. What had cored him was the extent of her preparedness to go. Clearly she had been planning for months.

They were drunk. There were tears. He should not have been driving. He was aware of not knowing what to say. He was holding her hand. A Garda car blurred by, its blue light flashing towards Wicklow.

They had somehow begun to kiss and it had quickly become passionate, probably, he thinks now, because they had been drinking. He remembers unbuttoning her jeans, her fingertips on his wrist. They had driven home afterwards in silence. His seven-year-old nephew was staying the weekend with them. The neighbour's girl who babysat said he'd been restless, disobedient. They paid her and she left and Senan Mulvey locked the cottage gates, for there had been trouble with drunken teenagers on the waterfront.

She had taken off her jeans and top when he came in from the yard and was on her knees by the empty fireplace in her underwear. She had a joint in her hand: he did not know how she had come by it, but she offered it wordlessly, as though it was a token of something, and he took a deep, obliterating pull. Her mascara was smudged: she was cleaning it off with a tissue. Nothing was said for what seemed a long time. The television was on but the sound had been turned down very low. They made love at some point – he does not remember everything. She was kneeling, he was behind her, kissing the hardness of her shoulder blades. And the mascara-stained tissues in the fireplace.

In the morning she told him, again, that she would leave at the weekend. What had happened last night was goodbye.

His father opens the glovebox and fetches out the road map, while the wipers cut steadily through the drizzle.

'We're lost,' he mutters worriedly. 'We should've gone left back the road.'

'We're not. It's down here. Just give me a chance to find it.'

'We should've turned left at Annamoe.'

'Then why didn't you tell me?'

'I thought you knew.'

'If I'd known, I'd have turned.'

'I couldn't see with the rain. I'm after forgetting my glasses.'

'For Christ's sake, Dad. Do I have to do every fucking thing for you?'

He drives on abruptly, headlights turned full. The newsreader comes on at half-past midnight; there is an item about a fund for the missing firefighters and police officers of 9/11, the fathers never seen again. He switches channels quickly; a classical music station crackles. Since the separation, he has found it unbearable when stories of sudden bereavement are recounted. It terrifies him, what they make him feel.

When he was married it had seemed that the world was distant, that its tragedies and evils were at a remove, like the darkness beyond the gleam of his headlights now, as he guns the heavy car through the mud. You regretted them; Christ, yes, you had a stake in the future; and the thought of having to explain them to the children you might one day have to protect was grotesque; but you didn't truly dwell on such horrors too long because someone needed you not to. Since Marie-Thérèse has gone, the world has lurched closer. Nobody needs him now.

Hedgerows flit past. A signpost for Arklow. A line of Travellers' caravans under dreeping trees. Pearls of bright rain in cold yellow halogen. He realises that his father is crying.

He brings the car to a halt. A donkey peers over a fence. Rain spatters on the windows and roof.

'I'm sorry, Dad. I didn't mean it. I shouldn't have spoken to you that way.'

'You're all right. I'm the one who's sorry. It just took me aback.'

'I don't know what's the matter. I've been finding it hard to sleep.'

'You're upset. It's Marie-Thérèse. I shouldn't have told you she rang. She asked me not to let on to you. She knew you wouldn't like it.'

'I'm taking this medication. It's for depression, anxiety. I don't know. I feel knackered all the time.'

'She's worried about you, Senan.'

'So I noticed when she left me.'

'She mentioned – it's none of my business – but she mentioned, just in passing, that she'd heard there was trouble for you at work. I don't know who told her. She didn't want to say what it was.'

'There isn't any trouble. She should mind her own business.'

'So, what is it, son? Is everything all right? If there's a way I can help you, or you want to have a talk . . .'

'There's nothing needs to be talked about. She'd be better not gossiping.'

'Would you not move back in with me for a while? I've asked you before. Your room is there, empty. It's a sin to see it wasted.'

'Okay,' he says abruptly, and drives on into darkness. The moon is visible through the trees.

* * *

In the car park of the pub the walkers are circled around a brazier, their oilskins gleaming in the rain. They look buoyed, expectant, like children on Christmas Eve. One of them is passing around sandwiches.

'Can you give me a dig-out with the stuff? I've one of the lads' rucksacks in the back.'

'Yes,' says Senan Mulvey. 'It looks heavy.'

They aren't prepared for the wind, which rushes up against them like a wave, making his trouser legs flap, and he shivers. A gust slaps his back like a hard-swung pillow. His father introduces him to a few of the walkers; there are jokes about the weather, their folly. He feels like a parent leaving a son to school. His father will soon need friends.

It is nearly one o'clock. It is time to go. He fears that he will break down if he stays.

'I'll be seeing you, Dad.'

'On Saturday. Yes.'

'On Saturday. Right. Good luck.'

They shake hands rather formally. His father is not a hugger. Anyway, the walkers are watching.

'You're a great lad,' his father says. 'Thanks for tonight. I'd have been up the creek without you, that's the truth.'

'I just want you to know: everything is okay for me, Dad. Don't be worried about anything. All right?'

'Are you sure now, Senan? There's nothing going on?'

'You're not to go thinking anything bad. Everything is great with me. Everything is very clear. I know you sometimes forget things but I want you to put this in your mind. I'm really at peace with everything.'

'You just look a bit stressed. I don't know. Not yourself. Would you come with me, do you think? On the walk?'

'No, Dad. I'm tired. I've work in the morning.'

'Wouldn't it be a bit of crack? One of the lads here could kit you out. We all bring spare kit on a night like this. And I'd love to have your company along.'

'I can't. There's the car. I wouldn't want to leave it.'

'Sure what about it, when you think? Isn't it only a car? We could get a taxi down for it tomorrow in the morning. It would only take an hour. Would you not?'

Father and son stand in the drizzle. The walkers are watching them. He is picturing the apartment, the coil of hosepipe on the table, the masking tape, the sedatives, the four notes. He has written one to Marie-Thérèse, saying it isn't her fault, he has always loved her, wishes her nothing but the best, is sorry for having done such a violent and cruel thing, but life has become unbearable now. There is a note for his father, and one for his sister, and one for his troubled and favourite nephew, this one not to be opened, he has written on the envelope, before the boy reaches the age of sixteen. If he has forgotten him by then, his parents are to destroy the note. Whatever they think is best.

'Starter's orders,' says his father. 'The lads are getting going.'

'You were a great father to us, Dad. I don't know if I ever said it. I know it was hard for you when Mam died. And before. You're a wonderful man. I could never thank you enough for what you did for us.'

'God bless us, there's a spake,' says Eamon Mulvey.

'I mean it, anyway. So now you know.'

'Would you not come with me, son? We have to get on while it's not too bad.'

'Another time, Dad. Not tonight.'

'Well, there'll be other nights again. Drive safely. God bless.'

'God bless, Dad. Thanks for everything. I love you.'

He drives slowly across Wicklow, through the sleeping suburbs of the southside, pausing a few minutes by the harbour at Dun Laoghaire. Everything is quiet. The lighthouse beam glints. He walks halfway down the pier, down as far as the old bandstand, where he smokes two of his last three cigarettes. The security camera at a garage captures him at a quarter to four, buying chocolate and a bottle of water. Shortly before dawn, he returns to the apartment. He waits for his neighbours to go to work.

October-Coloured Weather

Dublin, 2011

Allgood's Hotel had been on her mind for some months. She had noticed it one numb afternoon around the time the bad news had been given her. The place had seen better days, she thought now, as she crossed quickly from Heuston Station through the damp, cold air of a Dublin October evening. Posters for the Presidential election flapped from the lamp posts. She couldn't face her family. She couldn't face the train. She would stay in the city tonight.

The building appeared weary, as though about to fall into the street. But she was not one to judge. Probably she looked that way herself. Mixed feelings. Yes. There was no point in denying them. But mixed feelings were better than none.

The Asian man on duty explained that there was only a king-sized double left. Her face grew suddenly hot; she half turned away from the counter towards the breeze from the revolving door. She would take it, she told him, and handed over cash.

'Grand,' said the man. 'Room 10. Third floor. Lift over there by the bar, love.'

Alone in the room, she felt weary, cored out. In the mirror, she gazed at her reflection. Maybe her husband was not just being polite and salving his conscience when he told her she was still attractive. His guilt for what he was secretly doing would be appalling, she knew. He was not a bad man at heart, not nearly as bad as he wished to be. He was the sad kind of Irishman who finds his own decency an embarrassment. She thought about what might be going on around her, in the rooms above and below, and in those on either side.

She went to the window. The river was muddy, full of oily-looking swirls and eddies. Gulls flew at the surface as though attacking it. Here and there, a branch or battered bough sped past madly rotating in the foam, the result, she told herself, of the recent autumnal storms.

The room was small and far too hot. It smelt of dust, stale cigarette smoke, laundered but not thoroughly dried linen. She lay on the bed and peered at the ceiling. Beneath the thick cream-coloured gloss paint she thought she could make out the ghostly outlines of the original plaster orna-mentation, palm, myrtle, willow and citron motifs, harps and Irish shamrock.

Maybe she would go to a play at the Gate or the Abbey. But it was already seven-thirty. Too late. There might be a concert on the radio. Perhaps just take a walk by the river. But it wasn't that kind of river any more. There were junkies on the boardwalk, everyone said it; there'd been letters in the *Irish Times*. And so many of the buildings were empty since the downturn. The cinema in Smithfield had closed.

She lay very still, eyes deciphering the shapes. A line from Keats came to her. *What struggle to escape.* She had recently covered the poem with her sixth-year English class. First thing on Monday morning, her favourite group of the whole week, the upturned, curious faces still raw with weekend kisses, as hungry for poetry as they were ever going to get. Peckish, at any rate. What good would poems do them? She had often faced that question. What use will poetry be to us on the dole queue, Mrs Connolly? Haven't you heard there's a recession? This country's, like, over. Yeats won't get us a job.

She had contended that poetry was sustenance for the soul, a way of talking about the moments in every human life that conventional language couldn't encompass. In her heart, though, she feared that her students were right, as the young almost always were these days. Was there even one employer in Galway city would want to know what her girls felt about the sonnets of Patrick Kavanagh. (Perhaps her husband, actually, but then he was unusual. Few men, even in Galway city, would choose as their lover a recent former pupil of their wife.) She had a sudden sharp image of herself standing in front of her class, a foolish middle-aged woman burbling second-hand explanations, rigorously anatomising the images that maddened young men had mined from the depths of longing. Her husband's jowly face loomed up at her then, an image from some recent dinnertime argument, followed, a moment later, by the grim picture of his pendulous sweating arse between the outspread thighs of a teenage girl to whom she had once taught the definition of pathetic fallacy. He might be inside her now. He would be shaking as he came. He was always so sweet when he was coming. They would be in his car, perhaps, parked there by Lough Atalia. The dusk so beautiful by the lake.

She thought about Galway, Atlantic rain on the laby-rinthine streets of the old city. It seemed far away from her now.

In the shower, soap stung her eyes and caused her to wince. She remembered the pleading voice of her son on the telephone earlier. Could the family go to Florida next summer? The traffic outside the station had been so loud that it was difficult to talk. In a way, she was glad. Talk would have been cruel. She couldn't have brought herself to tell him the truth: that for her there would be no next summer.

'There's a tree on the line, love. I'll have to stay in Dublin.'
'What?'
'I won't be home tonight, pet. There's a casserole in the freezer.'
'But Ma—'
'My credit's running out, pet. I'll see you tomorrow. Make sure and do your homework. I love you.'

She dried herself in a half-hearted way but did not dress. Instead she lay on the bed again, her hair dampening the pillow. The face of the doctor on that bright afternoon came back. She thought about her body and how it was failing, how nothing could be done; it would do what it must.

Now, through the floor, she thought she could hear a radio playing that old song by Oasis, 'Wonderwall'. Her fifth-years that spring had been mad about it for some reason; she had allowed them to have a special class where they discussed and analysed the lyrics, even though she herself was not sure what exactly a wonderwall could be. The wind threw a handful of leaves against the window. Her mind began trying to recall the words of the song, though she didn't really want it to. After all, you're my wonderwall; what on earth could that possibly *mean*? – but nothing after this line would come. The forgetfulness annoyed her, but then a different song started downstairs, or in some other part of the hotel. She felt heavy, sleepy, as she listened to the new melody. Her fingertips strayed to her sex. Some minutes later, as though emerging, startled, from a trance, she realised she had been quietly crying.

She sat up and began to dress, pulling on her slacks and top. She looked at the telephone on the table beside the bed – it was a modern phone, a gleaming slab of plastic with a keypad that seemed far too detailed. She told herself she should call her son or daughter again. But she needed a rest from their neediness.

Three months now since she had been coming to Dublin every Thursday, supposedly for treatment at the clinic. When the oncologist had told her there was no point in continuing, that the tumour had gone too far for there to be any hope at all, she had found herself unable to tell her family the truth. There weren't the words. Her children were too young to be motherless. She continued leaving for Dublin every Thursday morning from Galway, the train trundling heavily across the featureless Irish midlands. Alone in the city she would walk for the day, or visit the National Gallery, or sit in Stephen's Green waiting for night to fall. At seven she would return to Heuston for the western express. Everything had gone well, she'd say.

In the lift, she noticed her reflection again. Pale, admittedly, a little frayed around the edges; but not like a woman dying. Was it true? Was it a dream? How could it be true? Her cancer a larval eel. Sharp-fanged. Blind. Pathetic, in its way. Seeking only to live. Coiled deep in her lung like a question mark. It would grow until it could spiral itself tight around her spine. Every time she ate, she fed it, too. She had seen with her own eyes the cloudy shadows on the X-rays. She was dying, the specialist had told her. She had maybe ten months. Her instinct had been to apologise, to quietly go away. He was twisting one of his cufflinks as though he were embarrassed. She was sorry, she'd said, that he'd had to give her the news. It must be hard for him to give out a diagnosis like that. Yes, he agreed. It was hard.

In the lobby, a party of savagely tanned Americans had congregated around a noticeboard. A smaller group was converging on a stocky handsome man who seemed, from the way they jabbered and poked at him, to be somebody. Was he a tour guide, a person from their travel company, perhaps? Outside the wind was gusting so hard that the revolving door was slowly turning as though placed in motion by some invisible god. She smiled to herself as she overheard one of the tourists, a doughy-faced old man in a turquoise golf jumper, asking the barman, 'Hey there, sir, let me get an Irish coffee without the whiskey?'

The small dining room smelt of grease and disinfectant. Staff were moving between the tables, setting them for breakfast. Two middle-aged priests, one small and thin with a horsey face, the other as large as a rugby player, were seated at a circular table in the middle of the room. Although they were murmuring, she could just make out their Dublin intonations. They looked easy with one another, happy and relaxed; their privacy so quintessentially male that she felt ashamed of herself for eavesdropping. She glanced around the room, at the poorly done charcoal portraits of famous Irish writers on the walls; she recognised Joyce and Brendan Behan, Swift and Bernard Shaw.

The ancient waitress had a flattish nose with prominent purple phlebitic veins showing through the flesh.

'We're closed,' she said.

'Oh, could you squeeze me in, love? I'll be very quick, I promise.'

The waitress gave a plangent sigh and beckoned her towards a booth, making a great show of shaking loose the conically folded serviette. The menu was plastic – she noticed, with a small shudder, that it offered 'a bowel of fresh soup'.

She opened her magazine but could not concentrate. A ridiculous thing to be reading. Celebrities and their platitudes. As ridiculous as eating, or showering, or remembering. All of it, a waste of time. The stocky man she had seen in the lobby and thought to be a tour guide came strolling into the restaurant. He caught her eye, smiled, nodded with strange formality in her direction. The waitress approached and led him to a table. She wondered why *he* had not been told that the restaurant was closed. She felt a little aggrieved. But what did it matter? The horsey-faced priest leaned in close to his colleague and began to speak in a confidential whisper she couldn't hear.

When she turned to attract the waitress's attention she noticed with a start that the tour guide seemed to be smiling across at her. He had a kindly, florid face, thick but tidily cut light grey hair, eyebrows that almost met above his long straight nose. He pointed at her.

'She used to run around with Bryan Ferry,' he said. 'Isn't

that right? Bryan Ferry, the guy from Roxy Music? You remember that group?'

His accent was New York, his voice soft as a new dishcloth.

'Jerry Hall,' he said. 'The model.'

'Did she?'

He smiled again. 'I'm sorry. I just saw her there.' He pointed again. 'I mean on the cover of your magazine. And for some reason that came into my mind.'

'The fact she used to go out with Bryan Ferry out of Roxy Music?'

'Yeah.'

'I see.'

'Just as well they didn't get married, isn't it?' he said.

'Why's that?'

'Well, cause then she would've been called Jerry Ferry, wouldn't she?' His crimson cheeks crinkled into a grin.

She couldn't help laughing.

'My kid told me that once,' he chuckled. 'Killer, right?'

'It's a good one, yes.'

Something about his timorous smile was encouraging. He looked, she thought, partly like a small boy, but also like a man who was genuinely comfortable with women.

'Won't you join me this evening?' he asked. 'If you're dining alone?'

'Oh, no thank you,' she said. 'I wouldn't interrupt you.'

'You wouldn't be,' he said. 'As you see, I'm alone too.'

Before she had quite made up her mind on his invitation he had stood up and was pulling out a chair for her.

'Please won't you?' he asked again. 'You'd be doing me

a real favour. I hate to eat alone. It makes me feel such a loser.'

He was called Ray Dempsey. When she gave her own name he repeated it several times – 'Maureen Connolly, Maureen Connolly, how lovely.' His handshake was warm and firm, like an athlete's. How inky-black his eyes, and how white his small, straight teeth. He was from Brooklyn, he told her. Yes, she was correct, he was a tour guide. He had worked in many countries, had taken Spanish in high school. But he loved Ireland best of all, Connemara especially.

'The Becketty nothingness of it,' he said, 'is a line I read in a short story. A story by John Updike, I believe. But it sums up Connemara, though, doesn't it?'

'Yes,' she said, startled by the rightness of the phrase. 'Yes, it does.'

'The Becketty nothingness of it,' he repeated, and smiled. 'Man, I love a good description in writing.'

Her mind was racing during the minutes they spent looking at the menu. And yet, at the same time, she felt comfortable with him. It was something to do with the largeness of his hands, the incipience of his gestures, the slight clumsiness in the way he held himself, always seeming to abandon a movement halfway through. She told the waitress that she wanted plain sole, grilled, and a side salad, nothing more. The American ordered a large rare steak, with mashed potato, carrots and extra fried onions.

'We're lucky to get fed at all,' she said, when the waitress had gone. 'They told me they were after closing.'

'Oh, they usually make a little allowance for me,' he explained. 'One good thing about being a tour guide. Hotels look out for you. And I'm glad, because boy, am I hungry tonight? I have an appetite here.'

He beamed at her. 'Tonight is a big feast night actually, for Jews. I'm a Jew.'

'Really?' she said. 'That's nice.'

'Well, kind of. I'm Jew-ish, more than a Jew.'

'So what's the festival?'

'Oh, well, today is the first day of Succoth. The festival for the close of harvest. It begins on the fifteenth day of the Jewish month of Tishri, in the fall. Lasts eight days if you're Reform. Nine if you're Orthodox.'

'And what are you?'

'Well, my family wasn't Orthodox.'

'Oh,' she smiled. 'Neither was mine.'

He chuckled. 'Right. Whose was?'

'But tell me more about your festival. I'd like to know.'

'Well, the final day is Simchat Torah – Rejoicing of the Law. It's when the yearly cycle of reading the Torah gets going again.' His face took on a mock stern expression and his eyebrows went up and down as he waggled his finger.

'Amid much dancing and singing,' he intoned, and his face creased into a laugh, crow-lines appearing at the corners of his eyes. 'That's what the rabbi used to tell us as kids. Like he was ordering us, you know? Judaism is the only religion I ever heard of where you're actually licensed to have a good time. On pain of death.'

'Catholicism isn't like that, I can tell you,' she said.

'Right,' he grinned. 'My dad was Irish Catholic.'

'Oh?'

His father was a native of County Mayo, he explained,

and had emigrated to New York in the twenties. He had worked for a time on construction sites and in bars, and, briefly, as a longshoreman on the Hudson. He had met himself a Russian girl, converted to Judaism and married her, to the consternation of the folks back in Swinford. After their marriage he had tried to join the police force but had never passed the tests, mainly because he had bad feet. He told the story of his father's feet with a charming fake-seriousness, pausing from time to time to ask if he was boring her. She kept saying no, he was not, which was almost true. His voice was beautifully gentle. Listening to him talk even about a subject as seemingly uninteresting as his father's podiatric distresses reminded her of being in the warm shower earlier, the delicious water pouring down over her. She noticed, while he talked, that he had the American habit of adding a superfluous question mark to the end of most sentences. She found she didn't mind, although it demented her when her children or students indulged in it. 'Yes,' she kept saying. 'Yes, I see', when usually she would have remained silent in a conversation with a strange man about his father's feet or almost any of his father's appendages.

When the food came, plates almost fizzing with microwave heat, he continued to talk about his father. 'He had this weird thing about Ireland? This love–hate thing? He'd say "Don't talk to me about that island of hypocrites and donkeys, I'd rain bombs on the priest-ridden dump if I could." But when he was drunk it was different? I don't know why. It was Up the IRA and three cheers for Michael Collins and bury my heart in Swinford. He used to get these Republican newspapers mailed over from Belfast and read 'em. "I'm a Democrat every damn place in the world, son," that's what he used to say, "but in the occupied North of Ireland I'm a goddamn Republican. And you should be, too. Yes, sir."'

He looked at her. 'But enough,' he said. 'I don't know what's got into me tonight. Boring you to sleep like this.'

'Oh, no, you weren't really.'

'You're kind,' he smiled. 'But tell me something about yourself?'

She thought about his request as she pushed the food around her plate.

'To be honest, there's nothing much to tell,' she said. 'I've had a very uninteresting life compared to yours, I'm sure.'

'Well, what do you do, Maureen? Are you a working lady?'

'I'm a teacher, for my sins. In Galway city.'

He nodded. 'Oh, you teach. Beautiful. High school or college?'

'Fifteen-to eighteen-year-olds. Girls. English literature.'

'Oh, that's great. That's so wonderful. Do you enjoy that, Maureen?'

Nobody had ever asked her this, as far as she could remember. 'I suppose I do, yes. I mean, the kids are fantastic. They'd keep you on your toes too, these days. They're so aware. They grow up too fast now, I feel sorry for them sometimes.'

'Really,' he said. 'I have an eighteen-year-old myself. Trying to keep up with her drives me just about nuts. So I can imagine how challenging that must be for you. Yes, sir. You have kids yourself, Maureen? I'm getting the feeling you do.'

She paused for a moment and looked across at the window. 'I do,' she said; then, 'a boy and a girl.'

The hotel manager stalked up to the table like an executioner and asked if everything was all right. They both nodded and murmured a few words of satisfaction, although in truth the meal had not been well cooked. The manager peered down at their plates, then moved away with a bow.

His officiousness amused them. When he had left they allowed themselves a small and secret laugh at his expense. But her companion seemed like a man who could laugh without being cruel or superior, and she liked that about him. After the dinner a new waiter appeared and poured coffee and tea. She noticed and found it oddly moving that her new acquaintance was so polite to the waiter, in the American way, and said 'please' and 'thank you kindly' and addressed him as 'sir'. People were always saying New Yorkers were loutish and abrupt. Compared to any Galway teenager, they were Mother Teresa.

'Maureen,' he said, with a nervous expression, 'I have something a little naughty I'd like to ask you now.'

'What?'

'I have a guilty secret. You promise you won't tell?'

'I suppose so, yes.'

He leaned forward.

'Would you mind if I stepped out and smoked a cigarette?' he said. 'I'll tell you the truth, I have a weakness for a cigarette with my coffee.'

'Not at all,' she laughed. 'Smoke away, please.'

He grinned. 'You looked worried there.'

'My God, did I? Well, I didn't know what you were going to say.'

Chuckling, he took a packet of Marlboros from his jacket pocket.

'Oh, my gosh, I'm sorry, Maureen. Would you join me? Do you smoke?'

The eel stirred, gnawing. She closed her eyes and willed it away.

'Do you know what?' she said. 'I think I will actually, Ray. I haven't in a while, but I feel like the one tonight.'

Stepping out into the smoking porch, he handed her a cigarette and lit it for her, almost brushing against her knuckles as he curled his long fingers around the flickering flame. She dragged hard, sucked the thick smoke deep into herself. The waitress brought the bill, placed it near the ashtray on a table.

'I'd be honoured to get the check, Maureen. Make up for boring you to death about my dad?'

'Oh, no, I couldn't possibly let you do that, thanks. And it wasn't boring at all.'

'It would be a privilege to treat you. Won't you please say yes?'

'No, honestly. I'd rather you didn't. We'll go Dutch. But thanks anyway.'

'Well, then, would you allow me buy you a drink, maybe? A nightcap?'

'I don't know,' she said.

'Oh, well, if you've plans. Totally understood. But thank you for your company over dinner. It was a delight to meet you, Maureen. You're ever in New York City, here's my card, look me up? Or you'll find me on Facebook. Ray Dempsey.'

She glanced at her watch. Her husband would be getting in now. She knew his routine better than he did himself. He would come in to the kitchen, say something obscene about the government or bankers, go straight to the sink and thoroughly wash his hands, as always.

'Well, all right, then,' she laughed. 'I could go for a quick one, I suppose.'

He beamed. 'Damn the torpedoes. Only live once, huh?'

They came back inside and walked across the lobby towards the public bar. Behind the reception desk a radio was playing a song she thought she recognised from her college days, but she couldn't think of its name. Years ago Frank had bought the LP for her as a birthday gift. Was it shortly after they had got engaged? Or married? He had brought her to an expensive restaurant on Barna pier and given it to her over a glass of champagne. Strange that she could remember the beautiful way he'd wrapped it, in blue and silver paper and tied in a bow, but not the actual title of the song.

She asked the American about it.

'That's "You're So Vain" by Carly Simon,' he said.

She squeezed his arm. 'So it is, so it is.'

'As a matter of fact, I think just about my favourite singer is Carly Simon,' he told her.

'Really? Mine too.'

Maureen Connolly, she said to herself, what an unbelievable liar you are.

They entered the small bar and moved slowly through the crowd. It was almost completely full – people seemed to be drunk and someone was attempting to start a singsong – but as if by preordination there were two high stools empty by the counter and they went and sat on those. When he asked what she wanted, she said she would have a glass of dry white wine. He called for this, and a tonic water and ice for himself.

'Penny for your thoughts, Maureen?'

'Just Carly Simon,' she told him. 'Brings back a few memories.'

'Me too,' he said. 'Before all this rap stuff, huh?'

'You're not into the rap? The girls in my class seem to love it.'

He chuckled.

'I hear it, Maureen, you know, with my own kids around the house. But I got to say, I don't get it. To me personally, I mean. All that Eminem stuff drives me just about nuts. And Lady Gaga? That's a lady needs a shrink, in my book. I prefer "You're So Vain". But then I guess Carly's just my era. The Jurassic era, that's what my kids say to me. Damn brats.'

'Did you know she was engaged to Bob Marley once, Ray?'

He peered at her. 'Wow, really? I did *not* know that.'

She felt herself blush. 'No, no. It's a joke. Carly Marley, you see.'

'Carly Marley?'

He threw back his head and laughed. They clinked their glasses.

'You got me,' he said. 'You got me there, Maureen. Slam dunk.'

He drained his glass in one long slug, checked if she wanted more wine and called for another tonic water. 'So don't you like to drink?' she asked.

'Oh, no, no, it isn't that.' He put his finger into his tumbler and stirred the ice cubes around. 'Actually there was a time in my life when I liked it too much. So I don't drink any more. I'm an alcoholic in recovery.'

She felt stupid and embarrassed. 'Oh, I'm sorry, Ray.'

'Hey, don't be sorry, it's fine. What are you so sorry about?'

'I'm mortified now, joking you like that. You must think I'm dreadful.'

'Of course I don't.' His eyes stayed on hers for a moment.

The flirtation unsettled her and she glanced away from him to collect her thoughts. What was the name of that restaurant in Barna? She couldn't recall it now. After dinner they had walked the length of the pier and looked out at the Aran Islands. The words 'the end' had been daubed in whitewash on a broken wall. They had joked about it together. She remembered the sound of his laughter echoing on the water. They had driven into Barna Woods and made love in the car.

'I've an uncle an alcoholic,' she said.

'Oh yeah?' The American nodded. 'I must look him up in the directory.'

She laughed and slapped his hand.

'I didn't mean it like that,' she said. 'Don't be nasty.'

'I'm only bouncing the ball a little with you,' he smiled. She felt the memory of smoke burn the back of her throat. 'But why did you give up the jar in the end, Ray? Do you know?' she asked.

'You remember where you were the moment you heard the Twin Towers got attacked?'

'Of course,' she said.

'I don't.'

'Really?'

'No,' he said. 'I'm kidding.'

'Why then? Really? May I ask?'

'My drinking cost me a marriage. Yvette – that's my first wife – she left my sorry ass in the drunk-tank and took our two girls with her. Not that I blame her, you understand. I did some bad things. She was a lady and a half. Kind-hearted, compassionate? But marriage to a drunk is a full-time job. I guess she hadn't signed on for that.'

He took out his wallet and removed a creased Polaroid photograph of his daughters, the taller of the pair wearing an academic gown and mortarboard. 'That's Lisa on the right, and Cathy on the day of her graduation. She took a degree in Business Journalism, Baruch College, Manhattan. That's one day her old dad felt proud.'

'They're beautiful-looking girls.'

'Yeah,' he said. 'They take after their mom.'

'Do you ever see her?'

'No, no. She's married again now to a nice quiet feller raises horses. Lives in Port Angeles, Washington. I guess we lost touch over the years.'

He put the photograph back in his wallet and took a sip of his drink.

'And so you married again, Ray?'

'Yep, Cupid hit me another time.'

'Well, that's nice for you, isn't it? Doesn't she mind you travelling so much?'

'She passed away, I'm afraid. Three years ago now. She was killed in an auto accident near our home.'

'Oh, Ray, I'm sorry. That's dreadful.'

He shook his head and said nothing.

'How truly awful for you.'

'That hurt, yes,' he said. 'I'm here to tell you, that hurt.'

His eyes ranged around the room and took on a mystified expression, as though he wasn't sure how he had got there.

'I guess life must go on,' he said. Then he stared at his fingernails. 'Well, I don't know that it must. It just does.'

It made her uncomfortable, the sudden darkening of his mood, the downward curl of his mouth. He took out another cigarette and tapped it on the bar before realising he wouldn't be allowed to smoke it. He held it between his middle finger and thumb and rolled it to and fro, staring all the time at the tip. For a few moments she could think of nothing to say. 'And are you a religious man, Ray? Would that be a consolation for you?'

He peered into his glass. 'No, Maureen, it wouldn't. Not really.'

When he glanced up at her, she saw that he was trying to smile, although now she was horrified to see that there were tears in his dark eyes. 'I hope I'm not offending you, Maureen, but as far as religion' – he paused – 'to me it creates fear where there's nothing to fear. And it gives you hope when there's nothing to hope for.'

'I never thought of it like that,' she said.

'No. Well anyway.' He pinched the bridge of his nose and suddenly smiled again. 'No politics or religion in the barroom, right? Isn't that what the wise man advised?' He brushed non-existent ash from the knees of his jeans. 'So are you married yourself now, Maureen? May I ask you that?'

'Well,' she said, 'I'm entangled.'

He nodded diplomatically, as though he had been fully

expecting her answer. 'One of those complicated situations.'

She pondered his phrase. 'Well, I suppose so, yes. One of those complicated situations. Would you mind if we didn't talk about it?'

'I've been divorced. I understand the pain of that. The pain of being left. But there's a pain in leaving too, right? It takes courage to say goodbye.'

'I suppose it does.' She swallowed a mouthful of wine and glanced around the bar.

'I believe I need to visit the restroom now,' he said. 'Would you excuse me, please, Maureen? Don't go away.'

She watched him walk out the door. The bar seemed to grow hotter. Two policemen appeared outside in the lobby, their luminous yellow night-jackets sleek with rain. She felt light-headed, panicked. Suddenly she noticed that the priests she had seen in the dining room were in a corner near a slot machine. Neither was speaking. They looked drunk.

Somewhat to her surprise, Ray came back from the bathroom. He sat down, drank what was left of his glass in one go and said he thought there had been an incident outside. He had overheard the police in the lobby say something on their radios about suspecting that drugs were being sold in the nightclub downstairs. Just at that moment, as if to confirm what he had said, the manager appeared in the doorway. At his nod the staff moved quickly to make a great show of closing the bar. They snatched the glasses from the tables in the window bay where an office party was going on. Two revellers stood up shouting and began to square up to a barman.

One of the policemen strode in, followed by the manager,

who raised his hands in the air and clapped them together. The lights came on. The conversation faded.

'This premises is closed as of now,' the Garda announced.

A low groan came back at him.

'Is the residents' lounge still open?' someone shouted.

'Only to residents,' the barman replied.

'Is it too late to book a fukken room?' the same man called, and everyone near him laughed.

'It'd be as well for yourselves,' the policeman said, coldly, 'if you'd head yourselves to bed or the residents' lounge beyond or wherever else it is you're bound for. Because otherwise I'll take a statement from everyone here. And I amn't in the humour for smartness.'

Grumbling, people began to get to their feet and shuffle out, some with glasses or bottles concealed beneath their coats. The lobby was cold and draughty. Ray had a washed-out look in his eyes. He stared around as though trying to think of something to say.

'The licensing laws in this country,' he finally did say.

'Yes. It all makes for a sudden goodbye.'

He checked the time on his phone. 'I guess,' he agreed. 'Unless you feel like a trip to the famous residents' lounge.'

Her heart seemed to whomp. Her face felt hot.

'I don't know,' she said. 'Would you like to come to my room for a while? For a cup of tea or something? I think I saw a kettle up there.'

He pursed his lips and refused to meet her eyes. 'Okay, sure,' he said. 'Why not? What the hey? Maybe we've had enough of bars for one night.'

In the lift they said nothing. She thought about what her husband would say if he could see her now. He would be asleep at home, in the bed where their daughter had been conceived. The cup of tea he rarely finished would be growing cold on his table, beside his watch, his phone, the VAT returns from the shop, and the bottle of blood pressure tablets. He would have the radio on, as he always did when she wasn't there. She found it attractive about him that in her absence he couldn't sleep without the radio playing. He'd maybe stir in the night and put his arm around her pillow, and the clank of the radiator they had never got around to fixing would wake him when it came on in the morning. Walking down the corridor she found herself hoping that she hadn't left her underwear lying on the floor. She needn't have worried. The room was as neat as a cell. She filled the kettle and told the American to sit down wherever he wished. It occurred to her that she couldn't remember the last time she had been in a hotel room with a man. He ambled over to the window and stared out for a while as though something specific and unusual had taken his attention.

'You know,' he said suddenly, 'you were asking me about religion earlier. I have a buddy who's religious. A Catholic priest. I was thinking just now, it's funny as hell, but he's actually the one responsible for turning me into an atheist in the end. Indirectly.'

'How?'

'He was involved with this born-again thing in New York. Prayer groups. I don't know. Back when I was having a hard time with my drinking he persuaded me to come along one night. And that was what turned me off for good.'

'Why was that?'

'You don't want to know.'

'I do, Ray. Tell me.'

'Well, let's see.'

She handed him a cup of tea and sat on the bed.

'Tell me,' she repeated.

He gave a short laugh. 'Well, it's a real hot summer in New York. The water's running short and people are going crazy. Everyone's slithering around in these cycling shorts, looking pink and moist. Like miserable chickens. And this night, me and Noel Gallagher, that's my pal, Father Noel . . .'

'Father Noel Gallagher?'

'Yeah. It's a kick in the head. Anyways, I've decided I'm going to this prayer thing. I mean, what the hell, right? Sometimes you'll try anything. And it's in a hairdresser's salon. Because where they usually have it, the air conditioner's broken down, so – one of the group, the leader, Luis his name is, he works in a hair salon on the Lower East Side where the air con's okay, so the meeting's relocated there at the last minute.'

She laughed into her tea. 'Go on,' she said.

'Well, we're the first to arrive. Me and Father Noel. There's coffee and sodas beforehand, even some cold cuts and sandwiches. Regular little party they got going. Fifty bucks' worth right there. Pieces of cheese on cocktail sticks. We're not in Hoboken. It all kicks off with a tambourine playing and guitar strumming, you know. What I'm saying is it's harmless enough. No big deal. But it's when the speaking in tongues starts up that I get to feeling, Jesus, I want out. This is no way for a grown man to be spending his time.'

A grown man, she thought. You poor deluded thing.

'What I remember is sitting there thinking about the TV news? I'd seen the CNN news that afternoon in a bar. Something about Northern Ireland. That made me think about my dad. He'd died the year before. And something about a satellite that was lost – the news anchor said if it crashed into the earth it would leave a hole the size of Manhattan. I remember too, I was thinking about the war in Iraq. Crazy. Go figure. Like a confusion, I guess. It was so strange to me, Maureen. I had no one over there. But I was thinking, kids in Iraq are getting maimed and killed right now, and I'm sitting here half drunk in a hairdresser's salon, not feeling right or normal in any way much talking about. The heat, for a start, it's the kind of heat you can get feelings about. If this air con is working, I'm a monkey's aunt. I keep feeling, if I put my feet in a basin of water these clouds of steam are gonna come fizzing out of them. There are middle-aged people all around me; I'm saying people my age. But they're coming on like beatniks. What can I tell you? There's this one guy across from me and he's sitting in one of these old-fashioned barber chairs? And he's praying away. But this guy has a head like a racehorse. Seriously. You're laughing now, Maureen, but you should see this piece of work. And the woman beside him, she's cosying up to me on the coffee table and she's clearly in need of some kind of medical attention. She's rolling her eyes and going. "Praise you, oh, praise you, Jesus," in this weird voice. You know what I mean?'

'Yes,' she said. 'I know what you mean, Ray.'

'God sent his son to die. That's what Luis informs us at this point. Yeah, right, I'm thinking, but not hair dye, pal. And I don't feel great, Maureen. I feel mother soul alone. There's this strange light in the room, that sodium light oozing in from the street through the slats in the venetian blinds? And something about this light is making me feel nauseous. I'm looking at the way it glints on the domes of the hairdryers. And there's this hairdressing smell too? That metallic smell you get with hairspray? The pine-scented shampoo? You know? It don't smell like pine, it's like a committee's idea of what pine smells like?'

'I know exactly what you mean,' she said. 'I hate it too.'

'Right. So this broad's sitting beside me, with the Little Richard eyes. And right there in front of her, I mean *right* in front of her on the coffee table is this big stack of women's magazines? And I can see the words SHATTERING ORGASMS in heart-attack pink on one of the covers, stamped across this picture of some actress in a black bikini. I hope that doesn't offend you, me saying that, but there it is, that's what it says, SHATTERING ORGASMS. Right there on the cover.'

'It doesn't offend me, Ray.'

'Shattering orgasms. When we're supposed to be praying. Am I wrong? And I'm looking at this shiksa beside me and trying to figure if she's ever had a shattering orgasm herself, you know? And I'm here to tell you, I doubt it. And then I wonder if *I* have. And I don't really think so. Man, if I ever had a shattering orgasm I don't remember it now. But then I'm not so sure I'd want to, whole hell of the truth. An orgasm that's actually shattering, I don't know if I'd want.'

'Who would, Ray?' she said. 'Who would?'

'Right. So Luis, the *Presidente*, he starts again with the praying in tongues. This is one big mother I'm talking about here. Puerto Rican. Likes to eat. Ain't slim. He got the wifebeater vest and the shorts going on and the Dalai Lama sandals with the socks. But he opens his mouth and lets this *wail* come out. And then the whole crew of these individuals start doing the same thing. Making this noise, going nuts, bobbing backwards and forwards. Father Noel, he's warned me, but now it's going down. Luis is really doing it. The man is *lowing*. Ay, caramba! I'm saying Houston, we got a problem. Send the cavalry.'

She did her best to laugh.

'And the noise, it's like, I dunno, all vowels. And I'm trying to feel pious but it sounds to me like the chorus of some doo-wop song. He's going, "Join in, people, if you feel the Spirit moving, move *with* it." And awopbopaloobop is what comes into my mind. Hand to God, Maureen, that's the literal truth. Awopbopaloobop alopbamboom. Here's Luis is saying, "Go with it" again. And I'm thinking, tutti frutti, oh fuckin' rootie. Pardon my language.'

'Go on,' she said. 'I hear worse every day of the week.'

He stood up from the windowsill, went to the chest of drawers and poured some more milk into his cup. When he had finished he lit a cigarette, took a long drag and sat beside her on the edge of the bed.

'Raymond Joseph Dempsey, take a long look at yourself,' I'm saying. 'And then, when you've really and truly sized yourself up? Take a look around you. The Jesus people. Because I feel like I'm watching them on some kind of screen. Or maybe through a lens. Like a movie. Or maybe through an old window that's steamed up and dirty. And then they start again with the singing. All these people, they're singing hymns. Not old-fashioned hymns, you know. More like folksongs. "Bridge Over Troubled Water", for instance. "He

Ain't Heavy, He's My Brother". I mean, these things are *hymns* now. What are you gonna do? "You're So Vain" is gonna be a hymn before these pinheads are finished.'

She lay flat on the bed, kicked off her shoes and stared at the ghostly fruits on the ceiling. She began to get the feeling he was inching towards her. He loosened his tie and undid the top button of his shirt.

'They say the Lord moves in mysterious ways, Maureen? So does Luis. I'm looking at him lurching around like Tina Turner with a beard. He hands me a tambourine. "Bang it for the Lord, brother." I'm not kidding, that is exactly what he lays on me. "Bang it for the Lord". Out in the street this burglar alarm's going off. The sound it makes – I'm thinking of a person crying. The sun is setting down now and everything is bronze outside. It looks mysterious, beautiful. Through the blinds I can see these black kids wearing baseball shirts and caps. They're playing soccer, except they're using a tennis ball? I see it clearly, still. Every once in a while, the ball bangs against the window and it makes this loud rattling sound. When that happens, all the kids crack up laughing.

'Luis asks me to speak. Well, what are you gonna do? You don't want to be impolite to the man. He's trying to help you. I say "My name is Ray Dempsey." And just then the crashing sound of the tennis ball hitting the shutter comes again. And to give me time to think I whip around and take off my glasses and look at the window, like that's going to achieve something wonderful. And here I can see the sun now, deep orange in the sky, and the sky is this wonderful shade of purple like you never saw in your life. Then I turn back and look at these upturned faces all around me. As a drunk, I should be used to being the centre of attention, right? But I'm not. For some reason that I don't get, I find myself feeling teary all of a sudden. And I mean, I haven't cried in years.

'I tell them my name again, where I'm from, all the works. I tell them I'm forty-nine years old and I work for a travel agent. My wife died recently. I loved her. And she died. This God of yours, this loving power, see, he took my wife away. For no reason. For nothing. *Por nada*.

'I feel my face twisting up as I try to swallow down the tears. Someone gives me a napkin. I'm really crying now. Luis comes over and puts his hands on my head. He starts going, "Forgive, Ray, forgive, Ray." Keeps saying it, over and over. And after a while I can't actually figure out whether he's saying I should forgive somebody, or I should be forgiven myself. That's all he says. "Forgive, Ray, forgive, Ray." Over and over. Then what he does, he puts his hands on my head again and starts pressing down so hard that it hurts my freaking shoulders. Next thing I know he's going, "Do you feel it, Ray? Do you feel it? Oh, tell me you can feel it, brother. I *know* you can." And I guess this is the point of the story, Maureen. Because funnily enough, I did feel something.'

'What did you feel?'

Wind whistled outside the window. He stared at the ceiling. He was silent for what seemed a long time. When he began to speak again his voice came steady and calm. 'What I feel, really for the first time in my life, as an absolute, ultimate, undeniable certainty – that there's nothing out there, never was, never will be. And that this is okay. That it don't matter at all. So why be afraid? What does it matter?

That the salon, the bottles of shampoo on the shelf over there, the barber chair, the mirror – that this is all there is. The kids banging their tennis ball on the shutter outside. And nothing else. No vengeance. No punishment. These people, yes. Their hopes for a God, yes. But no great Being out there. No terrible thing. There's this conversation, this moment and that's all there is. Here and now, for example, there's only this room, there's you and me talking in a room, in this hotel, in this city. We never met before. Tonight we met and talked. Five minutes either way, it wouldn't have happened. But it did, see. That's the sacred moment. If there's a sacrament, that's it. And wider than that? The things that happen in our lives. Our memories. Our desires. The work great artists do. Patrick Kavanagh or Whitman. If we have children, then our children. And all those we love. Maybe all those we ever loved. But nothing else. We go around one time and then it's over and done. Man, that's all she wrote.'

'And no afterlife?' she said.

'No,' he said. 'Not for me, Maureen. Because to live just once, that's miracle enough.'

He stood up slowly and walked to the window, leaning his face against the glass. She looked at his reflection. The call of gulls came from the river. A grey moon had emerged from the clouds over Smithfield. An ambulance sped along the north quays, its blue light flashing, reflected in the turbulent water.

'It's late,' she said.

'Yeah,' he said. 'It is. I'm sorry, Maureen. I don't know why I wanted to tell you all that ridiculous stuff. I got carried away. I talk too much. What can I tell you? I'm Irish.' He glanced at the clock on her bedside table and pulled a face. 'I better go.'

He turned to look at her.

'If I've offended you in any way, I'm sorry,' he said. 'It's probably all crap.'

She took a step towards him and kissed the side of his face. He touched her hair.

'I guess this isn't such a great idea,' he said.

'You made me laugh tonight, Ray.'

'You made me laugh too. Really.'

'Can I tell you something? I needed a good laugh more than you did.'

'Why's that?'

She touched his lips. 'It doesn't matter. Something difficult has happened in my life. Something very painful. I don't want to talk about it. Even my family don't know. Not the full extent of it. But you made me laugh and you moved me. You're a lovely, tender man, Ray Dempsey. I hope you know that, really. I'd run away with you given half the chance.'

'If you could, right?'

'If I could.'

'Well, why couldn't you?'

'Because there wouldn't be any future to it, Ray. And that's the truth.' She kissed him softly on the mouth and held him until he had fallen asleep beside her.

The mournful whine of a vacuum cleaner outside in the corridor woke her just after half-past eight. The damp sheets were wrapped hard around her thighs. The room was airless and stultifyingly hot. Her tongue felt as though she had swallowed a cake of salt. When she sat up to take a drink of water she saw the note on the pillow.

> Gone to Newgrange, back 6pm. Would like very
>   much to see you then?
> Please? Will put do not disturb sign on the door.
>   Happy Succoth.
> All best, Ray. PS. Thank you for everything.

She took a long, cool shower and then sat naked on the king-sized bed for a while, where she found herself pondering the word 'king-sized'. What did it mean, really? A king could be any size. Richard III, for example, was technically a midget, whereas Henry VIII was six foot in all directions and had to be winched into Catherine of Aragon on a pulley. She smoked two of the three cigarettes left in the pack she found on the carpet, while she stared down at the river, its whorls and pools blurring in her eyes, and she thought about the meanings of words.

Downstairs, the exhausted-looking night porter was standing like a sentry by the doorway of the restaurant; it was almost as though he had been expecting her. When she went to enter the room he stepped into her path and regarded her disapprovingly. 'You're the lady was late for dinner last night,' he said.

'Yes, I am. I'm sorry.'

He tapped on his watch. 'Well now, you're after leaving it very late again, missus.'

'I know,' she agreed. 'I slept in.'

He shrugged. 'Breakfast's over at nine. That's the rule. We're short-staffed.'

'I understand. But maybe . . .'

He held up his hand like a policeman stopping traffic. 'It wasn't me made the rules. But the rules is the rules. I was never asked my opinion on them. But there they are, all the same.'

'But do you think . . . do you think just one last time . . . that you might be able to make an exception for me?'

He stared at her for a moment, as though what she had asked was preposterous.

'Please,' she said. 'I know I'm in the wrong, I do see that.'

He sighed and rolled his eyes, indeed his whole head. 'I suppose anyone can make a mistake. Come on so. We won't let you starve. But just this once, mind. The rules is the rules.'

He stepped out of the doorway and beckoned her towards a booth with a wave of his grubby white cloth. The small room sang with light. She thought about her husband getting up, putting on his fresh clothes, the lemony musk of his aftershave. She pictured him leaving the house and driving into work. He would listen to the end of *Morning Ireland* on the radio. He would stop at the petrol station on the way into town to buy the *Irish Independent*, a packet of cigarettes, two tickets for the weekend Lotto. He could get them in his own supermarket just as easily, she was always telling him, but no, he had always bought them in Lafferty's garage on the roundabout and he liked cursing the government with Mr Lafferty. He was a creature of habit. It was one of the things that annoyed her about him, but also one of the things she loved. She tried to imagine how he would even begin to cope when she was gone. They would have to talk about it soon, the inescapable fact of her going, the absurdity and yet the truth of it, the onset of her final winter. He needed to be told. It would have to be faced. The thought stirred tears but she blinked them away. The porter brought her a bowl of cornflakes and a cup of greasy-looking tea.

'That's absolutely all I can do for you,' he said. 'If it was known I even done that much I'd be out on my ear. I'd be crucified. Not joking you.' He drew a finger across his throat.

'Thank you, that's lovely.'

Five minutes later he brought her a rack of hot, soggy toast, a basket of bread rolls, a little silver dish of marmalade.

'Thank you,' she said. 'You're very kind.'

'Indeed and I'm not.'

'You are. You're a godsend.'

He pantomimed a scoff. 'I've been given a lot of abuse around this place but that's a new one now.'

'Could I ask your name?'

'Jimmy, pet. I'm always here. Ask for Jimmy any time.'

He glanced furtively over his shoulder, as though he thought somebody important might be listening. Nobody was there. The lobby was empty. The revolving door was slowly turning but everything was quiet now in Allgood's Hotel. He ran a fingertip around the collar of his shirt, which appeared too tight.

'Just don't be leaving it so late next time, love,' he whispered. 'That was all was meant.'

'No,' she said. 'I won't. Scout's honour.'

He walked away and began to set the tables for lunch.

She considered going out to the lobby and telephoning her husband in the supermarket, just to say she had missed him, that they needed to talk, that the time for mercy and forgiveness had come. But it could wait. She would see him tonight. She would book a table somewhere. Maybe the restaurant on Barna pier. She sat alone in the dining room, watched the traffic through the window, knowing she would never see Dublin again.

Figure in a Photograph

'I never thought I was gonna live to 30. I only planned
it out till I was 28. I figured at 28, the black dress,
the gutter in Paris, I had it.'

PATTI SMITH

Sean Hyland enters the dank basement shop feeling awkward, out of place. In his arms, his infant daughter is restless. Trance music thuds from the wall-sized speakers. Around him stand the teenagers, sullen in their baggies. It's June 2010 and Dublin is too hot today, although rain has been pestering the city for weeks. Last night he quarrelled with his wife, one of those foolish marital spats that don't do serious harm but which he has come to find exhausting. It's their son's birthday on Saturday. He forgot to get the present. Lately he hasn't been sleeping.

He approaches the counter cautiously and waits to be noticed. This being the Irish summer, he has the worst cough of his life. Last week he saw the doctor, who didn't smile as she said to him: 'Why didn't you come to me before, Sean?'

'Because I'm a man,' he tried to joke.

She didn't smile, again. Shame and antibiotics make a powerful prescription. He resolved to do better in future.

He feels terminally middle-aged as he waits for the youth behind the counter to finish his phone call. Who can he be talking to? And why is he speaking in that American accent they all have these days?

'I'm like, whoah, and she's like, that's cold, and I'm like, whatever, and she's like, my shorts, and I'm like, butt out, and she's, like, so lame, and I'm like talk to the hand, bitch, 'cause the face ain't home. And shove it up your whole world round.'

'I'd like to buy a skateboard,' he interrupts.

'Uh-huh?'

'For my thirteen-year-old son.'

'Cool.'

'Do you think you could, like, help me? When you're finished your call?'

'What kind yeh want, like?'

He explains that he wants, you know, the kind with wheels. And a board.

The assistant regards him with withering tolerance, his hair like a plate of cold tagliatelle, a tattoo reading FUCKED across his knuckles.

As he leaves the grimy shop, package under his arm, he finds himself thinking about his son. Lately Joseph has been difficult: surly, unapproachable. He's a bright kid, bookish, so at least there is that; but the music he listens to is so desolate and joyless. You don't want to go turning into one of those miserable bastards who forget they were ever young, but he has the sense that he has come to be seen by his son as an embarrassment. He didn't think that would happen. And it hurts.

And there's a girl, Ciara says. A year older than Joe. Ciara's worried that their relationship is too heavy for a teenager. She's not a bad kid, but she's had boyfriends before. She dresses in those crop-tops and low-slung jeans, sends him arch little sexualised texts. One of them mentioned blowjobs, with asterisks for the o's. Another had a photograph attached. But when Sean Hyland went to his son's bedroom to make an attempt at a talk, he met only resistance dressed up as indifference, a sarcasm so contemptuous it could have peeled the Death Metal posters off the wall.

'I don't need the facts of life, Dad. Spare me, okay? This isn't the 1300s like when you and Mum were kids.'

'Come on, Joe, don't be like that. Let's be mates here, okay? I was kind of afraid of my own dad. I'd hate that for us.'

'I'm not afraid of you, Dad. Nobody is.'

'Mum says Jenny sent you a text that was a bit inappropriate.'

'How?'

'You know what I mean. I'm not getting on her case. I understand it's only messing but you can see how Mum would be worried.'

'You know what I think, Dad? I think you're fucking jealous. *Now close the fucking door when you leave.*'

The sound of his hand striking his son's pallid face. The thing he had thought would never happen. The raging shame and anger, and Ciara's shocked silence. For weeks afterwards, she had barely looked at him.

Midsummer's Day. The dawn birds chirping this morning. He had drunk too much last night. Ciara dressing in the darkness of the room before she left. He had watched from the bed as she fumbled through her drawer for a bra, had wanted to ask her to stay. Once, she would have. Now that wouldn't happen.

'It's gone six,' she'd whispered. 'Are you sure you'll be all right?'

A weekend over in London. Her brother's Civil Partnership ceremony. Sean Hyland had insisted many months previously that of course she must go. He'd be fine with the baby and Joe. No problem.

'If she won't sleep, just comfort her,' Ciara advised. 'Rock her. Soothe her. Speak to her gently. If she really won't stop crying, try a half-teaspoon of Dozol.'

'I'm a bit old to be taking Dozol,' he said.

She departed with a look. The quiet clunk of the front door. The taxi pulling away through the half-light.

After she went he was restless. He got up and shaved, found *Morning Ireland* on the laptop; made breakfast for Joe. The news was of the banks, a post office robbery in the midlands and a volcano threatening to erupt again in Iceland. Sweet Christ. Wouldn't you think the Icelanders had done enough to us this year already, what with wrecking the international economy and permitting the release of another album by Björk, without buggering up everyone's summer as well? Not that he and Ciara will be taking a holiday. Money's too tight since he lost his job. Maybe a week with her father down in Wexford. Maybe not. Suddenly he feels weary as an anchor.

Ciara loves Björk. Modern operas. Fusion jazz. Anything you couldn't dance to, unless you were demonstrating to an audience the distressing effects of either rabies or narcolepsy. His own taste in music, old ska, old punk, she doesn't understand or connect with. He pictures her in the ferry terminal, cool in her sunglasses. And he pictures her on the deck of the SeaCat as it eases out of Dun Laoghaire harbour, out past the Muglins, past Howth and Ireland's Eye. Then walking through London, past buskers and shop windows; the summer sunshine making a swelter of the city.

He woke the baby at seven-thirty and gave her the morning bottle. A ghostly memory of Ciara's mother in the little one's features. Strange how that happens: a haunting. Some days they look like you, or your other half, or both of you. And then suddenly one morning you are holding one of your grandparents: small, frail, needy. Who else does this child look like? How can Sean Hyland ever know? Hylands who died four hundred years ago, maybe. Others who are not yet born. To them, he will be a phantom, a figure in a photograph: Great-Great-Uncle Sean who lived in a suburb of Dublin in the years of the Second Great Depression.

So quiet when he returned from dropping Joe into soccer camp. He checked his emails. Did the hoovering. Switched on the TV. Chat shows. Soaps. Repeats of programmes he disliked the first time around. Scousers screeching at one another on Jeremy Kyle. He watched for a while before falling asleep on the sofa. In his dream, he was voted out of the Big Brother House. When he awoke, the baby needed changing.

He took her to the park. Home again for lunchtime. Jedward on the radio. He couldn't find his iPod. Now he's walking through the city where he was once a teenager himself, with a skateboard under his arm and a baby in a papoose. The headache is bad. His glasses are of a kind promoted by opticians as suitable for parents of toddlers. Designed by geniuses, tested in a wind tunnel, advertised by astronauts, they are guaranteed unbendable. The Swiper in the Diaper whips them from Sean Hyland's face, does something fast and deft with her clever little hands and tosses them triumphantly on the footpath. They look like an ampersand. Sean Hyland's daughter has a future in origami. Or vandalising car aerials.

He drifts into South William Street, the old alleys and laneways. Porn shops, head shops, adult boutiques. A nation recently reassured that it's okay to play with yourself has taken to it with the zeal of the released. He's never thought of himself as a prude, but Jesus Christ. In his teens, a copy of *Mayfair* smuggled from London by a schoolmate might circulate around the upstairs of the bus. Its centrefold of a former Bond girl draped in gauze on a chaise longue could be rented for a Mars Bar per night. When he was fifteen, he had a photograph of Debbie Harry in a tight white dress pinned above his bed for perhaps three months, until sleep deprivation made him feel like one of the Birmingham Six and he replaced her with a Boomtown Rat. These days they can download an orgy if they want. He hopes it's making them saner. But he doubts it. A walk down Dawson Street. He looks in the bookshop windows. It's said that in the ancient times, to appease the anger of volcano gods, the natives would make a human sacrifice. He wonders if this worked. It's tempting to think so. Perhaps the Icelanders could get together and drop Björk down the crater? That would take care of several problems at once.

The poster photograph for Patti Smith's memoir brings New York to his mind, though it's fourteen years since he was last in America. Shocking to count the years. Their marriage had not been in good shape at the time of the trip. Sean Hyland remembers that weekend.

They had wanted a child so painfully. The strain it had

put on them. Other people's thoughtless remarks, barbed Irish quips. Those jokes so cutting, though they are meant to make light. 'Married all this time – shouldn't something be happening?' Sean Hyland and Ciara had laughed with the rest. The Good Sports you can never imagine grieving.

The pain of occasions like Father's Day and Mother's Day and Christmas. The long, long childless summers. Children in the park on warm July evenings. Fathers pushing buggies by the willows. News of friends becoming parents became difficult to hear, and you hated yourself for that, for the black weed of envy, but there were nights you were unable to crush it. And the ads full of toddlers, and people phoning radio shows to complain about youngsters these days, when Sean Hyland and his wife would have given anything for their problems. And six weeks after they returned from that trip to New York, she told him tearfully that something had happened. She was late. She had done a test at work that lunchtime. It was positive. She was sure. She was pregnant.

He thought it important to remain calm. He made her do another test. Stress could make her late; it had happened before; she had been working too much overtime. He remembers driving through the rain to the all-night pharmacy in Earls Court Road; the news on the radio in his car. There had been a bomb scare in Belfast; people in the shop were talking about it. A woman crying among the shop-girls; her daughter lived in Belfast. The chemical brightness of the aisles as he walked them. Muzak over the speakers.

He went to work the next day but could not concentrate. He was frightened, not happy. He wanted to talk. She had miscarried four times. It might happen again. But there was no one to talk to about something like this. He felt like a man in a boat in a tornado with the tiniest candle in his hand. He felt, in short, like a father often feels; as his own father must have felt, but would never say directly, for an Irish father didn't talk in that way at that time or others would have laughed at what he said.

At lunchtime he left the office and walked in the pedestrian precinct. A thunderstorm began. The streets emptied. He wandered into a church where an organist was rehearsing and some homeless people were keeping out of the weather. His clothes were wet. It was many years since he had entered a church. And Sean Hyland knelt and prayed.

At the supermarket checkout now, the beautiful Estonian girl smiles and compliments him on his daughter's handsomeness. He makes a mental note to tell Ciara. They are a couple who make jokes about infidelities.

It is not the happiest marriage. She says they don't go out enough any more. But it is sometimes companionable. They have found a way of being together. She had a relationship for four years before meeting Sean Hyland. It ended badly, untidily; she was hurt by it. At moments he has a feeling that he and Ciara do not belong; that the rebound that brought them together will push them apart in the end. He wonders if other couples ever feel like that. He finds her unreachable sometimes.

They have quarrels about money, especially since the recession started. These worsened when he lost his job. They paid too much for the house, they can't afford the mortgage, should never have returned from England. But he has the sense that this is a camouflage; that they are secretly arguing about other things. He wishes he could walk away before an argument escalates; but he finds that he can't, and he wonders why. Perhaps a couple are rarely as close as when they're arguing. Perhaps arguing is a kind of sex.

They don't make love as frequently as they used to. They both say they would like to; that it's just something that happens. In the two years since the baby, he has gained weight, grown unfit. And in one row, a bad one – they had drunk too much at a wedding, the only one they have attended since their daughter was born – she had told him she didn't think they had a future together, and Sean Hyland had aggressively agreed. They never spoke of the quarrel again but it flowed between them like underground water.

Everyone should try childcare with a hangover. Once. Chocolate down the bib. An ectoplasm of snot. His daughter looks like a poster girl for some campaign. Sean Hyland finds himself thinking about the man inside Barney. Four years in stage school. Now you're a fucking dinosaur. But well paid for something extinct.

Crossing Stephen's Green, he hears a busker singing an old London ballad. *I saw my love on Limehouse Dock, all on her way to Woolwich.* A memory of Bayswater arises and follows him like a ghost. They had lived there five years. He'd gone there for work. It was where Joseph was born. Their flat was by the canal. Happy times, mostly, days of hope and lightness in the Little Venice Ciara had loved. Money was always tight. The city was ruinously expensive. London was a place where you went out in the morning with sixty quid in your wallet, didn't take a taxi or buy a lunch or a newspaper, and yet, by the time you got home that evening, the sixty would have evaporated to a fiver in change, your clothes sticky and smelling of the Tube. A junior accountant in a computer multinational didn't make much, and he was supporting his divorced sister, to Ciara's unspoken resentment. But there was always the hope of promotion one day. In the meantime, they had one another and the baby.

So memorable, the months following the birth of their first child. Walking in Hyde Park. The Regent's Park Zoo. The morning they took the baby to visit the Iranian brothers who ran the dry-cleaner's on Westbourne Grove. A night her brother and his boyfriend came to sit for them and they went to a gig by The Beat, a recollection of her smile as she danced with him. But when Joseph was a few months old, a better position had arisen at the Irish office. Sean Hyland was wanted in Dublin before the start of Christmas week. The plan had been for Ciara and the baby to fly, and he would take their rusting, decrepit car on the ferry. But in the exhaustion of new parenthood, they had left it too late to book the flights. There was nothing for it but Holyhead. Sweet Christ.

He remembers driving across England in that cold mid-December, through fog and sleet and ice-glazed scenery, the wipers relentlessly fighting the grists of hail, and the crackle of the broken radio. The car was older than their relationship, and at some point he had spilled a pint of milk on the floor, which had left an unkillable stench. But you couldn't open the window – literally couldn't, in the case of one of the windows – because being face-whipped by a hailstorm as you're driving past Stoke isn't everyone's idea of a good time. He had actually tried to sell the car in London as a prelude to re-immigration, telling the dealer it had been valued at five thousand pounds. The salesman took it out for a brief test drive before handing back the keys. 'Facking key ring's worth more than the car.'

Ciara was in the back, with a toaster on her lap, a portable television beneath her feet, and her pockets full of cutlery. She seemed to be wearing almost every garment she possessed because it was so cold and because they had no room for another suitcase. He had entrusted her with his records, and in his memory these were balanced on the top of her head, in the manner of a Bedouin woman carrying a water jar from an oasis, but in fact she was holding them in her mitten-clad fingers, whose tips were turning blue. The baby was there too, strapped into a safety seat, but a safety seat whose workings neither of the parents had full confidence they understood because they didn't have a degree in Engineering. Into the crock's boot had been packed the remainder of their worldly goods, total value nine quid, Ciara joked crisply.

A strange worry had gnawed at him about returning to live in Ireland. His happiest years had been spent in London. But Dublin was booming; almost everyone said it. Emigrants were coming home. Life was good. The English Sunday supplements had photo-spreads of Temple Bar, articles on Irish playwrights and bands. The President was a woman. Full employment had arrived. There was even talk of peace in the North. The only dissenting voices had been those of her brother and his boyfriend. Ireland would never change, they had quietly asserted. You could give it a facelift and pump it full of Botox but you couldn't fix its cruelty, its fearfulness. The Irish might replace the Virgin Mary with Mercedes-Benz, but it would always be a frightened place where the wrong things got worshipped. They weren't buying the hype. They'd be remaining in London. It saddened them to say it, but once bitten, twice bite. He quoted them at some stage during the drive, which resulted in an argument. He didn't speak to her for an hour. Well, he didn't like to interrupt.

It was the midnight sailing. They rocked across the Irish Sea. A dreadful night, the worst crossing he'd ever known. Through all of it, the little one slept soundly in a carrycot on the floor of the lounge. Around them ranted a mob of beer-fuelled young men, roaring, carousing, slapping one another on the back, singing carols with obscene or facetious new lyrics, and trying to strangle one another with lengths of tinsel. There were rebel-yells and mawkish choruses, screechings, cursings. 'Fairytale of New York' was sung so often and so badly that he came to hate it with a genuine passion. Every time a massive wave hit the ship, they seemed to rise a hundred feet in the air before crashing back down again with the viciousness of a hanging judge's gavel. The gnash of glasses breaking. The moans of vomiting en masse. He couldn't believe the baby was so tolerant of the punk rock ambience. This was a kid who could sleep through 'The Fields of Athenry'. Their gripe water bill would be low.

By six in the morning the party had ended, mainly because most of the celebrants were by now unconscious. Close to dawn, the baby was still sleeping, and Ciara asked him to get her a bottle of water. After he'd done that, he asked her if she wanted to go out and get some air. She didn't really want to – she was exhausted and cold – but she suggested he step out himself.

Everything was calm. It was a cold, clear morning.

Remembering it now, as he crosses a midsummer Dublin, he doesn't think he has ever seen a sky with so many stars. Certainly, he never has since. You felt you could reach out and touch them, stir them around in the blackness. There was an unearthliness about the beauty and the stillness. He walked around the decks for a while. People were gathered here and there. And as he rounded the stern of the ship, there was an elderly couple sharing a flask of tea and listening to classical music on a radio. He once tried to get it across to a friend, the strange beauty of that scene: being far out at sea, in the dark and the cold, with haunting music being played on a radio. He stood near the old couple for a while. He was smoking, which Ciara didn't like. What happened next, he'll never forget.

A piece of music they recognised came on. And he recognised it too. They turned it up a little louder and poured themselves another cup of tea. An extract from Handel's *Messiah*. The choir on the radio began to sing. And the old couple hummed along.

> For unto us,
> A child is born.
> Unto us,
> A son is given.

He is not a man who cries. But when he heard those words, he stood in the dark and wept. Dawn began to come on. The clouds turned red and gold. The ship was approaching Dun Laoghaire, the town of his childhood. He could actually see the waterfront where he and his schoolmates used to hang out on summer evenings, the steeples and the shopping centre, and the hills in the distance, the office blocks silhou-etted against the impossibly scarlet sky.

On the Luas, among the strap-hangers and the homeless people and the weary, he seems to see it all again: those stars; that dawn. And he pictures a teenage boy, so sullen and hard to reach, turning pirouettes on a skateboard. He will watch. That is all. He will watch and say nothing. His son's growing body, its mysteries, its discovering the strange adventure of itself. Once, he could hold him in the palm of one hand. So hard to let go, in the end. But the sun will turn the windowpanes golden as he watches. He will watch, grateful even for the loneliness he didn't know would come with fatherhood. And there might be the tiniest instant when his son turns and waves, or grins, or says nothing at all. Or skates down the pavement into the shadows by the bridge, lost in the alleluia of his headphones.

The Wexford Girl

I don't know if you know the village of Glasthule, near Dun Laoghaire. To be honest, there's no reason why you should. Glasthule is a small place. Not much happens. Plug in your fukken kettle and the street lights dim. That was my father's favourite joke about Glasthule. But more of my father later.

Glasthule is more like a little town down the country than a part of Dublin. It's on the sea, which makes it nice, if you don't mind that word. My father used to say the sea was good for people. He said the nearer they were to the sea, the saner they got. He said that was why Dubliners were great people altogether. And that was why people from the midlands were mad. They were too far from the sea. It wasn't good for their minds. It was why so many gangs of culchies came cantering up to Dublin. They needed to get themselves nearer the sea, the poor bastards. Even when they did, it mightn't help them.

He didn't actually believe that. He wasn't an idiot. But it was the kind of thing he liked to come out with for a laugh. It would vex my mother because her family was from down the country. Her home place was near Athlone, in

County Westmeath. Athlone is in the exact dead centre of Ireland. It's about as far from the sea as you can *get* in Ireland. So he said that on purpose, to annoy her. It worked.

I don't know what Glasthule is like now. But when I was a kid in the village, you could smell the sea in the summertime. The smell was in the streets, even on your clothes. It was a town full of old biddies and sad, stray dogs. Funny little shops that sold rashers and bottle of gas – dark, drab places that always looked closed. Dead flies and dead bees in the windows. There was a pub, the Eagle House. And a barber's, Paddy Connolly's. There used to be a little picture house too, the Forum Cinema, on the main street, beside the undertaker's shop. But it was closed not too long ago and all boarded up, and last time I was passing through Glasthule I noticed the Forum had been demolished. There's a supermarket there now, on the site where I had my first kiss, halfway through *Saturday Night Fever*.

Glasthule was where I grew up, but it's not where I live now. These days, I don't even visit. In some ways that's good. You have to move on in life. But in other ways it's a sad thing to pull up your roots. A place can get deep into you, right into your bones. And when you leave it behind, you leave part of yourself. But that isn't the story I'm telling.

My father's family lived more than a hundred years in Glasthule. My great-great-grandfather went to work there in 1848. He was from the tenements of Bride Street, in an old part of Dublin city, the Liberties. He was a working man all his life, a stonecutter by trade. He helped to build Dun Laoghaire pier. He was part of the huge team of men who blasted the stones out of Dalkey Quarry. They'd sleep in tents on Killiney hillside, maybe a thousand navvies and labourers, and the cutting teams would use sticks of dynamite to blast out the boulders. They would hammer a hole in a wall of granite with a chisel, then squeeze in a stick of dynamite and blow the rock to pieces. Then they'd cart the chunks of stone down the hills to Dun Laoghaire through these narrow bits of laneways they cut alongside the train tracks. The laneways are still there today. People in the area call them 'the metals'. But nobody knows why. It's just a name.

Anyway, my great-great-grandfather married a Glasthule girl in 1852, the year the lighthouse on Dun Laoghaire pier was built. And it's a funny thing about that lighthouse, because, believe it or not, that's exactly the spot where my father met my mother. It was one summer night in 1961. She was going for a walk down the pier with her friends from the factory where she worked, when my father asked her if she had a light on her. He was a bit of a lad. Bit of a man for the ladies, they say. He shapes up to my mother and asks for a light. Then he gives her a wink. And he asks for a cigarette. Three months later they were married.

She often said she wished she hadn't gone walking the pier that night. Or that she hadn't stopped to talk to him when he asked for the light. But they had their good days too. Not many. But some. I believe they were happy enough around the time I was born. I don't know why I believe that. But I do.

It's a strange thing to think about, but it's true all the same. If she hadn't had a box of matches in her pocket that night, I wouldn't be here to tell this story. A box of matches can change everything.

My father loved to walk the pier with me, all the way

down to that lighthouse and back. On summer nights we went often. It was a peaceful walk, with the sun going down on red water. He would show me the little holes in the massive blocks of stone. From where the workmen had bored the sticks of dynamite all those years ago. When they were blasting the stones out of Dalkey Quarry.

Some of the blocks were bigger than I was. Some were even bigger than my father. It was a strange feeling to look at a dynamite hole and to think that my own great-great-grandfather might have made it. His name was Patrick. Like my father's name, and my name. It made me feel happy. It gave me a kick. To think one of my own people helped to build Dun Laoghaire pier. My father acted like he *owned* that pier. And he acted like he was *king* of Glasthule.

But my family have all moved away from there now. The area changed. Gangs of yuppies moved in. The price of houses went mental, half a million for a labourer's cottage. The old shops are gone. The old families too. I find if I have to go down that way at all now, I try and avoid Glasthule altogether. A place can bring back memories you don't want.

The year of my story is 1975. Where we lived, the young-ones used to dress up like Bay City Rollers. They'd have tartan shirts, tartan hats, tartan down the sides of their jeans. If they could have bought tartan knickers, they would have. I knew this one girl who lived on York Road and everyone said she'd done just that. I don't know if it was true about her tartan knickers. But she certainly had tartan wallpaper on the covers of her school-books. That was the kind of family she had, the kind where the parents put wallpaper on your books. In mine, they didn't even put it on the walls.

Apart from the Bay City Rollers, and *Starsky and Hutch*, it's hard to remember what else was going on. There was trouble in Northern Ireland. There usually is. Bombs going off. But I don't remember the place names. Petrol was scarce a lot of the time. The country wasn't doing well in 1975. And that turned out to be a very big year for my family. Although we didn't know at the time that it would be. It was the year my mother went away to England. All sorts of things got turned upside down. It was a year you wouldn't wish on too many people. And when it was over nothing was the same any more.

I won't lie to you, my parents weren't happily married. My father used to joke about it but it wasn't too funny. 'Me and the wife have had nine wonderful years,' he'd say. 'Trouble is, we've been married fourteen.'

He had all sorts of awful jokes about my mother and his marriage. He never got tired of telling them. 'Me and the wife were happy once. Then we met.' 'I'll tell you the truth, I don't like the word marriage. In fact marriage isn't a word, it's a whole fukken sentence.' All the old biddies in Glasthule used to love him to bits. I don't think they knew his marriage really wasn't good. They thought he was only messing. He'd pull faces and tell them jokes. They'd laugh when they'd see him. They'd fall around laughing.

'Here he is,' they'd say. 'The comedian.'

He'd be made up when they said that. It'd give him a kick. He'd put on this stupid gobshite face or this beefy smile he had and tell one of his thirteenth-century jokes. 'Marriage is a wonderful institution, ladies. But who wants to live in an institution?'

Most people have a dream in life, a fantasy that keeps them going. My father's was to be a comedian. He loved to tell jokes and to make people laugh. He was never happier than when he was doing that. I think he would have liked to do it full-time. If his life had turned out differently, maybe he would have. Though not with material like that.

In those days there was a television programme called *The Comedians,* fairly late on a Saturday night. If my father and mother weren't fighting, my father used to watch it. He'd have a beer or two and watch it, laughing his hole off. He had a loud rough laugh, like the bray of a donkey. There'd be times when my mother was after going to bed, he'd let me sneak down and watch it with him. There'd be comedians like Charlie Drake and Jimmy Tarbuck on the programme. Tom O'Connor would be on, and Bernard Manning. Little and Large. Cannon and Ball. Nearly all of them were shite. Tommy Cooper wasn't bad. Another one was Dave Allen. He was funny. My father liked Dave Allen a lot. Dave Allen was his hero. He liked watching Dave Allen because Dave Allen was from Dublin. I liked watching him because he had a missing finger.

'Look,' the father'd say. 'Would you look at your man, son. He has it made, so he does. Over there in England, on the pig's back so he is. Earning millions for telling jokes. The women hanging out of him. A man with nine fingers. Jammy bollocks.'

People were always telling my father he was funny as fuck. People in Glasthule would have said that to him often. Maybe not in so many words. Once a month there was a talent night in the Eagle House pub. A prize of twenty pound for the winner. Ten for second place. In 1975, I'm not joking you, that was serious shekels. You could have bought the whole of Ireland for about forty-two quid with the Isle of Man thrown in. Everyone said if my father entered the competition and told his jokes, he'd win. He'd win for sure. No doubt about it. Everyone said that, except for my mother. But he never did enter it.

Him and my mother really didn't get on at all. There were reasons, but I don't want to go into them. He drank a bit sometimes, but it was more than that. They didn't have a lot in common. Maybe they married too young. He was eighteen; she was nineteen. You change a lot in your twenties. Maybe they grew apart. You see that happen to a couple.

They look happy enough, mind you, in their wedding-day photos. A happy young couple, smiling and kissing. I still have one of the photos somewhere. They look a bit older than eighteen and nineteen. It's a queer enough thing but people tended to look older in those days.

'I never knew what happiness was, until I got married. And then, of course, it was too fukken late.' That was another one of the father's jokes. He loved that one. He really did. He'd be killed laughing. He'd nearly wet himself.

One night Dave Allen was on the *Late Late Show* being interviewed by Gay Byrne. He said the secret of comedy was never to laugh yourself. To tell your jokes without laughing at all. You'd have to keep a straight face when everyone was laughing around you. But my father could never do that, no matter how he tried. He laughed at his own jokes. He didn't care. He'd embarrass you, laughing like a fool.

My father was a trawlerman out of Bullock Harbour.

That was his work. Catching fish. He'd land them on the quay and the women from the chippers in Dun Laoghaire would come down to him there, for the ray or the cod or the whiting. There was a Mauritian man had a restaurant up in Killiney village; he'd buy lobsters. There were nuns in a convent on Coliemore Road. The father'd always give a bargain to the nuns. What he didn't sell, he'd put in a pram and sell door to door. A banjaxed old pram he found in a skip. He'd fill it with broken ice and away with him, then. His round would have been from York Road up to Ballybrack or so. All around the new estates in Sallynoggin and Monkstown Farm. The king of the road. That's what he said about himself. 'Paddy O'Meara, king of the road. A job where you travel is great.'

At nights, if he needed the extra, he'd stay out until dawn. Near the end of the week, or if Christmas was coming, or he needed to make the monthly payment on the boat. He'd radio in to the house and I'd say goodnight to him from the kitchen. I'd hear the crackle of his voice and the sound of the waves over the CB. He'd tell you not to be worried, he was looking at the mermaids. 'Say a prayer for me, Sailor. I'll be home in the morning.' I'd lie in the bed thinking about him, alone in the bay. I'd pray for the storms to stay in England.

One night I heard him crooning a song over the CB to my mother. 'Oh my true love she is fair, and my true love she is bonny, with the ribbons in her hair, ah my darling gentle Annie.' She was laughing at him, gently, sitting there at the table. I never saw it again. But it stayed in my mind. It's the way I try to remember them.

Sometimes in the summer he'd take me out in the boat. He wasn't supposed to. It was against the law. There'd have been heartburn on the arse if the authorities ever found out. Though I never knew why. It wasn't as if his boat was dangerous or anything. It was tiny, for a start, and so slow, it was like a toy. A little one-man trawler, you used to see them around Dalkey and Irishtown. They've gone this good many years. My father's was called *The Wexford Girl*. He wanted to name it Red Rum, after the horse that won the Grand National, but you can't change the name of a boat without arse-ache so he never got around to it. 'There wouldn't be power enough in that engine to work your missus's vibrator.' That's what my father used to say to the other men on the harbour. And he'd laugh to himself. And he'd pull a funny face. 'The lord of the high seas. In me speed machine. But, sure it'll have to do me. Till I get the hundred-footer. Like Onassis.' And all the old grannies would be chuckling and giving him the eye. And I'd be thinking, what the fuck is a vibrator?

I loved going out on the boat with my father. I often did it in the school holidays or on a Saturday morning. I wasn't much of a one for school, to be honest. The teachers didn't like me. Feeling was mutual. Pack of snobs in dog collars, that's all they were. You came from my street, they'd label you already. They'd single you out. They'd be sneering in your face. They'd humiliate you in front of the others because your clothes were second-hand. They'd imitate your accent. They'd want you to cry. It wasn't even the beatings; it was the way they'd take your dignity. Every one of them was from the country. They hated Dublin children. I wouldn't even be bothered talking about those men. I hope they're in Hell today. God forgive me. But I do. If there's justice, they'll have got what they deserve.

So there'd be mornings I'd spin him the yarn that I had the day off. He'd know I was lying, but he'd let me all the same. You maybe have an opinion on something like that. Wouldn't blame you. I'm not saying you're wrong. I'd regret it sometimes now, all the days I bunked off. Back then, I didn't care. I was working with my father. And I'll tell you the truth, though you mightn't believe it: I learned more from that man could barely write his own name than I ever learned off a Christian Brother. I'd go up with him to buy the diesel for the outboard in the village. Then we'd get the broken ice from a publican he had a deal with. He'd let me help him carry the nets, the crates for the catch. He'd carry the big ones. I'd carry the smaller ones. 'Look at us,' he'd say. 'Little and Large.' He'd be teaching me the names of the fish, showing me their markings. Gurnard, codling, dab, flounder, coalie, rockling, thornback ray. I'd be amazed listening to him talking, how he knew every species. Long spine scorpion, bass, starry smoothhound, ballan wrasse, dragonette, conger, shanny. There's people find poetry in words on a page. My father pulled it out of the sea.

It was a good feeling for a kid to be helping his father. The old biddies would sometimes give me money, especially if I was polite. One of them was in charge of the bakery in Dalkey and she'd bring us down a treat on a Friday. I liked the lovely smell of the hot, fresh bread. It made me feel warm. It was a nice safe smell.

Late at night, I'd be listening to them fight each other downstairs. And I'd be crying to myself. I'd be afraid, I suppose. The way a kid can be. She'd be saying she was going to leave. He'd be saying that too. I would sit on the top stair and cry while I listened. Sometimes Helen or Sheila would come out of their room and sit beside me. They'd be crying as well, more than me.

I'd hear them smashing plates or glasses downstairs. I'd hear them screaming all sorts of things, pushing each other around the kitchen. And what I'd do then – I'd get back into bed and pull the covers up over my ears. And I'd try to think about that smell. Often I would dream about it. I still do. The smell of hot, fresh bread. Funny thing, a man told me once you can't dream about a smell. But I know you can. Because I have.

There were two boys and two girls in our family and I was the eldest. So I was the only one of us could remember happier times. The times when my mother and father didn't fight each other. I don't remember those days so much now, to be honest, but I know they must have been there.

Another thing I remember was praying to Jesus to send my brother Rory to us. He was the youngest. I prayed for him to be born. I think I was sick to death of having sisters. I wanted to have a brother so I could teach him to play football. Helen and Sheila didn't like the football much. No girls did, back in those days. It was Bay City Rollers or nothing.

Rory and I used to play football up the gypsies' field. Or we played it out on the street. Anywhere we could. He was Chelsea, I was Leeds United. I was Germany, he was England.

Rory and I never see each other now. He was in trouble a few years back. He got mixed up with a bad crowd in town. There were drugs involved. He did things he shouldn't. There's no point in talking about it now. I'm not using his real name here, because it was in the papers at the time, and you'd remember what he did if you saw his name written out. What happened meant I had to move away from Glasthule. But that's another story.

I'm not saying it's up to me to judge him. I love him still. It's just I can't be around him. It would wreck your head to be around him. I wouldn't even know where he lives since he got out of prison. Being honest, I wouldn't even know if he is alive right now. It's a sad thing to have bad blood with your only brother. But me and Rory do. And it won't change now.

Still, back when we were only kids it was different. I was mad about him. I prayed my mother would have a boy and she did. I was thrilled. A baby brother, what a gas. An answer to my prayers. We'd play soccer out on the road. He'd want to be Leeds or Germany, but I made him be Chelsea or England. I used to tell him: 'If it wasn't for me, pal, you'd never have got here. So you're England. And I'm Germany. So shut your fukken gob.'

I remember a very cold Sunday in the winter of 1975. It was the kind of day where your breath turns to steam. We were just standing in front of Glasthule church on that freezing morning, the auld-lad and Helen and Sheila and me, and little Rory in the auld-lad's arms. We were blowing on our thumbs to keep our hands warm. I suppose we were thinking about what we could do. Although we were too young to be able to admit it, we didn't want to go home. We didn't want that at all. This was because the worst fights in our house were always on a Sunday. And they always ended with my father putting on his jacket and leaving the house. And not coming back until it was late. There'd be nights he wouldn't come back at all.

My father looked at me on that Sunday morning. I could see he knew what I was thinking. His lips were cracked and pale. He kept chewing at the skin there while he stared around.

'Da,' says Sheila. 'I'm cold.'

'I know you're cold, Teapot,' my father says. 'But think of the poor people in Africa. In the desert. The backsides roasted halfway off them. Think how much they'd like to be here in Glasthule now.'

'I don't care about the people in Africa,' she says.

'Do you know how hot it is in Africa? You sweat so much you have to carry yourself home in a bottle.'

'I wish I was there now, instead of here,' she says.

The auld-lad laughs. 'So do I. If you want to know the truth.'

This sad look comes over Sheila's face then. When she was a kid she had a look that could break your heart sometimes. She wasn't a kid who could hide her feelings.

'Will I tell you a joke?' he goes. 'To cheer you up?'

'No,' she goes. 'I don't want to hear a joke.'

'Once upon a time there was three bears,' he goes. 'And now, there's bloody millions of them.'

My father laughed. But Sheila didn't.

We stood in front of the church until all the people were gone. Until the man who sold the newspapers had packed up his stall. This young culchie priest came out the front gates, kind of hugging himself because it was so cold. He went in next door to his little house. I could see him in there. In his neat front room. He was sitting at a fire, eating his dinner. And I remember wishing that I was a priest who had a little house. A place where there'd be no parents, no brothers, no sisters. Nobody to love. Nobody to cause you trouble.

'Ah, to blazes,' my father goes suddenly. 'I feel like a bit of gas today. Come on, we'll get the bus down to Bray or Greystones. Some culchie place where they eat their young.'

'Do you mean it?' we go.

'Hundred per cent. Let's mosey.'

This was great. Now we wouldn't have to go home until five or six o'clock. Now there wouldn't be as much time for them to fight each other. I remember feeling nearly wild with happiness then, because that Sunday might turn out all right. But it didn't.

There was a bad fight that night. My father went out. I remember walking around the village, looking for him, not being able to find him. I went into the Eagle House and a man there told me he'd seen him half an hour before, going into a flat in Glasthule Buildings, a little narrow street, in behind the Forum Cinema. There was a woman who lived there whose name I won't mention. She has people still alive. It wouldn't be fair. Let's just say you'd hear her name during the fights in our house. We grew up hearing my mother scream it.

The street was dirty. There was a burnt-out car turned on its side. Someone had spray-painted UP THE PROVOS on a broken wall. And THIN LIZZY RULES OK. And MARY MOORE WEARS TARTAN KNICKERS. You know what youngfellas are like. Little bastards. I waited for a long time but he never came out of that woman's flat. Maybe he was somewhere else. I don't know.

Late that night my mother came into me and Rory's

room. She sat on my bed for a while and she smoked a cigarette. She said my father would come home, I wasn't to worry. And she didn't mean what she'd said about my father during their fight. She said my father was a good man. And she didn't want me to turn against him. In case I wouldn't want to get married myself when I grew up. I told her I didn't ever want to get married. 'I want to stay with you, Mammy,' I said.

She laughed. 'You won't always feel that way.'

'I will so,' I said. 'Why can't I marry you?'

'Because one day you'll meet a girl,' she goes. 'And you'll fall for her. And that'll be that. Your goose will be cooked.'

'It won't,' I said.

'It will,' she told me. 'That's what happens. When you fall in love, that's a wonderful thing.'

'Like you and my da,' I said to her, then.

She looked away. Took a drag on her cigarette.

'Yes,' she says. 'Now go to sleep and don't be worrying .'

My mother wasn't religious at all. Never bothered with it. Never. She said religion was all lies and hypocrisy and rubbish. And you didn't hear that in Ireland much at the time. The place was scuttling with Carmelites and rosaries and scapulars. But my mother was different. She'd talk about it very bitterly. But one thing you could say about my mother was this – she hated all religions equally.

What I'm saying is, she never went to Mass, Which was a pity, because you'd see a good side of my da on a Sunday. He'd be charming the women, holding open the church door, saluting all the neighbours and the priest. There was an ancient old biddy without a friend in the world. My da would make a fuss of her after Mass. She's dead many years now. I don't remember her name. Maybe it was Bridget or Agnes.

She had never married. When we asked her why not, she used to tell us she was still waiting on the right fella. Then she'd rock with laughter, wiping her eyes. 'God forgive me,' she'd say. 'I'm a terrible rip.'

Her favourite possession was a signed photo of Charles Haughey. Taken the day he came looking for votes in Gasthule. Smug smile on his face and his eyes half-closed, like a sugar-coated pineapple chunk had been shoved up his arse. One arm around the parish priest. The other around Agnes. His suit would have cost more than a year of her pension. She adored him. Go figure it out.

'If only my Charlie was forty years older,' she'd go. 'I'd give him a right run for his money, so I would. I like a man with a bit of go in him, so I do. Not them weaklings who think they only have it for stirring their tea.'

'Agnes!' my da would go, pretending to be shocked. 'You're an awful woman, Agnes. Charlie Haughey's a married man. You're an awful auld whure, so you are.'

She would laugh like a nutcase then, and so would he. And we'd all laugh too. Me and Helen and Sheila. Even though we didn't know what a 'whure' was.

Then one night we were sitting on the landing, listening to them fight each other downstairs. And I heard my father call my mother that name.

'You're a womanising bastard and a liar,' she screams.

'And you're a heartless fukken whure. You always were.'

She started crying then. So did he. A door slammed hard, I remember that. It was like a gun going off, it was so loud in the house. I knew the neighbours would be able to hear. They'd be listening through the walls. It was like a blast of dynamite.

I could hear them, crying downstairs, in different rooms. And I knew what the word meant then all right.

A word can go into your heart like a bullet. But a bullet goes right through you, and a word stays inside. It stays in your heart till it turns your heart sour. But I didn't know anything about that at the time. That's because I was a child. I was too young to know.

On a Saturday we'd sometimes buy ice creams in this shop called Teddy's near the public baths. We would sit on a bench and talk for a while. There was a man who was down on his luck, he'd been raised in an orphanage and things hadn't worked out in his life. My father would give him a few little mackerel or a fillet of cod. One time, for some reason, the man cried when he did that. After he went, I asked my father why.

'It's hard to help a proud person,' he told me. 'But you should always help them anyway, if you can. Because you never know the time when you might need help yourself in life. And you should never judge another person. Not until you've walked a mile in their shoes.'

'But why can't he buy his own fish?' I asked him. 'Is he poor or what?'

'Well,' he goes. 'He's not the Aga Khan.'

'Are *we* poor?' I asked him then.

'Don't ever let me hear you saying that,' he goes, 'when we have enough never to be hungry or cold. That's more than a lot of people in this world will ever have. It's a terrible thing to be lonely in life,' he goes. 'You could have all the money in the world. But where would it get you if you've no one to love? Nobody is poor if they have that.'

'Do you love my ma?' I asked him then.

'Yes,' he goes. 'Of course I do.'

'Then why are you always fighting?' I asked him.

He looks away from me, then, and out at the sea. He puts his hand up over his eyes, as though the sun is in them.

'That's only a little game,' he goes. 'Don't you worry about anything. I'd never wrong your mammy, I swear on my life.'

'But what kind of a game is that?'

'It's like when you and Rory are playing Cowboys and Indians,' he goes. 'You let on to be fighting but you don't mean it.'

I couldn't think of anything to say.

'It's football,' he goes. 'Your mammy's Germany. I'm Brazil.'

I can still see him saying that, as though it was yesterday. The way he was trying to smile.

I remember another day. It was in the autumn of 1975. The 26th of October. We all went on the bus to Bray after Mass. My father and me with Sheila and Helen and Rory. The sky was clear and the sea was blue. All along the seafront the bumper cars were rattling. There was a sweet smell of candy-floss in the air. We bought orange ice-pops and looked at the waves for a while. A woman on the promenade said the waves were the souls of the angels God really loved. She said God let them dance around on the sea, to thank them for being so good.

'Some fukken thank-you,' Sheila said. Under her breath.

'That was the best day ever,' my da said, coming home on the bus. 'That was great gas now. We'll do it again.'

But that wasn't true. Not the way things turned out. As we walked back that day, my father didn't know that the days like this were over. Everything was about to change.

When we got home the house was empty. That was unusual. My mother never went out on a Sunday. In fact, by then, she hardly went out at all. I think it was Sheila who found the note in the kitchen. 'Daddy,' she said. 'Mammy's gone.'

'Don't be dense,' he laughed. 'She's gone out for a walk.'

'No,' said Sheila. 'You're wrong.'

She gave him the note she had found on the table. She was crying now. Her face all squeezed up. The note said that my mother had taken enough. 'Go to her,' it said. 'Let's see how long she stands you. You broke my heart. Break hers.'

My father stared at this note for a long time. He was holding it very lightly in his hands. As though the piece of paper was on fire. He sat down on the stairs and he read it again. And after a while he looked up at us.

'That's lies,' he said. 'Don't be minding it. That's nothing.' He rolled the note up into a ball. He put it in his pocket and went out to the yard. He stayed out there for a long time.

I wasn't very upset. I knew my father was, but to be honest I couldn't see why. All I could see was that now there would be no more fights. When you are the age that I was then, you don't see the pain of being left. Or the pain of leaving either. Because there is pain there, too. You are just too young to know about these things.

When Sheila and Helen had stopped crying, my father went out to get chips and burgers in Dun Laoghaire. He was gone an hour. When he came back he had a smell of beer on his breath. He told us that 'a really gas thing' had happened. He had run into a friend of my mother up in the chip shop. She had told him my mother was just gone away on a holiday. She was after going down the country to see her relations. She would be back in a few days' time, he said. Everything would be grand then. Everything would be fine.

'So you see?' he smiled. 'I told you there was nothing to worry about.' He put the chips out on to plates and he looked me in the eye.

'You believe me,' he said. 'Don't you, Sailor?'

'Yes,' I said.

'Of course you do,' he said. 'You know your old da wouldn't tell you a lie.'

'Yes,' I said. 'You wouldn't do that.'

And I was happy then. I really was. Because I'd said what he wanted me to say.

A week went by and she didn't come back. Soon it was two weeks, and then a month. Christmas came. We got great presents. The best we ever had. Rory and I got new football boots. The girls got dresses and dolls and toys. I hadn't a breeze how Santa Claus could afford them. We'd always been told before that Santa wasn't flush. But that year, we asked no questions.

The new year began. Still there was no word of my mother. Sometimes at night I would look out my window. My father would be standing on the path. He'd be looking

up and down the street, as though he was waiting for somebody to come along. One night I asked him who he was
waiting for. 'Oh,' he said. 'Just this man I know. Don't you
worry about it. Everything's rosy.'

And then my father stopped going out in the boat. He
wanted to be there when we came home from school. He'd
get chips for our dinner. Some days he'd get pizza instead.
Then he started learning to cook, out of this book he got
one Saturday at a sale of work. He burned the arse out of
every pot in the house. Sheila said our mam was never
coming home now.

'You don't have to come home early,' I told him one day.
'We can look after ourselves.'

'Don't worry about that,' he'd say. 'Eat your chips.'

One day I was coming home from school when a
strange thing happened. I turned into the street and got
a surprise. Outside our house, a thin man in a suit was
talking to my father. I had seen him before. I knew he
worked at the Munster and Leinster Bank. I knew they
held the loan on my father's boat. He'd pay them every
month, never fail.

Beside the man was a fat policeman. The copper's neck
was thicker than his head. As I got closer I could hear that
the bank-man and my father were having an argument.

'Ah, now,' the policeman says to my father. 'Don't be
talking like that now, Paddy. There's no need at all for that
class of language.'

Suddenly my father takes a step forward and pushes the
man from the Munster and Leinster Bank. 'Don't you *dare*
say that to me ever again, pal,' he goes. 'Or I'll put you
through that fukken window, so I will.'

He goes into the house and slams the hole out of the door. The copper and your man in the suit look down at me.

'There you are,' the copper goes.

'What's the matter?' I ask him.

The bank-man says something quiet and fucks off in a hurry. The copper sighs and ruffles my hair.

'You're a great little warrior, aren't you? What are you going to be when you grow up? Would you like to be a policeman? I'd say you would.'

'I wouldn't,' I go.

'Would you not like that? To be a policeman and catch robbers?'

'My father says all policemen are culchies,' I go.

'Does he now? He's a gas man. A right comedian.'

'I want to be a priest,' I go.

He looks at me in a funny way. It's like I told him I was Jesus or something. There was an awful smell of stew off him.

'Well now,' he goes. 'That's a great thing for a boy to want to be.'

He gives me tenpence and fucks off. The big fat culchie. He walks like a duck. Fucking prick.

I go into the house after my father. He's by himself in the kitchen. His shirt is off. He's just standing there, silent, going spare in his vest and trousers. He doesn't say a thing. Not a single word. He gets a pint of milk out of the fridge and drinks it down in three gulps. He doesn't look like our da. He wipes his face with his vest. He leans his hand on the kitchen table as though he suddenly weighs a ton. He's staring around the kitchen like he's never been there before. He's got the face of a man who needs to sleep for a week. He goes over to the CB radio and flicks it on. There's a crackle. He switches it off.

'Why was that bank-man here?' I ask him.

He says nothing. I've asked again.

'He was messing,' he goes. 'He was having the crack. That was only a little mess we were having for a while. Come on out now and we'll go for a saunter.'

We walked all the way down to the end of the pier. Down to the lighthouse. Like we often did. But my father was in a quiet mood that night. He didn't want to talk. He'd get like that sometimes. And you didn't really mind. We sat on the benches near the lighthouse. The six o'clock ferry was leaving for England. There were people on the deck, walking up and down. They looked like they were having a great old time.

'Were you ever in England?' I asked my father.

'I was going to go once,' he said. 'When I was young.'

'Why didn't you?'

He took out a cigarette and lit it.

'I might yet,' he said, in a quiet way.

'I wouldn't like that,' I told him. 'I wouldn't like you to go away, Da.'

He didn't look at me. He reached out and took my hand. We sat like that for a while. Not saying anything. While the beam of the lighthouse swept over the water.

'Is Santa Claus real?' I asked him.

'Of course he is.'

'That's good. I wasn't sure.'

'Everything you think is real is real,' he goes. 'And everything else is shite.'

One day not long after that I found a letter in his bedroom. From a cunt who was a local politician for the Fine Gael party. He'd been in touch with the bank, he wrote.

They'd told him they knew things were difficult at home. But the back-money my father owed them would have to be paid right away. Or else there would be serious trouble. They didn't want to cause problems. Didn't want to take his livelihood. But the money must be paid without further delay. I don't know what happened after that. No one ever told me. But when my father came home to the house the next afternoon, he never went out on *The Wexford Girl* again.

The bailiff sold her in Killybegs. That's in County Donegal. There's nights I still see her in dreams.

Not many people came to my mother's funeral. Just me and my father and Sheila and Helen. And little Rory in my father's arms. There were a couple of neighbours but most stayed away. It was a year since we had seen her. She'd been living in Birmingham. I don't want to go into the details.

My father gave a pound to the gravediggers. He said digging graves was hard work. A thing that wasn't easy for anyone to do. They nodded and said they were sorry for his trouble.

It was a sunny day, but windy. So the priest's white lace robe kept blowing up into his face.

The night of her funeral I couldn't sleep. When I came down the stairs it was late. My father was sitting in the front room, in the armchair. He was still wearing his black suit and a shirt I didn't know he had. His shoes were off, and his toes were sticking through his socks. My father looked broken. He was crying.

This wasn't the first time I had seen him cry. And it wouldn't be the last. But it was the worst of all the times I ever saw it. He sat with his head in his hands. Sobbing. Breathing hard. Saying my mother's name over and over. As though my mother's name was a poem, or maybe a prayer. And I wanted to cry too. Not just because I was upset. But because I wanted to cry with my father.

'Da,' I said. 'Don't be crying. I'll mind you.'

He was shocked to see me standing there. I don't think he knew what to say for a while.

'I'm not crying,' he said. 'Why are you up?'

'You are,' I said. 'I saw you.'

We went into the kitchen. There was a packet of burgers sitting in the fridge. We fried them up with slices of stale bread. We sat in the front room, watching *The Comedians*. He drank a can of beer and I drank milk. He kept wiping his eyes with the back of his hand.

Whenever he finished a cigarette, he'd light another one on the end.

'Mammy's in heaven now. We've a friend with the angels. The main thing is not to be worrying about anything,' he goes. 'You're too young to be worrying about the big things. We'll just keep the flag flying here. And things will work out for the best in the end.'

'I won't worry,' I said. 'I promise.'

He nodded and looked around the room.

'Do you know what I do when I get worried?' he said.

'No,' I said. 'What do you do?'

'I think about your great-great-grandfather. I think about the way he worked. All those huge stones. The rocks the size of cars. It must have been awful. Really and truly. There must have been days his back was half broken. But in the end, it was worth it. It was worth all the work.

Because in the end, he was able to stand on the pier. He was able to say, "Look at this. I wasn't nobody. I'm a man who did something with his life.'"

The rain began to fall, softly against the windows of our house. Out on the street a car alarm was going. The dogs were barking at the thunder.

And we sat in each other's arms then, watching *The Comedians*. Even when it was over we didn't move. We listened to the sound of the rain, falling softly on the street. I suppose we must have been thinking about all kinds of things. But all I remember is the sound of the rain. And me, holding on to my father very hard.

He got a job washing cars and doing odd jobs around the village. He'd go around the rich houses up in Killiney and Dalkey. He'd wash cars, he'd cut grass. Anything for a few pound. A retired judge up in Dalkey paid my father to weed out and tidy his garden. It took him nearly three months to do it properly. Sometimes on Saturdays me and Sheila would go and help him.

The job was so good that the judge paid my father to come back once a week and make sure the garden was all right. After a while, word got around and he was asked to do other gardens too. Funny enough, that was work he seemed to like. He seemed to have a talent for it. He lost a bit of weight. His face got suntanned. He went to night school in Sallynoggin and learned about plants.

After a while he met a woman. She was a big fat biddy from down the country and she laughed a lot. Her husband died in a fire, I believe. My father and herself used to go walking the pier together. She drank a bit, but so did he.

Some people said that was what kept them together. But talk is cheap. And nobody knows.

All I know myself is that she seemed to understand him. I think she made him happy. It's just my impression. The rows they'd have sometimes? Jesus, don't be talking. But they always made them up in the end. She wouldn't be behind the door when it came to a fight. She'd skin the living hide off you with her language, so she would. I wouldn't repeat it. She'd go through you for a short cut. She used to sing when she had a few drinks on her, which was most of the time. These sad country-and-western songs about cowboys leaving waitresses. You wouldn't be able to stop her. She had a terrible voice too. And I've heard some squawkers in my time. The father said she had a voice would peel a fukken carrot. She was 'a two bucket woman', he'd say. She could drink two buckets of Guinness and come back for more. She'd suck the sweat from a dipso's vest.

The last time I saw them together was at my sister Helen's second wedding two years ago. After dinner, the father gets himself up to make the speech. He had everyone in stitches. He really did. His eyes were shining like little lumps of sunshine.

'But marriage is great. It's changing, of course. These days, there's even talk of marriage for gay people. And personally I'd be in favour. You have to be fair. Why shouldn't they be as miserable as the rest of us?'

People laughed. And he started to laugh himself. I think he must have got a fit of giggles. A thing a comedian should never do. You never laugh at your own jokes. Any comedian will tell you that. But that day, for some reason, he laughed. It was like he was happy, he really didn't care. It was as though he had never had a worry in all his life. He laughed until he was red. Everyone laughed back. He laughed more. He roared with laughter. Everyone howled. Then he took a step backwards and fell right over. And everyone went mad, laughing and clapping.

They thought it was supposed to be funny, part of his routine. And that's the way he would have wanted it, I'd say. You could say my father died laughing.

The church was packed with little old biddies for his funeral. The priest was new, a bit nervous, a culchie. He said he had never met my father himself, but that everyone said he was a great comedian. In his work as a fisherman he'd helped a lot of people. He was known all the way from Dun Laoghaire up to Ballybrack. From Monkstown Farm over to Sallynoggin. The king of the road. That's what he was. He was known for his kindness everywhere.

Nobody was saying he was a perfect saint. There was nobody saying he never made a mistake. But Paddy O'Meara had a kind word for the lonely person. The neighbour who was down on their luck, in trouble. He had been visited by tragedy. Only God knew why. There was a reason for everything. Now there would be mercy. To many in Glasthule, especially the poor, Paddy O'Meara was more than a trawlerman.

'Paddy, like Jesus, did miracles with fish,' the priest said. 'To some in this parish, he walked on the water.'

'Only because he couldn't swim,' someone called, down at the back. And everyone broke their holes laughing, even the priest.

Sometimes I think I see him in the street. When I get the smell of the sea, he'd come into my mind. And now and again, at night, I think about him still. When I'm tucking my own kids into bed. For some reason I'd think of him then. I'd remember saying goodnight to him over the radio at home. The crackle and the wash of the waves through the dark. 'Say a prayer for me, Sailor. Don't worry your head. I'll be home in the morning, never fear.'

Or whenever I see a comedian on the television, telling jokes and pulling faces. Sometimes just the sound of laughter brings him back. Like a ghost. Like someone in a song.

I think about him walking Dun Laoghaire pier. Down to the lighthouse, looking out at the boats. Wishing he had gone away to England.

And then I picture him walking slowly back up. Along by the seafront wall and back towards Glasthule. Laughing his head off at the madness of the world. Laughing away. Always laughing.

Where Have You Been?

A NOVELLA

I

Scenes from a Hurricane

Dublin, 2010

S everal years after his divorce, as his thirties came to a close, Cian Hanahoe spent five weeks in hospital. What had happened was referred to as 'an episode' by the consultant psychiatrist, a scrupulously courteous, slightly eccentric Ulsterman who stirred his coffee with a biro that looked as if it had been given free with a boys' comic, in that it had a plastic eyeball in place of a clicker. Cian Hanahoe had little to say. It didn't seem to matter. The season began to change.

The monks who cared for the patients asked no questions about the past. He found them wise, admirably realistic, secretive. One of them, a Brother Lauri, facilitated an informal writing group for patients, after which he would encourage them to play CDs or tapes. He had a theory that traditional songs were actually short stories. If a patient volunteered to sing, which happened surprisingly often, he had a habit of scribbling down the lyrics. An inner-city Dubliner, he was forty and had tattoos on his forearms. In his cowl, which he only wore occasionally, preferring jeans and a hoodie, he looked like a middleweight Rasputin.

He was a gruff, nice man, so it seemed to Cian Hanahoe,

and had the kind of belief in God that gives no offence to those with less certain positions. He would even mutter 'Merciful Christ' when irked about something small, like the coffee-vending machine in the day room being out of order again or one of the red balls on the snooker table being missing. It was rumoured of him that he had once threatened to have a pompous psychiatrist sectioned under the Mental Health Act, an incident that had greatly increased his stock among his charges.

In the evenings, when the hospital was quiet, Cian Hanahoe would make an attempt at writing. But it was difficult to know what to write. The brief for the class was to begin with a short piece of memoir, to fix on one remembered incident from childhood and simply describe it as it had occurred. The piece should be no more than one side of foolscap and the event need not have special significance. The task was to write it down quickly, using the first words or expressions that came to mind. But how to begin? Where did any event begin? He would walk the paths and groves of the hospital grounds, trying to enter the past. One morning in the showers an incident came to him so completely that he felt it was what he had been waiting for. By the time he had returned to the ward, the piece was composing itself in his mind. Scared that he would lose the words, he scribbled them down so quickly and aggressively that the pencil-lead snapped as he scrawled.

My name is Cian Hanahoe. I'm living in Dublin. I'm a Property Loans Manager with an Irish investment bank. As a teenager I used to go to this disco in the rugby club in Donnybrook on a Saturday night. There was a night I was on my way home and I was walking past this old house on Nutley Lane to get the bus. I don't know what got into me but I was mad keen to see the house close up. I went in through the gates and about halfway up the drive when this dog starts howling and I ran like fuck. When I got home, it was about half eleven and the police had been called to our house. My father was upset. I think he was in tears. One of the neighbours, this quiet man who did something in the Irish Hospitals Sweepstakes, was standing in our front garden looking frightened. My mother was screaming. The window in the hall door was smashed.

My father put us into his van, myself and my brother, Paul. We nicknamed him 'Pablo'. He's two years younger than me. My father drove away from the house pretty fast like he never wanted to see it again. I was happy we were going. We drove a good few hours northwards, Pablo stopped crying and fell asleep. It was the middle of the night by now. After a while I nodded off too, the van was warm and kind of consoling. When I woke up, the van wasn't moving, my father was sitting at the wheel and just staring out at the road ahead of him as though he didn't understand it, like he'd never seen a road before. This would have been four or maybe five in the morning. He was fond of fishing, my father, and he was wearing his fisherman's jacket. I don't know why I'd remember that.

I said: 'Are we going to Donegal, Daddy?' Because we sometimes went there in the summertimes. My father was in the drapery business; he'd go to Donegal to buy tweed. It was a place he seemed to love.

He said to me: 'Would you like to?'

I said: 'Yeah, I would.'

'Would you not miss your mam?'

'No.'

'Mammy isn't well, love.' (My father sometimes called me 'love'.) 'You're fifteen. It's hard. There's things you don't understand. But we'll stick together, Cian, and all will be grand. We'll be in on the first count. Do you believe me?'

I said: 'Yes.'

'That's good. You're a great lad altogether. Sure your dad would be lost without you, so he would. Come on so, we'll head home to Mammy.'

He read over it a few times before tearing it up. And when later in the day he opened his notebook again, it was not to write anything of his life, his own memories, but to draft out a letter to a Dublin newspaper, one of whose columnists had written a scathing piece about bankers. They were little better than traitors, the article said. They had wrecked the whole country. Turned it into a casino. They had all known the facts. None of them cared. A strange rage invaded him as he penned his response. He crumpled it and threw it away.

His line manager visited weekly. They were difficult occasions. It was hard to know what to say, what to leave unsaid. Mainly they spoke of the weather or sports, little incidents at the office; the trees in the hospital grounds. If there was anything he needed, he had only to say. But he couldn't think of anything to ask for.

He was often asked during his consultations if he had heard of bipolar depression. He answered that he believed his mother had suffered from it all her adult life and that he did not think this was his condition. He had none of the symptoms he had seen in his childhood: the irrational laughing highs, the sudden crashing lows.

'But you've self-destructive thoughts?'

'No, I haven't. Not seriously.'

'Cian–'

'I said a couple of stupid things on the first night you saw me. I've been stressed-out at work. That's all that happened, honestly. Things got on top of me a bit because I hadn't been sleeping. I told you, I didn't sleep at all for four nights. I'm feeling calmer with the medication and the therapy has helped too. I just needed a rest. I'm planning on taking a holiday with my brother and his family. They've a place they often go to in Portugal.'

'Cian, we really have to work on this. I can't help you if you're evasive. Even before this incident, you were hospitalised for an overdose.'

'Calling it an overdose is a bit much.'

'So what would you call it?'

'I took a sleeping pill I hadn't been prescribed and had an allergic reaction with antibiotics. I don't feel I need help. I'd like to sign myself out.'

'Son, you've had what used to be known as a nervous breakdown. It isn't something you run under the cold tap.'

'With respect, I understand that. I'm the one who had it.'

'I don't advise you to leave us. Have you someone at home?'

'I'll be staying with my brother,' he lied.

'I obviously can't agree to your checking out until I'm satisfied you're no danger to yourself.'

'I can wait until you are. That's fine.'

He returned to work. People were quietly welcoming. It

was clear they knew everything, although nobody made any reference to what had happened. He was asked to move temporarily to the Public Relations Department; they needed extra backroom help, he was told. It became evident to him that colleagues were quietly organising the tasks that came his way so that they would not be overly taxing, would run with the things that interested him. Their decency and discretion moved him but it could not be acknowledged. He was asked to write a speech for the Chairman of the Board who was presenting a sports prize the bank sponsored for underprivileged schools. Since the downturn, it was important to get these things right. There had been unhelpful and damaging publicity.

One evening when he was working late, the Chief Executive came into his office unannounced. He was one of those bourgeois Irishmen who affect a working-class accent as a means of asserting fellow feeling.

'How's the man? No, don't get up, you're grand, how's tricks? It's good to have you back, Cian. I just wanted to drop in.'

'It was thoughtful of you to send the card, Fergus. It was appreciated; thanks.'

The Chief Executive gave him a gaze of amiable incomprehension. He looked like one of Fagin's gang grown up: affable, a bit hungry, in need of a plate of stew and a cuddle. It was Aifric who had once referred to him as 'The Artful Dodger' and the image had never quite faded.

'When I was in hospital,' said Cian Hanahoe. 'The card.'

'Oh, the card. Sorry, I'm jacked. I remember it now.' He stared strangely around the office, as though its furniture had emitted a sudden noise.

'And you're back on the straight and narrow, Cian. That's the main thing, says you.'

'Yes, Fergus. Much better. Being busy at work helps.'

'Sound. That's great. The auld stress is an awful bastard, isn't it? It's fierce hard relaxing. And then it all mounts up. There's times I'd nearly wonder if we weren't better off in the old days. Do you know what I mean? Before everything got so busy.'

'I know what you mean, yes.'

'You'd be admired here, Cian. I wanted to say that to you. I'm not good at putting a thing sometimes. But I'd want you to know that. Because we've all had ups and downs; there's none of us didn't. I'm not putting it very well. I wouldn't have the gift you'd have yourself that way with words. But I hope you know what I'm saying. There'd be a regard for you here.'

'Thank you, Fergus. It's very generous of you to say that.'

'Not at all. But I'm being a bit gay. We'll say no more about it. But if there's anything I can do, you just let my people know. Don't be bothering with these fuckers down here, just have a word on the q.t. with one of my girls above. By the way, that was a massive speech you wrote for me there the other week. For the function I did in Manchester. Got a fabulous reaction so it did. I'm after getting one of the girls above to make photostats and send them to everyone was there. "We are no petty people." That was ace. The way you put it.'

'I'm afraid I can't take the credit, Fergus, it was something Yeats said. In his speech to the Senate about divorce.'

'Go way?'

'I'll dig it out for you if you like. I have it on the computer somewhere.'

'I'd a lump in the throat reading it. It really hit me. You know? Just the way you laid out all the history and the poetry and everything. On the plane coming home, it was in my mind all the way. I don't know why. Just night-thoughts, I suppose. We were coming in over the Wicklow Mountains and everything dark and I couldn't get it out of the mind. You'd be thinking about Pearse and Connolly when you'd read something like that. And the poor fuckers in the Famine, God love them. And all the people had to emigrate. If they saw the carry-on of us now, they'd be amazed by the place. It'd nearly make you wonder, wouldn't it?'

'Yes, it would.'

'Sure there it is, I suppose. Anyhow, I've to head across to the Merrion for a pint with a shower of gobshites up from Cork. Would you join us? Sure you know where we are.'

When the Chief Executive had left, Cian returned to his work, but the invitation to the Merrion began to nag at him. Unsure as to whether or not it had been sincerely meant, he was equally uncertain if he should accept it. Perhaps it was a summons, perhaps just a politeness – sometimes, with the Chief Executive, it was hard to decipher subtleties – and there was no senior colleague around whose advice might be sought. In the end, he went across to the hotel but there was no sign of the Chief Executive in the lounge or the restaurant, and the concierge assured him he hadn't been in that night, indeed rarely came in at all.

'But the Minister for Agriculture is here,' the concierge offered helpfully, as though an invasion force had been sighted in the Irish Sea and any important personage that could be sobered up at short notice would suffice to rouse the nation to militancy.

'I'll leave it. Thanks.'

'As you wish.'

It was several months later when a co-worker told him there had been a phone call while he'd been out at lunch. From a woman called Catherine Dwyer, a Londoner here for work. She had been given the bank's number by a librarian in Arklow. She was Production Designer for a major television series that was to be shot in Ireland, a remake of *Wuthering Heights*. The project had received funding from the Irish Film Board. She was based at Ardmore Studios in Wicklow.

'What's that to do with us?'

'Haven't a breeze, Cian. She didn't say.'

An older colleague chipped in: 'We've some painting she wants to have a look at. Apparently it's downstairs. She sent someone a fax but I can't find it.'

'The painting or the fax?'

'Neither of them, actually. Would you give her a shout, Cian? I'm up to my eyes at the minute.'

Her mode on the phone was clipped, a bit harassed and disjointed, as though several conversations were going on at the moment and she wasn't sure which one she belonged in. He was surprised, when she came into the bar of the Shelbourne Hotel, by the Principal Boy litheness of her look. He had expected someone older. She might have been thirty. She was taller than Cian Hanahoe and seemed at ease in the room, and since walking into a new room tended to make him feel ungainly, he found self-possession a sort of beguilement in others. It was raining very heavily as she hurried in from Kildare Street so that her hair clung in straggles to her forehead. There was a stud in her nose. She was wearing lace gloves. There was something buccaneerish going on with the coat. His father would have said she 'cut a dash' or 'had a nice figure'. She pulled her mobile from her pocket and looked at it resentfully.

'Is it Catherine Dwyer?'

'You must be the man from the bank? So sorry I'm late.' Her handshake was firm and quick.

'I got in before the crowd,' he said. 'I've a table over here?'

'Do you mind if we stand? I'm in a bit of a rush. Bugger of a taxi-man overcharged me. Slightly *distrait*. How are you?'

'I'm fine. Would you like something to drink?'

'No thanks, just water. Are you from Dublin yourself?'

'Well, Dun Laoghaire, really. It's about eight miles south.'

'That was called Kingstown, right? In the nineteenth century?'

'The same.'

'When our lot were in charge.' She gave a playful grin. 'With a name like Dwyer, you're surely one of our own.'

'Only about an eighth, I'm afraid.'

'You'll have to forgive me,' he said, 'I'm not quite sure what a production designer does.'

'It's how the show looks, really; the locations, the sets. I so wish we were allowed to smoke. Do you smoke yourself?'

'I'm trying to give them up. We could stand outside if you like?'

'Oh, not with the rain. Shall I start pestering you now? How dreary at the end of your day.'

'It's my pleasure. How can I help? My colleague didn't say.'

'I'm interested in the paintings of the Irish artist Seán or John Keating. Are there some in the bank's collection? A colleague at Ardmore told me there were.' She waited for a communal roar at some sporting event on the television to die down before she continued. 'I'm on the trail of anything large-scale featuring County Wicklow in particular, just thinking of different handles on landscape. There's one I've been trying to dig up, called *Scenes from a Hurricane*. Nobody seems to know where it is.'

'I don't know that particular one. But yes, I believe we've a few in the collection. I can look it up and get back to you if you give me your email. Have you tried the National Gallery? And there's an excellent private gallery, Whyte's. They're just down the street here. They'd often have work by Keating and their catalogue essays are good.'

She started making notes of what he was saying and he found it oddly arresting to watch her, perhaps because she knew old-fashioned shorthand. She had worked as a features reporter in London, she explained, before giving it up for art school at the age of twenty-five.

'Late starter, I'm afraid. Everyone else was about seven. They're all making millions in fashion now.'

'You won't believe it,' he said, 'but as a child I actually met Keating.'

'No way?'

'We have a television programme over here called *The Late Late Show* that's been running since the 1960s. Keating was a guest on it one night – it must be thirty years ago or more. He'd have been an old man by then. A son of his, Justin, was a politician here. Well, my father happened to see the interview and was taken by him, I suppose. He arranged for our portraits to be done by him, mine and my brother's, just little charcoal sketches. I hardly remember him. He lived in this shadowy old house up in the Dublin Mountains that had a watermill and cats and trees. Fierce looking man, sort of red-eyed and monkish. But very kind too. Like Santa Claus.'

'How amazing. What a guy.'

'Keating?'

'No, your dad. Did he work in the arts?'

'He was a draper here in Dublin. He's retired a few years.'

'But he had your portraits commissioned?'

'I never thought of it as unusual. But maybe it was. My mother took an interest in the arts. She was a librarian before she was married.'

'Do you still have it? Your portrait?'

'Yes, she left it to me when she died. It's a simple little thing. He would have done it in ten or fifteen minutes; it's not in oils or anything. But it's a nice memento to have. Do you enjoy working in television? It must be a fascinating world.'

'Full of absolute fucking tossers, if you'll pardon my French. Was your degree in commerce?'

'Maths and history. And I've a H. Dip., a teaching diploma. Why?'

'You don't seem a typical man from the bank.' She had taken out a compact and was reapplying her lip gloss as they talked.

'I sort of drifted into it. It was meant to be a stopgap, and then, I don't know.'

'Can I be your assistant?' she deadpanned. 'It sounds pretty cool to work in a bank.'

'You'd find it fairly unexciting, I can assure you. We're not too popular these days.'

'Yes, you're somewhere between paedophile priests and corrupt politicians, according to the papers over here.'

They kept talking and he gave her some pamphlets he

had brought as an afterthought, about forthcoming exhibitions and lectures. He told her of wild places in Wicklow she might wish to see – a forgotten glen near Imaal, a ruined village close to Curtlestown – scribbling directions and guidelines to landmarks on the photocopied Ordnance Survey maps she produced from her briefcase. There was an easiness about her companionship; it was like being with someone he already knew. When she begged a sip of his coffee, it didn't seem strange to be sharing the cup. After an hour she mentioned she was hungry and it occurred to him there might be a chance to continue the evening.

'We could maybe have something to eat, if you're free? There's an Italian on Dame Street. It's a little place called Nicos, kind of a Dublin institution.'

'Oh I'm meeting someone, sorry. He might pop by in a minute?'

'Of course. Well, anyhow. I'd better be heading on.'

'Another time though if you'd like? I'm in town now and again; sometimes I have to come up to the National Library or Trinity. Maybe you'd let me drag you away for a sandwich and a fag.'

'That would be grand if you're at a loose end. I've rarely anything on at lunchtime.'

'Oh look, here's my date coming now.'

An absurdly handsome man in his late twenties stepped out of the crowd and approached them with a sodden umbrella. His long coat was splashed and muddy and he was wearing a furry hat that made him look like a Russian cavalry officer.

'Christ, Catherine, sorry I'm late.' He spoke with a Galway accent.

'Hi, Kevin. God look at you. This is Mr Hanahoe, he's a man from the bank. He's tremendously important and he's also very helpful. He had his portrait done by our friend when he was a lad – isn't that amazing?'

Nods were exchanged and brief pleasantries traded. A certain amount of collaborative mockery was made of Catherine Dwyer, since her date's name was not in fact 'Kevin' but a Gaelic version 'Caoimhghín', and he revealed that she had once asked him if it began with a 'Q', a letter not existing in Irish. She chuckled in mortification as the anecdote was told, touching its teller often and fondly on the arm. His face was freckled and broad, his smile deeply good-natured. 'I don't mean to be clock-watching but we'd nearly want to be making tracks, Catherine. The table's booked for seven-thirty.'

'It was nice meeting you, Cian. Thanks very much for the pointers. Let me give you my number and maybe you'd bell me if the picture turns up?'

'Of course. Have a nice evening.'

'Call me, okay?'

'I will.'

They shook hands as she left.

II

Wintertime in Wicklow

He gave in his notice in October, was permitted to leave without serving it out in full. There was 'a medical context', his superior had explained, and whoever needed to agree had agreed. He was asked if he would like a gathering of some kind – maybe drinks in Head Office or a small dinner with colleagues. It would have to be small. Times had changed. He replied that he wouldn't like anything at all. Really he just wanted to go.

He left the premises for the last time on a drizzly Wednesday at lunchtime. On his way towards the DART station he pushed unnoticed through a crowd of reporters and television cameramen that had gathered by the gates of Government Buildings. The delegation from the IMF had arrived in Dublin to put the bankrupt country on life support.

The motorcade came up Merrion Street flanked by Garda motorcycle outriders. He watched the journalists pushing closer to the limousine, microphones thrusting out. It was raining heavily by now and some of the cameramen and reporters were dressed in sou'westers, like fishermen. He felt a strange, intense sympathy for the men from the IMF. But it was probably the benzodiazepine kicking in.

Someone had organised a collection to buy Cian Hanahoe a parting gift: a hundred-euro book token for Easons. The card had been signed by almost everyone in the department and even by the Chairman of the Board. He was congratulated on his 'escape from the lunacy in here', his 'flit from the madhouse', 'the Bedlam'. One colleague, a quiet man, close to retirement himself, had written 'I will miss you greatly, Cian' and a short couplet of Yeats. He had never realised the older man thought of him as a friend. Maybe he didn't really, but it was a compassionate thing to have written.

Immediately, he sent letters to schools in Dublin, and to the dormitory towns in Wicklow, Louth and Kildare, saying he was an arts graduate, mathematics and history, with a H. Dip. in education, had worked since leaving UCD in various branches of mortgage-related banking but now wished to change to teaching. Most principals did not reply. Of the ones who did, few had anything they could offer. But one of them, a nun who managed a school in the north inner city, said receiving his letter had been fortuitous. A young part-time teacher had announced she was leaving in the new year. There might be a few hours available. Had he any recent experience? Could he come in some time for a talk? They were looking for someone to take pass-level maths and civics for the Inter Cert classes. A former bank employee might well have insights.

Against all he might have predicted, it became a winter of hope. He began attending the gym, slimming down. In the evenings, he would drive into Wicklow and meet Catherine Dwyer at Ardmore. She was scouting night-shoot locations that would be accessible for a crew, and finding it difficult to come up with them. ('Bloody *Wuthering Heights*,' she'd say. 'Every other scene happens in darkness. What were those Brontës *on*?') It became a pleasant challenge to help her, a means of companionship. He was doing nothing else, he assured her. He had the feeling she was lonely in Ireland, for all her bonhomie and avowed contentment, had few confidantes on the production and no friends in the city. Perhaps she didn't get the codes of Irish professional camaraderie, with its subtle mix of mockeries, resentments and fondness. She laughed a great deal when she told him stories from the set. The sense grew in him that hiding your hurt was a thing she'd respect, a hard-won, important victory.

There was a new arts centre in Bray. They sometimes went there to watch a film or hear music, dining afterwards in one of the little cafés on the seafront. Or they would walk the forlorn promenade, past the amusement arcades and kebab shops, as heavy metal blasted from the windows of the hotels. Working-class English, kids with Damien Dempsey on their ghetto blasters, boarded-up guesthouses and burnt-out chippers and IRA graffiti on the walls. Squeezed-out tubes of spermicide and sunscreen in the bins, with puked candyfloss and unwanted shooting-gallery prizes. It was a wonderful place, she said, not entirely ironically. She really did seem to like it.

He showed her Wicklow: hidden lakes, the ruins of old mines, bog meadows, Raven's Glen, the waterfall at Powerscourt. She was a reason to visit again the places of his childhood Sundays, their names sounding beautiful in her London accent: Djouce Mountain, Tonduff, Carrickgollagan. Knocksink. Aughavannagh, Glenmalure, Annamoe, Lough Nahangan.

The grave of the painter Paul Henry in the churchyard at Enniskerry, not far from Lover's Leap rock. She asked him to show her his favourite view of all; he brought her hiking up a steep-ditched switchback path above the reforestation project at Kilmolin. On the eastern horizon they could just make out the peaks of Snowdonia, the bald drumlin of Holy Island at the entrance to Holyhead.

They drove south to Brittas Bay, ate grim sandwiches in the dunes. The ruins of a fairy ring near a housing estate at Arklow, still transmitting its menace a thousand years after it was made, according to the kids supping cans nearby. A corporation worker had tried to bulldoze it eighteen months previously, so they said; his JCB had burst into flames the moment he entered the rath and he was dead before the engine cut out. 'That's as true as jaysus, mister, I seen it myself. You don't be fuckin' dissin' the fairies.'

'Way to fuck, you fuckin gowl,' scoffed another lad, whispering to his girl. But the first boy, aged about twelve, sunburnt to the shade of his Man U shirt, insisted on the veracity of the story. 'I'd no more cross that circle than piss on a grave. They'd come after you so they would. They're cunts. An oul tinker used to be at the tarmackin' told me ma the fairies took his wife. An you seen him yourself you'd believe it, mister. Your head'd be wrecked thinkin' about it.'

She returned to London for ten days over Christmas. He found that he missed her, wanted to collect her at Dublin Airport and had set out in the car to surprise her before realising it was too loaded a gesture, the kind of thing lovers did. He pulled into the breakdown lane on the side of the M50, sat there almost an hour trying to sort his thoughts. He watched the planes coming in. She would be on one of them, he knew. To approach her across the arrivals concourse, to embrace her, take her bag? Would she be happy to see him there or find his presence unnerving, more than would be expected from a friend? In the end he sat so long that she must have landed by then, was probably in a taxi back to the hotel, or to Ardmore. She had mentioned there would be a very late script-meeting that night. Money People were coming in from Los Angeles.

For several days she did not call. Often he had the phone in his hand, but some reluctance he couldn't fathom made him unable to dial her number. He had begun to give up hope, but one night when he returned to the apartment, having been to a film alone in the city, his answering machine was flashing a red '1'. For a while, his apprehensiveness had made him incapable of playing it. He made coffee, took a shower, opened a beer. The couple in the neighbouring apartment were having an argument. He watched part of an old movie on Sky. He never looked at the RTE evening news any more. He was almost afraid of it.

'Cian, it's Catherine Dwyer.' Her saying his name. The message was briskly genial, like an affectionate sister's. She had been busy; it was crazy; had he been well, as she hoped? It had been good to see London; she had visited her parents. 'It was nice for my mother to be able to get on my case.' If he'd like to have a new-year pint she'd be clearer after the weekend. 'But I expect you're probably busy, no pressure.'

They met in what used to be the Elphin Hotel in Dun Laoghaire and was now some sort of gastropub with gas heaters outside. She was tanned, relaxed, with her hair tied back, and was wearing a leather jacket he hadn't seen her in. Some of the gaffers at Ardmore had been teaching her bits of classroom Irish as a joke. *'Ciúnas. Suí síos'*: Silence. Sit down. *'An dtuigeann tú?'*: Do you understand? *'Ma's é do thoil é'*: Please. *'Cait ní Dubhuir is ainm dom'*. Catherine Dwyer is my name. *'An raighfá thar claí liom?'* He laughed.

'What's funny?' she enquired. 'Isn't that: *May I please be excused?'* He had to explain that it was actually *'Would you go over the ditch with me?'*, a time-honoured Gaelic invitation to al-fresco sex. 'How do you say 'You fucking bastards' in Irish?' she asked him. 'Ah, that's easy,' he told her. *'Englishmen.'*

One night they went into the city to see a production of *Juno and the Paycock* at the Abbey. He loved sitting beside her in the darkness, being close to her. Not to be alone in the pews of the theatre; to have someone to share a programme, a murmured joke between acts. The sense that she might touch you during a scene change if she wanted something small explained. At the interval he found himself hoping someone he knew would be in the foyer; he would have liked to introduce her, to be seen with her in public, and for word to go around that she was beautiful and amusing and smarter than anyone in the room. She couldn't begin to see what he liked in the play, found it burlesque, full of clichés, the dialogue ridiculously florid and the women characters ruinously unconvincing. But afterwards, in the Flowing Tide bar across the street, some of the actors arrived, looking weary and cool, and like everyone else in the pub she was entranced as she watched them, moving conspiratorially among each other, swapping teases and embraces, like mariners returned from some forbidden adventure and sworn to fraternal secrecies. The girl who had played Mary Boyle was in ripped Levis and a tank top, her blue-black hair combed straight, long and loose, and she fought a running battle of imprecations with the long-suffering barman who kept insisting he'd put her out if she smoked. She was queenly, a chuckler, a drinker of Jack Daniels and ginger, and when she sang 'My Love is in America' at the end of the night it was as though this was the truer play.

They ate quarter-pounders and fries in a dive on O'Connell Street with the winos and the junkies and the night people. A flirtatious Russian security guard told him he was lucky 'to be marry such a beautiful wife'. On hearing it she laughed diplomatically, pushed her hair behind her ears, and in the almost painful brightness of the muzak-filled burger bar looked into his eyes for a second too long before returning to the coffee she said was hideous. He drove her back to Bray, the hotel on the main street, with Bob Dylan's *Street Legal* on the tape deck and the smoke of her cigarettes and her never-ending talk filling the space between them.

'I'll always remember tonight. But it was a terrible piece of rubbish.'

'I enjoyed your company, Catherine. Thanks.'

'Do you like it, really? The play?'

'I suppose I do, yeah.'

'I'd better go in.'

'Okay.'

'Should I have one last fag? Are you hurrying home?'

'No no, fire away, you're grand.'

'Would you like one yourself?'

'I'm kind of off them, but okay.'

'Funny character, that Russian. It's nice to have a husband who doesn't mind me smoking.'

'I'm tolerant.'

'Yeah. It's the reason I married you. That, and your money of course.'

At one in the morning she crossed to a kebab shop on the corner and got coffees and a bottle of water while he walked to the all-night petrol station down the street for cigarettes and the chewing gum she wanted. It was almost half-past two when she slipped from his car. Every Dylan CD in the glovebox had been played and no cigarettes were left. Their talk had been easy. There was a sort of freedom in the lateness and in sitting in a car, where you didn't have to look at each other face to face. The windscreen steamed. She carved spirals with her fingers, played Xs and Os with herself as they conversed. He told her stories from the bank, she told him about her parents' divorce. She had dallied with sculpture at art school, liked early Bowie, Shostakovich. She had had an abortion. She believed in God. The world would be meaningless if she didn't, she said, like saying you didn't believe in Emma Bovary just because Flaubert had made her up. There was one subject she refused to allude to but its deliberate absence seemed a presence, as though a passenger was sleeping in the back seat of the car and might be awoken if his existence were acknowledged.

It was obvious that there was someone in London but she never mentioned him directly, never offered details or a name. Neither did she ask outright about Cian's own situation, until one evening while they walking White Rock Strand, she said: 'Did you have children? You and your wife, I mean?'

'My wife?'

'Someone at Ardmore told me she'd been at UCD with your wife. Your ex, I mean. Is it Elaine?'

'Aifric is her name. No, we didn't have children.'

'You didn't want to? May I ask?'

'We'd hoped to. It didn't work out.'

She nodded. 'Understood. I'm very sorry. Let's leave it.'

'She was a great person. Aifric, I mean. What happened was cruel. You couldn't begin to explain it. When a marriage ends.'

'You're in touch, are you still?'

'Not really. She's moved on. We'd send cards at Christmas, nothing more. She had a baby a couple of months ago. He's called Robert. She's living in Manchester.'

He had never said the child's name aloud before. He lit a cigarette, took a drag. He had the feeling she was going to touch him out of something like sympathy and he didn't want that to happen. It loomed up at him, the night he had spent on the internet looking for a present on sites for babies' clothes, the care with which he had worded the email: 'From Cian – all the best of happiness.' Seven words in the end, after numerous hours of trying and so many redraftings that he couldn't bear to think of it now. To press 'send' had been hard, to receive the thank-you card harder. He had thrown it away after reading it only once.

'And for you, Catherine? There's someone in London? Do you mind me asking?'

'He's living in New York at the moment for work. But yes, there's someone. "Someone" puts it very well, I would say. He's someone called Paul. Paul Anderson.'

'What does he do? He's in television, is he?'

'His card says he's an entertainment industry lawyer. Whatever that means.'

'It's serious?'

'Four years. Well, we're on a break right now. One of those complicated situations. I'm not the greatest picker of all time, as it happens. I don't care for nice men. But there's been the occasional exception, of course. Actually he's very nice. He's like you.'

'I'd have been surprised if there was nobody.'

'How did you know?'

'Just you sometimes say "we". Like, *we* went to a concert. Or we were in Italy or whatever. I just noticed.'

'Did you love her? Aifric? What a beautiful name.'

He took a long drink from the carton of orange juice they'd been sharing while they walked. 'I really don't talk about it now. I've sort of made it a rule. I know I probably should, but I just decided not to. I don't mean to be offhand. I just find it works for me not to.'

'Do you have sisters?'

'No I don't. I've a younger brother.'

'I would have sworn you had sisters. Funny.'

He drove her back to the hotel and they sat in his car on the main street, while the young people darted in and out of the burger shops, laughing, shouting. It was the night before St Patrick's Day, he realised suddenly. Many of the kids were already drunk.

'Look at them,' she said. 'Do you wish you were eighteen?'

'I wish both of us were,' he said.

'Funny situation, this.'

'I guess it is, right enough.'

'You know what I think we should do?'

'What?'

'I think we should go into the hotel. Order a bottle of

– 238 –

vodka. Sit in the bar and drink it and talk about nothing serious at all. And whatever happens after that, never happened.'

'Okay.'

'You're sure? I mean it literally. Nothing ever happened.'

'I understand.'

'Okay then. Let's not bother with the vodka.'

Her room in the hotel was small and far too hot, and there was an untidy pile of papers on the table by the window, with her portfolios and rip-sheets and sketchbooks. A laptop showed a screensaver of her and a man at the Statue of Liberty. She checked her emails before powering it off. A blue dress he had seen her wearing was hanging in the bathroom doorway, in a dry-cleaner's polythene sack. There were several pairs of running socks drying in the sink, a couple of stacked paperbacks on the rim of the cracked enamel bath, and there was a make-up bag like a child's pencil-case sitting on the windowsill spilling a cargo of lipsticks and old DART tickets. He heard her moving about the bedroom as he washed his face and hands and when he came to her she had taken off her pullover and unbuttoned her jeans. There was a minibar set into a cabinet and its door was open, its humming yellow light illuminating a parallelogram of threadbare carpet. She was holding two miniatures of gin.

'Would you like a drink?'

'No thanks.'

'Are you scared?'

'A bit.'

'Me too,' she said. 'I've not done anything like this in a long time.'

'Would you rather we didn't?'

'I'd rather we did. If you're sure you're okay with it. Are you?'

Touching her, kissing her, unfastening her clothes, made him shake so badly that she whispered for him to be calm. But she wasn't calm herself as he opened her bra and touched her small breasts, her abdomen, her ribcage, the hardness of her collarbone, his hands finding the jogging shorts she had on beneath her jeans.

'Do you have anything?' she asked him.

'No, I'm sorry. I didn't expect–'

'Can we just kiss and touch, then? Do you mind if we don't fuck? It's not that I wouldn't like to, it's just–'

'No, of course.'

Down on the main street, the trucks hurtled by, throwing grids of white light up the map-patterned wallpaper. From downstairs came the muffled sound of a disco. She smelt of sharp, fresh sweat. Her appendectomy scar like a raised welt felt stippled as he kissed it.

'Can I show you how to touch me, Cian?'

'Okay.'

As she came, she kissed him fiercely, and when his own climax had shaken him, she lay quietly beside him for a while, before sliding down his body to take his wilted sex in her mouth but he was suddenly painfully aware of how overweight he was and he drew her back to his lips and then held her. He was conscious that he had wept during their lovemaking, something that had never happened to him before. He didn't want to see his reflection in the wardrobe mirror.

'Is everything okay, Cian?'

'It's been a very long time for me. I'm sorry I got upset. I wasn't upset. I don't know what happened. If I scared you or anything. I don't know.'

'You're very gentle, the way you touched me,' she said. 'I think you must have been a girl in a previous life.'

'Some girl I'd make.'

'It was lovely. I can still feel your mouth. You're very passionate.'

'It must have been the running shorts. They're an impossible turn-on.'

'You perv.' She laughed. 'Your hand felt good inside them. I'd planned a laundry day tomorrow. You rather caught me unawares. As for the boxers you had on, it was nice to see an ancient Irish relic. They'd appeal to the knicker-fetishist in anyone.'

'Stop slagging me. Can I kiss you?'

'Oh, I think that would be all right. Are you always so polite in bed? I'm only teasing. Lie down, I love kissing.'

After a few short minutes, desire arose between them again, their fingers intertwining and breathing growing harder, and as he kissed her shoulders and throat he wondered if any of it was happening. Somewhere in the building an elevator churned violently. Her hair shone dark blue in the light.

'One of the girls from work has a room down the corridor. I could ask if she has a condom . . .'

'Okay.'

'Would you mind if I did?'

'If you're sure.'

She rose and took the tatty night-robe from the back of the bathroom door, returning after a couple of minutes.

'I have one.'

An ether of strangeness seemed to fill the hot room, the traffic speeding past outside in the rain, and it took a while to find a cadence, a way of being together now, where earlier it had been so urgent as to be easy. He managed to go slower; her pleasure aroused him fiercely. The words that spilled from his mouth, and from hers, and their sounds, and the way she thumbed his cheekbones as she clenched and kissed his eyelids.

For perhaps ten minutes afterwards nothing was said. Rain spattered the windows, flinging itself against the glass. A car alarm began an insistent bleat. He wondered if she was sleeping, her breathing was so steady. The radiator by the trouser press gave an irritable crank. She stirred, took his hand and kissed it.

'You've exfoliated me, mate,' she said. 'My face has been sandpapered.'

'I'm sorry. I should have shaved.'

'No, it's nice.'

She elbowed up to look at him, ran a finger across his chest, playfully spanning her hand as widely as possible around his chin as though making to touch both his earlobes simultaneously. 'Look at that feckin jawbone. Shure you're a horse of a man entoirly.' Her attempt at a rural Irish accent was not quite the worst he had ever heard; it had become part of their foolery in recent weeks.

'You're very beautiful, Catherine. To be with you like this—'

'Indeed and I'm not. Now you've seen all my cellulite. But then, beauty is the gift of the lover. Can you sing?'

'I'm not much of a use at singing in the nip.'

'If you sing me a song now, I'll be your mate for ever. I swear.'

'What kind of song?'

'"Dancing Queen" by Abba.'

'Fuck off,' he laughed.

'The Wolfe Tones?'

'Yeah, right.'

'I'd say you sing awesomely. You must have been told you've a sexy voice? Especially over the phone. You could charge by the minute.'

She was smiling at him as she reached out to caress his face, but she was one of those people whose smile includes stoicism deployed against the ghost of old hurts. 'You're a babe, aren't you really? So how come you're not taken? Should I ask? Is it a state secret or something?'

'Probably.'

She nodded. 'Stop pushing him, Catherine, he'll tell you when he wants to.' It was a strategy she sometimes deployed when she wanted to ask a question – spoke it aloud to herself, so that it could be dismissed as a joke if necessary. But it was a powerful way of asking all the same.

'The last couple of years were tricky enough,' he said. 'It got on top of me a bit. I don't know. I got stressed. Fucked-up, I suppose. There were problems at work. I made serious mistakes, took my eye off the ball.'

'Were you hospitalised?'

He laughed abruptly, accepted a drag of her cigarette. 'You've good sources. Yeah, I was. For a while.' He looked around the room, trying to find something to talk about. A pair of her boots in the opened wardrobe. Stacks of CDs on the carpet. Photographs torn from colour supplements or xeroxed from Wicklow guidebooks sellotaped to the dressing-table mirror. Scrawled yellow and pink Post-its forming a chessboard pattern across the door. A skirt folded over a chair-back.

'Angela, a girl at work, knows everything about everyone in Ireland. She's just one of those people that hoovers information. Once upon a time she'd have been burned as a witch.'

'Can I sleep here the night with you?'

Disquietude silvered her eyes. 'I don't think that would be wise. Would you mind?'

'Say if I threw all my clothes out the window over there. You wouldn't send me out in the buff. Or would you?'

She put a finger to his lips.

'*Ciúnas*,' she murmured. 'The Irish for silence.'

'Just this once. I promise. I'll never ask again.'

She looked at him. 'You're going to be trouble, aren't you?'

'I won't be, I promise. It never even happened.'

'Oh you menace. Leave me alone. Or don't leave me alone. Would you like to have another fag before you go?'

'I've to bring my dad to the doctor in the morning at a quarter to eight. I'll be gone before you even remember I was here.'

'Cian Hanahoe,' she said quietly. 'I like saying your name.'

'So does that mean I can stay? You could think of me as a Teasmade?'

'You're certainly a tease.'

'And you're certainly a maid.'

'Hardly.'

'Well, meet me halfway.'

'The disco can get loud. Downstairs. Do you mind?'

'I'm a seventies boy. I love disco.'

The rain began to thunder as she curled her back against his chest. From outside on the street they heard the young people shrieking. He sang quietly into the nest of her matted hair.

'*Fare thee well to the Moss House, where the birds do
increase,
At the foot of Mount Leinster, or some silent place,
And all Illinois I would give for your hand,
By the banks of the Claudy, in Wexford's lost land.*'

'I'm warning you, if you want any sleep, you better stop,' she whispered.

He stopped. And he started again.

III

Portrait of a Boy

Problems planning the film brought her to Ireland more often. Locations she had scouted proved difficult to nail down; there were negotiations with landowners and local authorities around Dublin. He admired her unflappable cool. Soon they were spending every other evening together. By day he would write letters to schools and cram-colleges in the city, or walk the Dun Laoghaire seafront or spend time with his father. Once a week he would drive alone to the hospital in Kildare for an outpatient session with his psychiatrist. He returned to daily swimming, a habit of his boyhood summers, arriving early at the Forty-Foot or at Scotsman's Bay, where leathery old men and women shared the water with harbour seals and issued warnings against being bitten to newcomers. In the evenings he would drive down to Wicklow, through Rathmichael, Enniskerry, the Scalp, Killegar, the Sally Gap. Mostly they went walking, ate cheaply in country pubs.

She was fond of *The Catcher in the Rye*, was putting together a design plan for a big London producer who had impossible hopes of filming it. She would splutter with gaiety on encountering favourite passages, reading them aloud in what she imagined was a simulacrum of the bored narrator's accent. As with her fake Irish brogue, this became part of their foolery. They would walk the cliffs near Greystones, exclaiming 'what a phoney, what a bastard', the private language of jokes an evasion of realities he imagined she didn't want to contend with. He didn't want to, either. He was happiest in silence, or lazing beside her in the hotel room. One hot Sunday morning, he accompanied her to church. It wasn't a religious thing; she just wanted to hear hymns. She wanted to sing, she told him.

Easter came. She bought him a boxed set of rare blues CDs. 'Instead of an egg,' she joked. It must have taken her some trouble to root it up – it was a French re-release she had found through a dealer – but she didn't seem to want to be thanked. It was her habit to write 'lots of love' at the end of notes or emails but she tended to sign off this way when writing to almost anyone and even to use the phrase when about to end a phone call. He wasn't at all sure where they stood.

She appeared reluctant to come to his apartment and he didn't push. But one day, when they had met for lunch in a café in Kilternan, he happened to mention it was not far away and she asked if they could go there 'just to see it'.

'That's you? In the picture?'

'Yes, it is.'

She approached the portrait silently.

'What a priestly little boy. You're angelic.'

'In Seán Keating's eyes maybe. In real life not so much.'

'Do you remember much about sitting for him? What was that like?'

'He talked a lot about America, I can't remember why. He was sort of abrupt. This red-weathered fierceness about him.'

'You've no other pictures. I was certain you'd have loads.'

'I never noticed. But you're right. I must get some.'

'Is that the bathroom?'

'Yes, it is.'

'I might give that a miss.'

'You're being typically sexist. The bedroom's over here.'

'So this is where the magic happens,' she said. She went into the room and crossed to a table piled high with books, examined them for a while, peered out at the Dublin Mountains. She had a habit of folding her arms around herself when she was assessing a potential location for a scene. He looked at her back from the vantage of the doorway.

'It's nice that you have trees.'

'I guess. That's Marlay Park beyond the fence.'

'It's funny being in your bedroom. Were you living here when you were married?'

'We had a house. It was sold when we separated.'

'Have many people been here? In your bed, I mean?'

She was touching the window, thumbing at a node of dried paint.

'No,' he said quietly. He felt the answer was important to her, and if she had no right to ask, it didn't seem to matter. They had drifted beyond the point of carefully respected entitlements and into a new land whose geography wasn't clear.

'Could we lie down for a while?' she said. 'I don't mean anything else. I'd like to lie in your bed. Look up at your ceiling.'

'Sure. Are you okay? You look a bit pale.'

'You wouldn't have a hot-water bottle? Only my period is due soon. It helps with the cramps. Or a Nurofen?'

'I don't think so. I'm sorry. I could go down to the chemist's?'

'Could you put your hand on my stomach?'

'Of course. Do you want to take off your jeans?'

She unbuttoned them and lay down. It was obvious she was in pain. She asked for a glass of water; did he have any alcohol? He had beer but no spirits and she never drank lager. He wondered if she'd like a joint but was nervous of offering. Lately it had become his sedative of choice. It was something she didn't need to know.

'I have stuff at the hotel. An analgesic for when it's bad.'

'There's a chemist down in the shopping centre. Can I get you something there?'

'It's a prescription thing, I'm afraid. I should have taken it with me this morning.'

'Would they give it to me, do you think, if I went down there? I will.'

'No, stay with me a minute. Let's look at the trees.'

They lay on his bed and drifted into a doze, the breeze moving the curtains, bringing scents from the park. A lawn-mower was grumbling quietly in the distance; from somewhere came the shrieks of a party for children. He and Catherine had drunk wine at lunch, only half a bottle of red, but it deepened the comfort of afternoon sleeping on a day when there was nothing to do. The sky was violet when he awoke. She kissed him on the mouth. She looked drowsy, fuddled, and the sleep had warmed her skin. She had taken off her T-shirt and bra. A bottle of mineral water was sitting on the table with a magazine she must have been reading.

'You looked sweet asleep,' she said, her voice slightly hoarse. 'It was good to have a chance to search the premises.'

'Did you find anything incriminating?'

'Nothing. So far. Well, a couple of dodgy CDs. I'm a Mahler refusenik, I'm afraid.'

'You don't know what you're missing. He's pretty good in small doses.'

'Oh, I opened your medicine cupboard,' she said quietly. 'I hope you don't mind. I was looking for a Panadol. You've an awful lot of sleeping pills.'

'I have trouble sleeping now and again. I used to take them too often. I'd forgotten they were there, to be honest.'

She nodded. 'Only, there seemed to be a few hundred. Not that I was counting. That's a hell of a lot of sleeplessness. I hope you won't mind me saying so.'

From beyond the window came the wail of the children's laughter and the tinkle of an ice-cream van's music. Someone slammed the fire door outside on the landing. She was looking away from him at the curtains.

'Did you rest a while?' he asked her. 'How are you feeling?'

'Better. I was dreaming of London. One of those flickery dreams. There's this street near the British Library where my mum worked in a restaurant when we were kids. It was like I was there with her as a teenager. It's called Woburn Walk, kind of pedestrianised and twee, with bow-fronted windows and dusty little bookshops. I used to hope I'd live there.'

'Maybe you will.'

'Oh, I doubt it. I'm not sure I'd want to any more. There was this guy in a black cloak – in the dream, I mean – and a stern emperor's face with a shock of white hair. He was sitting outside a café with a beautiful girl. He asked me where I was going and I said I didn't know. He was reading a book of poems. Deep, huh?'

'That's one for Oprah right enough. Do you fancy that cuppa now?'

'I'm starving. Are you? Is there a place we could order-in a pizza or something like that? Something really disgusting and messy.'

'There's a gaff down on the roundabout. I'll give them a ring.'

'Could I borrow your toothbrush and a T-shirt, do you think? Only the one I was wearing's nearly sweated to pieces.'

'God of course, help yourself, the wardrobe's over there.'

'Tell you what: you order the grub and I'll get the bath going, and we can scoff it like pigs in the bubbles.'

'I don't know if I've much in the way of bubbles, exactly.'

She grinned. 'We'll have to see if we can make some.'

At that moment, the doorbell sounded: a long, stubborn buzz. Neither of them moved. It came again.

'Cian?' said the voice on the intercom. 'It's me.'

'Who?'

'Daddy. I was passing and didn't I see your car.'

'I'm kind of in the middle of something, Dad. Is everything okay?'

'I won't stay two shakes, don't worry, will you buzz me in? I was coming home from Michael Kelleher's funeral and

I noticed your car. Can I come up and use the toilet? I'm desperate.'

'Catherine, this is my father, Colm. Dad, Catherine Dwyer.'

'Oh,' he said. 'I'm delighted, love. Delighted.'

'What a lovely surprise to meet you, Mr Hanahoe. I'm sorry to hear you were at a funeral.'

'Ah, I didn't really like him.'

She laughed uncertainly.

'Dad goes to funerals as a leisure activity,' Cian said. 'It's his bingo.'

'You're so tall,' said his father wondrously. 'What height would you be, Catherine?'

'Five eleven, I think. It seems to depend on the day.'

'You're so tall,' he repeated. 'God bless us, you're enormous. Is it hard finding trousers to fit you?'

'Dad, for God's sake . . .'

'Actually you're right about the trews, Mr Hanahoe. I can't get them just anywhere. Particularly here in Dublin. It's impossible.'

'No, you wouldn't. That's right. What's this is the word for you? Is it rangy?'

'That's one of them, yes. I've a niece who calls me Longshanks.'

'And you're English is it? Marvellous. Well, you're welcome to Dublin. *Fáilte* as we say. That's the Irish for "welcome". We're not the best in the world but we're the best at being ourselves. That's what I always say. Isn't that right, Catherine?'

'I expect it is, yes.'

'Yes. There it is. Sure I may as well sit down for a minute

now I'm here.' Something distressing involving gravity was going on with his comb-over hairstyle but he didn't seem to have noticed.

'And isn't it great the way a woman can wear trousers now? And nobody bats an eyelid. In my own day you wouldn't see it. Unless she was a gardener or a person like that. Or a woman on a farm. Do you know? And I heard a good one on Joe Duffy on the radio the other day. Do you know Joe Duffy's programme, Catherine?'

'No I don't. Is it good?'

'Do you not know it, really? Oh, it's an excellent programme. It's where people phone in and they saying whatever they like. I wouldn't dream of missing it. I tape it if I'm out. The things they do be coming out with and Joe Duffy a stranger. I don't know how that man sleeps at night, I honestly don't. And he's triplets. Himself and his wife.'

'He's . . .?'

'He has triplets. Joe Duffy. Wouldn't you wonder how he manages? And people talk about *pressure*. Well they're not Joe Duffy. I think you'd enjoy him, Catherine. He's a nice Dublin accent. I tape him if I'm gone up to the park with the dog of an afternoon. I declare to God if he ran for President he'd be elected.'

'The dog?'

'What's that?'

'I was making a silly joke. You know, about the dog.'

'No, I meant Joe Duffy. If he ran for President he'd be elected. He'd be in on the first count; you mark my words. And I'll tell you the one thing and that's not two: we'd be better off in this poor misfortunate country if he was. Oh he wouldn't be long licking us into shape, I can tell you. He wouldn't stick nonsense from anyone. "The live-line is open now." That's his catchphrase, do you see. "The live-line is open *now*." You'd want to hear it, Catherine. When it comes on, the dog does be going mad as a chimp. It's as though he *knows* the live-line is open.'

'It sounds marvellous fun. I don't know how I've missed it.'

'Catherine is working at Ardmore. At the film studios, Dad.'

'I should have known. And you so nice looking. And so tall. You're an actress?'

'Oh, nothing so glamorous. I'm a lowly production person.'

'A production person, God bless us. Boys oh boys, what? Wait till the neighbours hear. They'll think I'm Hollywood bound.'

'I could put in a word for you?'

'Oh by janey, you're a laugh. I could look at you all day. It's like looking at beautiful music. You've a beautiful smile, Catherine.'

'So do you, Mr Hanahoe, and a rather roguish eye.'

'God bless us but I'll have to come round here more often, so I will. And away with your "Mister", I'm Colm or Collie. And did you go to the university over beyond?'

'I did for a while, yes, at Saint Martins College in London.'

'Saint Martins College in London. Doesn't that beat Banagher. Aren't you the great girl entirely. Were the professors very hard?'

'No, they weren't too bad.'

'Now you're only being modest. Saint Martins College.

Wonderful. I'd an aunt had a powerful devotion to Saint Martin de Porres.'

'Did she?'

'Oh she did, God she did, Lord have mercy on the same girl. His remains were exhumed after twenty-five years and pronounced to be found intact, and exhaling a fine fragrance. There's a riddle if you like, isn't it, Catherine? *A fine fragrance*. Hah?'

'Crikey.'

'Tell that to the so-called atheists like scholar-my-lad here. What answer can they give you? They're bucked. God, you wouldn't be up to her for holiness. Aunt Freda, I mean. Well, we called her an aunt but she wasn't one really. And she bad with the nerves, the same poor creature. The sixth day of May, nineteen hundred and sixty-two. Eh?'

'I'm . . .?'

'Happiest hour of that woman's life. The date of St Martin's canonisation.'

'I see.'

'She gave me my first set of boxing gloves. In '51 that would have been. I still have them somewhere above in the house. I used to box as a youngfella. Cian's probably told you. I was never knocked out. Course, that was neither today nor yesterday.'

'I can tell from your build. You're a regular Mister Universe.'

'Parallel Universe, more like,' his son muttered.

'Isn't history a great thing, Catherine? Battles and dates, hah? I wouldn't have the grey matter upstairs for the history. But the son-and-heir here was a demon for the books entirely. You'd give him a book, he'd fairly ate it out of your hand. We couldn't keep up with him. Nearly bankrupted we were. He'd that many books read you couldn't keep up with him. It's a great thing, isn't it? An interest?'

'Yes it is. He's terribly clever, isn't he, your lovely son?'

'Oh, he's not the worst now. He's a clever mouth on him anyhow.'

'He certainly does,' she smiled.

'And I heard a good one the other day. What's this is the way it went? Paddy is up in Dublin from the country for a match, do you see, and doesn't he get nattering to this other auld bogman, call him Mick. Well, after the game, off with the pair of them down to Clery's in O'Connell Street where by coincidence both the wives is doing the bit of shopping. And says Paddy-Joe to Mick: "Jaysus, I think mine is lost." And says Mick: "By Chrisht, so's mine." And they wondering what to do. And they gawping at the watches. And says Paddy: "We'll have to search for them, so. What does yours look like?" And says Mick: "Well, she's a blonde and she's well-upholstered" – you can imagine the rest, Catherine – I don't want to tell it vulgarly – you can imagine the rest – "she's a blondie one with blue eyes and an hour-glass figure, shall we say, and she's nineteen and her job is modelling skimpy bikinis. And what about your own, boss? What does she look like?" And says Pat: "Feck mine, let's look for yours."'

Catherine's laughter encouraged his father, whose own giggle was like that of a malevolent schoolboy recently ordered to stop laughing by a nun. 'I hope that's not too blue now, Catherine. But we're all friends here. *Feck mine, let's look for yours.* Isn't it desperate? And what do you make of us at all, Catherine? Has this fellow of mine shown you the town? It would be nice to see a bit of it while you're over, so it would. In my own day you'd see everything in Dublin in two and a half minutes and a minute left over to get punched by some mugger, but sure nowadays there's every class of cafés and theatres and the rest.'

'Yes, he brought me to see *The Playboy of the Western World* at the Abbey last week.'

'Cian, is that the auld thing where the chap murders the da? Doesn't he brain him with the turf shovel? Isn't that it?'

'Yes, Dad. You'd wonder what inspired it, wouldn't you?'

'But in the heel of the hunt, he didn't kill him at all, Catherine. The way it is, he has you *thinking* this gouger done away with his father, only doesn't he tell you at the end *it never happened at all*. He's only making a *boast* of it, do you see?'

'Yes she knows, Dad. She saw it last week. You really don't have to summarise the entire–'

'*It never happened at all*. He's only acting the braggart. Because here's the da at the close and he fit to be tied and he bawling up meela murder. Man alive, the ructions out of him and what he isn't going to do. I didn't know where to look and that's the God's honest truth. I'd the rug pulled from under me, Catherine, and no mistake about it. It never happened at all! Fantastic.'

'Yes it's clever. I enjoyed it. Some of the acting especially.'

'Oh stop the lights, sure it's wonderful. I nearly burst myself laughing. It's a gift, of course. The way someone could *think up* a thing like that. A gift from the Man Upstairs. Putting *a twist* on it like that. I wouldn't be able to think of it in a million years. Aren't people a ticket all the same? Yes, people would amaze you. I'll tell you, whoever designed them would have made short work of the motor car. You're Catholic yourself are you, Catherine?'

'Dad!'

'I'm afraid I'm not, no. My mum's actually a Quaker. My dad's sort of Church of England at Christmastime.'

'Do you know what I always say, Catherine? In my father's house are many mansions. Isn't that what we're told?'

'I hope that's right.'

'Sure how would it not be right and it written in the Bible?'

'If we've done with the theology, would you like a cup of tea, Dad?'

'Do you hear this impudent chaw, Catherine, and his *like a cup of tea*. And me only dropping in because I happened to be passing. Sure if it's there, I'll drink it, and if it isn't, not to worry. Isn't that the best policy, Catherine?'

'Yes it is.'

'It would be an awful death, wouldn't it? Being brained with a turf shovel. Any way you look at it. God save us.'

'Just as well it never happened at all, when you think,' Catherine said.

'By janey, you never spoke a truer word there, love.'

'Joe Duffy,' she chuckled. 'The live-line is open!'

'No, the live-line is open *now*.'

IV

The Stolen Car

They walked up Killiney Hill on a cold day, dampness in the air, the sky grey as gulls' eggs, with an arc of smoky cumulonimbus stretching all the way from Howth Head into the mist-wreathed mountains of Wicklow. In the distance the tankers and container ships sat moored in the bay, and a red and white lightship was breasting its way out past the Muglins where a fog bank was beginning to roll in. The grey-green sea rolled slowly by Dalkey Island. A little trawler was making for Bullock Harbour.

They trudged around for a while, Catherine taking photographs and making notes in a folder, but a spatting shower started before they'd been ten minutes at the summit. They huddled close to the wall of the Famine memorial, plastic bags on their heads making the rainfall smack thunderously.

They shared a sodden cigarette, then a joint he'd been saving. The needling rain began to ease into drizzle. Yachts appeared near the pier, their yellow-white sails. From the cliffs came the rattle of the DART train. She was going to London soon for a long weekend, she said. She had a day of meetings at the BBC and an appointment with her therapist, and she needed to see the rental agency that was letting out her flat.

The trip was a nuisance, but it couldn't be avoided. He wondered if he was supposed to respond to what she had smuggled into the exchange. She had a mode of dropping revelations into otherwise unimportant conversations, like matters she wanted to get out of the way without a fuss.

'I didn't know you saw a therapist.' He tried to speak casually.

'You didn't guess? God, how cheering. I must be making fantastic progress.'

He managed a laugh. 'From what?'

'Oh, I had some issues when I was younger, isn't that what people say? Weight and loathing yourself and finding unemployable psychotics attractive. It's all in the past. But I guess I'd like to keep it there, so I see my lady every once in a while for a bit of an MOT. I actually *call* her "M'Lady", which always makes her laugh. She's rather fabulous. You'd like her. She's amazingly funny. All her male clients fall for her, probably some of the female ones too. She's married to a palaeontologist. Isn't that a beautiful word? Do you want to head back to the car?'

'Am I allowed to ask more?'

'How do you mean?'

'About what you went through.'

'Oh. Let's see. I think "self-harming" is the phrase. I had an eating disorder long before it was popular, really got in on the ground floor. I used to make myself sick. It isn't very hard. I didn't even have to shove my fingers down my throat in the end; I could do it just by thinking of Duran Duran. Joke. I actually like Duran Duran. But don't tell anyone, will you? Well, it started as a kind of dare with another girl at school. We'd cut the initials of these brutish

- 262 -

boys we fancied into our arms with our dads' razor blades. Only soon I was doing it even if I didn't fancy anyone. Which was most of the time, actually. Which is a whole nother story. Which we don't need to talk about because I wouldn't want to render you unconscious with boredom. I think the technical term is "losing your fucking marbles".'

'When you were a teenager?'

'Yeah. In the Pleistocene era. But I'm approaching my crystal anniversary of sanity. That's fifteen years, as you are doubtless aware. Pretty unexciting, though, isn't it – crystal? I'm looking forward to plastic. By the time I hit the menopause I'll be sane.'

It had been obvious to him for a while that how she dealt with difficult subjects was to avoid them or displace them by unsubtle attempts at irony. It had not been a problem. If anything, he was glad. But he wondered to himself now, as they headed down to the car park, if he could ever know someone employing such strategies. It seemed to him that she carried experiences not grieved for or even experienced. She was one of those people who would make sandwiches for a parent's funeral, being brave, unselfish, deflecting any question she didn't want, vacuuming around the altar in the church. She was good at redirecting. You barely noticed she was doing it until the subject of your conversation had moved on. And by then it would be bad manners to try to go back. It was a certain kind of English politeness, undeniably effective, but only if you bought into it yourself.

And why tell him now? Was it a milestone she wanted to pass? And why was he analysing it rather than letting it be passed? Such thoughts were about to disappear like snow off a rope. When they returned to the car park on the edge of the woods, rain was falling and his car was gone.

'Jesus.'

'Where is it?'

'I mustn't have locked it properly. Fuck.'

With her mobile she called Ardmore, asked someone to find the number for the taxi firm in Dalkey but the colleague rang her back a couple of minutes later to say Directory Enquiries had no such listing.

'What'll we do?' she laughed. 'Should we ring the cops or something?'

'We can't ring the fucking cops, they wouldn't be bothered.'

'Of course they'd be bothered. Will I call 999?'

'Don't be ridiculous, Catherine. It's not an emergency.'

'I'm not saying it's a bomb scare. But your car's been stolen, after all.'

'If you've an intelligent suggestion, I'm willing to listen. If you don't, then keep it to yourself, okay?'

'Don't talk to me like that.'

'I'm only saying—'

'No, *I'm* saying, Cian. Don't talk to me like that. Who the *fuck* do you think you are?

They walked down to the village through a heavy shower, made their way to the Garda station in silence. Later that night, the police found his car, abandoned in a backstreet in Dun Laoghaire with its ignition ripped out. Her laptop was gone. She joked that it was old. Indeed she seemed to feel the entire incident should be turned into a joke. 'Our first quarrel. What a milestone. You bad-tempered bastard.' But strangely, it was the start of the end.

V

South of the River

On the day she was going to London, he had some errands to do in Dublin and he arranged to meet her in a café for lunch. She was talking on her mobile as he entered slightly late and she beckoned to him as he came towards the table.

'Sorry about that, Cian, things are manic. How are you? Where have you been? Having fun?'

'Grand. I have an interview next week.'

'Oh that's great. At a school?'

'No, it's back at UCD. A kind of refresher course for teacher training. Have you ordered?'

'But that's brilliant. You must be chuffed.'

'Yes, I am.'

A fall of sleet began so suddenly that everyone in the café turned to look at the windows. Shoppers running through the street. A flowering of umbrellas.

'Where will you be staying in London? With your folks is it, Catherine?'

'It's a mate's flat in Bayswater, she's away for the weekend.'

'You'll be missed,' he said quietly.

''Tis fierce romantic you are, altogether.'

'I mean it,' he said, more abruptly than he meant to. Lately her default-mode jocularity had been perplexing him. He had come to wonder if it was not in fact, like all default modes, the result of careful manufacture over time.

She regarded him. 'So come with me.'

He laughed as though the suggestion was ridiculous.

'I can't go with you to London. Not just like that.'

'Why not?'

'You'll have people to see. I don't want to be in your way.'

'Oh yes. My way. Who'd want to be in that?'

'But . . . what time's the flight?'

'In three hours. We'd have to hurry.'

'I've no money on me, no bag.'

'Balls to a bag. A bag is twenty quid, couple of drawers and shirts, I'll sub you. Or you could always go commando. What do you say?'

'My passport is at home. I'm not sure it's even current.'

'You don't need a passport, it's only London, not Uzbekistan.'

'I can't. I've plans. But thanks.'

'It's the Notting Hill Carnival this weekend. A woman of my charms is practically throwing herself at him for a no-strings-attached flit to London and he can't. Dear God, ladies and gentlemen. What's the world come to?'

'Look, I said I can't, Catherine, okay?'

Again it came more assertively than he'd wanted and the mirth in her expression melted. The waiter brought their order.

'It wasn't a threat,' she said quietly, 'just an invitation. Relax.'

'I know. I'm sorry. I'm tired.'

'It's fine.' She gave a smile. But something between them had curdled. In a way, it was easier to be together now the feeling was less intimate; their talk came freely, of things that didn't matter, and if she began to look weary he put it down to the oppressive heat of the café, the noise of nearby conversations, the comings and goings. As in all eating establishments in Dublin, the tables were too close together. You could smell your neighbour's cappuccino.

'Look, I'd better get going, there can be queues coming up to the weekend. Oh Christ, I'm late already, I really have to run.'

They paid and walked up to the Green but there were no taxis on the rank. She slipped her hand into his without meeting his eyes. The air was sharp and cold, cleansed by the rain. He was thinking of her in London, the crowded noisy streets, an image of her walking across Trafalgar Square towards the National Gallery. Her wheelcase dragging behind her, through buskers and jugglers and exultations of tourist videographers. There was something uneasing him, which wasn't a surprise – there was usually something uneasing him, it was like weather you got used to. The girlfriend before Aifric had once told him he was the kind of Irishman who would eat his way through a light bulb rather than sit calm.

'It's great news about your interview. Do you have a nice suit?'

'It's a while since I've worn it. I could do with losing a few pounds.'

'We could all do with that. Don't you go to a gym?'

'I joined one a while ago but I sort of fell away.'

'We should go for a run together some time if you like. I usually go in the mornings, on the seafront.'

'I'm not at my best in the mornings, to be absolutely honest.'

'Oh, I wouldn't say that.'

He laughed.

'God, look at him,' she said. 'He's actually cheering up. Hold the front page. He's smiling.'

'I'm sorry I was narky. Wrong side of the bed.'

'You need a weekend in London,' she told him.

'I can't.'

'You can.'

'You're sure I wouldn't be in the way?'

'Don't be such a twat. Let's go.'

He found himself wondering what it would be like to say the words he sensed were coming. Perhaps that was why he said them. To see how it would feel. 'No, you go on ahead and I'll get a later flight. I've to see my dad this afternoon and take him to bloody Lidl and he'll have a nervous bloody breakdown if I don't. Then I'll nip home, get my stuff, there must be a flight at eight or nine. If you're absolutely sure now?'

'Do you want me to shoot you?'

'Okay, there has to be an Aer Lingus flight at eight or nine. If you give me the number of where you're staying, I'll ring when I land. I'll get a taxi or figure out the Tube. I know the Tube fairly well. What line is it on, do you know?'

'You don't ever get the feeling you might be overly Virgo, do you?'

'I was only saying—'

'You don't have to ring. Just pitch up. I'll be waiting.

– 268 –

Here's the address, it's West Two. Bayswater tube or Queensway would do it. Or the Heathrow Express and a cab.'

By the time he got back to the apartment, he was sorry he'd agreed. He showered, shaved, organised his clothes for the wash, opened several days' worth of post, paid some bills online. The thudding bass of a rock band sound-checking drifted over from the park. What did her invitation mean? Need it mean anything at all? And why had he lied to her about having to see his father? He noticed there was a message on his machine.

'Hi. It's me. I'm about to get on the plane. There's a flight attendant glaring at me. She looks like Dominique Strauss-Kahn in drag. I know you're having second thoughts. So I'm just calling to say you shouldn't worry about anything.' The public-address system in the background gave a dull metallic bong. 'So that's all I wanted to say. It isn't a declaration. I think it would be fun but if you're not into it, I understand. I'm not just saying it, I really do mean it; it's no *problemo*. But it would be cool if you wanted to. But it's cool either way. So my money's running out. And I've no credit on my mobile. The fright attendant is going to punch me if I don't get on the plane. If she smiles at me any harder her eyebrows are going to disappear into her hairline. So if I see you, I see you, and if not, please don't worry. I'll be back next week. Be good.'

Images from Irish history on the walls of the departure lounge. A dark-eyed skeletal mother, children in the folds of her skirt. A photograph of the customs station on Ellis Island, so massively enlarged that its pixels were the size of saucers. The reticent smiles of American Civil War soldiers, holding a banner reading OLD ERIN FREE. Even as the announcement came that the time had come to board, he was unsure if he wanted to go.

The plane was half empty, the cabin crew tired. The train speeding quietly through the western outskirts of London. A beautiful African man speaking French on a mobile phone. The backyards and lighted windows and doleful suburbs, as the Friday night city came into view.

It was almost half-eleven when he arrived at the friend's flat, which was in the basement of a Victorian town house that might once have been elegant. When she opened the door they burst into conspiratorial laughter, like disobedient schoolchildren putting a mischief into action. Even before it had closed they were unfastening each other's clothes.

'Now you've had me, are you buggering off or would you like to see the rest of the accommodation? It's even nicer when you make it past the hallway.'

It was a little place, almost windowless, low-ceilinged like an old ship, so narrow that the futon touched two walls of the bedroom. The flooring was old and wooden. Several televisions could be heard, none of which was in the flat.

There was Indian take-out, wine from the corner shop ('Château Seven-Eleven, le grand cru de Bulgaria') but she hadn't been able to find a corkscrew in the tiny, cramped kitchen. He tried forcing the cork into the bottle with a meat-skewer. ('Should have seen me when I was a student, I could do it with my eyes closed.') There was an all-night store on Porchester Road, she told him. Could he pick up some kitchen rolls too?

The night was blastingly hot, the last Friday in August. It was hard to credit the relatively simple reality that he was walking through London to a shop. People leaving a restaurant. Drinkers outside a pub. The half-moon was red. Girls in miniskirts and hipster jeans. Two mod-boys on Vespas watching them and smoking, polishing the mirrors on their bikes with their cuffs. Bluebeat and ska from a boombox on the pavement. A suedehead dancing a delirious, inebriated moonstomp with a girl who looked like a solicitor's apprentice.

They ate hungrily, often chuckling as they glanced at one another. Her flight had been atrocious; she'd been sitting beside a Corkonian drunk who had insisted on telling her the Famine was all her fault. Even though she had agreed and apologised heartily it had been difficult to calm him down. In the end one of the flight attendants had threatened him with arrest, which had rendered him quiet, at least temporarily, his patriotism being limited for the remainder of the flight to aggressive rustlings of his *Daily Mail*.

'Hey, nobody in the whole world knows we're here together,' she smiled. 'Isn't that just the coolest thing in the world?'

'The coolest thing in the world is actually you.'

She pulled a wince and mimed gagging and went back to her food but he could see the remark had pleased her. He felt happy.

They couldn't find the fresh sheets her friend's note had said were in the airing cupboard but agreed in the end it didn't matter. 'She probably doesn't have scabies. If she does, it's too late. You can use my toothbrush if you want, you probably forgot your own.'

'An anally retentive Virgo never forgets,' he said.

'Jesus, Mr Hanahoe, you're a scary mother sometimes.

I suppose you've brought a plasticised set of notes on what sights you'd like to see.' Being ridiculed by her was pleasurable because he suspected she didn't mean it. He found he was even enjoying his newly conferred role of geek-mocked-by-intrepid-lieutenant.

The sex that night was amiable, a bit drunken, but there was tenderness in it too, a generosity that liberated it into fondness. Neither of them felt adventurous. 'It's hard to fuck on a biriani,' she remarked.

Cars passed on the terrace. Booms of rap music and trance. Now and again she curled close to him, murmuring words he couldn't discern, her damp, hot hands around his torso, his back. And once he stirred muttering in the underwater of sleep, aware she had kissed his forehead, had whispered his name, had asked if he was all right – *I'm here, babe*. But he was too distant from her to be able to answer; it was a small, strange thing. He wasn't sure if he was sleeping or surfacing.

They awoke not long before dawn to the stutter of ragga from a passing car, made love without speaking. It was slow, very gentle, mouths tasting of salt and stale cumin, sleepfulness a kind of counterpoint to the raucous birds outside. There was a tiled patio with potted plants on it beyond the cool, dark bedroom and he saw that she had opened the doors but the metal security grille was still locked. A scruffy pigeon was watching them. She made him go and close the curtains. 'He might be under age,' she said.

After she left for her therapist, he slept a while longer, a dream of falling and starting and flickering purples. He was in the apartment back in Dublin, and then walking White Rock Strand, where a hawk-like man was prowling the cliffs, his dark wings raised as a cape. And suddenly, somehow, he was at Coney Island with Aifric, the sunlight making her blink as she gazed at him silently, the carousels behind her turning but no sound except for the sea. A hot sun shimmering on the quartz-white sand. Her face was continuously changing

The telephone rang sometimes; he allowed the machine to beep on but nobody left a message. He realised he didn't know even the name of the woman whose home this was, who owned this expensive furniture, those books and CDs, the little paintings and framed 1950s movie posters. He read for a while, made coffee, had a smoke; settled down at the desk in the living room.

It had occurred to him to try to write a little while she was out at her meetings. To be away from his apartment – away from Dublin – might free something he needed freed. Writing had been suggested to him again as a therapy but he'd found himself unable to enter his past. Perhaps he should try fiction, maybe an attempt at a play. He had sketched out beginnings of scenes. But nothing now would come. His scribblings had begun to appear to him entirely without merit, derivative, mawkish, stupid. He wondered if there might be a way of turning the botched play into prose – to *say* what was going on behind the mask of the dialogue. He went through a couple of the worst sequences, adding descriptions of the sky. Waste of fucking time and energy.

He couldn't get the television to work but there was a DVD machine hooked up to it and for a while he watched the only disc he could find on the bookshelves, an Italian opera he didn't recognise, subtitled in something like

Russian. He left it playing while he cleaned up, washed the dishes, swept the living room. Some of Catherine's clothes were on the bedroom floor, and as he was folding them into piles, a pocket diary fell from the pouch of a jacket.

He picked it up, placed it on the table where she had left her laptop to charge. It was wrong to look through someone's diary.

> *Meet NJ at Ardmore, 11 a.m. with notes.*
> *Meeting Cian Hanahoe (sp?), Shelbourne Hotel,*
>   *6 pm.*
> *KR for dinner.*
> *KR for coffee.*
> *Mortgage payment due. Phone bank re transfer.*
> *Dr Barnes re c. s. test. Ask her about headaches.*
> *M's birthday, send lilies, talk to Dad about meal.*
> *Paul calling from NYC. Our anniversary.*

Around lunchtime he left the flat, watched a steel band rehearsing in a school playground across the terrace. He took a taxi to the Tate Modern, but in his state of muzzy hangover the conceptual exhibition made no sense to him. And the sepulchral quietness of the gallery only intensified his fatigue, his longing for open air. He ate a sandwich on the steps, watching the tourists come and go, the open-topped buses disgorging crowds of the ardent. He walked with no purpose, no destination in mind, several miles into the city until he came to Broadcasting House. Workmen were cleaning the sculptures of Prospero and Ariel on the façade. He wondered what she was doing, where she was.

A strange yearning took him. He caught a tube

southwards to Greenwich. The narrow streets rowdy with schoolchildren on outings. Ships-in-bottles, framed posters of the *Cutty Sark* and Isaac Newton, artefacts involving bits of fishing net in the windows of antique shops. He and Aifric had spent part of a summer here the year before being married, and as he came to the shabby Edwardian house on the New Cross Road, he was astonished at how little it had changed. The front garden still unkempt, its rusted bathtub sprouting dahlias, and the door hadn't even been painted. A gay couple had lived in the largest of the flats, the older man a Greek Cypriot, his partner a divorced New Zealander. With a start, he saw now that their surnames were still on the doorbell label and he wondered if he should see if they were home. Folly, surely, after eleven years. He tubed back to West Two, strap-hanging now, for the night before Carnival was descending on London. It had been a day in which he found himself strange, uncertain of what he wanted, and as he walked back to the flat through the noise and diesel fumes of Queensway he was still burdened with whatever had sent him south of the river.

When she returned he had prepared a simple meal, salads and breads he'd bought in the supermarket, a bowl of raspberries he'd got from a stall on Porchester Road. Her meetings had gone well. She was stoked, full of talk. They took a shower together, went out to the little Victorian pub in a nearby side-street, watched old codgers playing darts and grumbling about Ken Livingstone and the heat of London in the summer. It was as though the left wing of the Labour Party had caused the humidity to occur, aided by lesbian collaborators in the media. From time to time she rose, went to the bathroom or the cigarette machine, and some of the oldsters eyed her with a sort of ruined and charming lust.

In the morning they drowsed late. It was almost eleven when they rose. She managed to get Radio 4 going on the impossible television while he straggled to the 7-Eleven for the papers. He watched her move about the flat in one of his shirts, her slim pale legs, her sunburnt arms; her hair in a towel that had seen better days. She had broken her reading glasses. He fixed them. It took time. To be companionable, doing nothing important.

He went out for a swim, the lido cold and chlorined, came back to find her still in his T-shirt, painting her toenails. She glanced up and smiled at him. 'Want to blow on them?'

She knew the area intimately, had grown up in an estate near the Westway, which her father, an engineer for McAlpine's, had worked on. It was not far from Walterton Road, where Joe Strummer of The Clash had lived in a squat. She told him this with a pride he found touching.

Almost eight years had passed since he had last been in London. He saw now, as he walked with her, that he had never truly known it. Muslim women in hijab; Rastafarians, rockabillies, African women in church clothes, Hell's Angels. She brought him to a Portuguese café she knew near Portobello Market; it was plastered with posters for Benfica, and the jukebox played only fado music, the entreaties of the mournful and full-throated torch songs doing battle with the laughter of late breakfasters. Hyde Park in the sunshine. Model boats on the lake. A Trotskyite at Speakers' Corner.

And the costumes of Carnival: birds-of-paradise, lions on stilts, women in head-plumes the height of a bus.

Thong-wearers, baton-hurlers, whistle-blowers, trumpeters. Children dressed as ladybirds and Caribbean islands and Apaches and pool balls and pirates. Floats inching through the pandemonium of Chepstow Road. People dancing on the roofs of apartment blocks. A statuesque woman in tiger bikini and mask hauled him out of the mill on the corner of Brickfields Terrace, grinding her behind against his crotch while the people roared approval and Catherine laughed at his efforts to calypso.

That night they ate Japanese in a front-room place off Westbourne Grove and went afterwards to see Joan Armatrading at Ronnie Scott's. There were people she knew in the club – a commissioning editor from the BBC and his partner. Cian was thankful, for some reason, she didn't know them well enough to want their company for more than a minute of pleasantry. The music was quietly powerful, full of secrets and darkness.

They couldn't find a taxi so they walked back to the flat. The streets around the terrace were thronged with carnivalistas. Soca came roaring from enormous speakers in the boots of SUVs. Pubs gibbered with drum-driven punk.

'Should we go home?' she shouted. 'I'll carry you over the threshold?'

'Would we not stay a while? The atmosphere's amazing.'

'You hang on if you like. I'll see you back at the ranch.'

He did not remain, of course, but her suggestion disconcerted him. He wondered if it meant something, as he made tea for her in the kitchen. Over-sensitive to think so – yet why would she say it? It was the remark of a travel companion. Was that what he was? In the hurry of Friday, he had forgotten to pack his medication. The want of it could make him edgy, mistrustful. She was in bed when he brought the cups; close to sleep, so she claimed. Muffled music all night to the dawn.

In the morning she rose early, went to a yoga class somewhere, returning an hour later with sarcasms against herself for the gym was closed on a Sunday. She looked tired, was overly cheery; kept checking her phone. By the afternoon he had come to feel that what had happened would not happen again, that a carapace was already forming itself around the weekend. It was the longest continuous time they had shared, a simulation of cohabitation, the little domesticities, during all of which she had hardly used the future tense. It was difficult to find a way into discussion of statuses – he wasn't sure he wanted to, was afraid of where he sensed it would lead. She had a way of ignoring the obvious, or of not finding it obvious. He wondered if he could ask about the lover in New York, if lover was the word any more. She was leafing through the pocket diary he had found in her jacket. The questions wouldn't come to his mouth.

'You okay?' she smiled.

'Sure. Are you?'

'I can hear cogs turning in your head.'

'It's nothing, honestly.'

'You seem a bit down?'

'Oh, probably just thinking about going home. No big deal.'

'Shall we stay here for ever and barricade ourselves in?'

'Yeah. Be a laugh.'

'Sure would.'

Looking back on it later, he would often have the feeling

that this had been the last moment to speak out. It had not opened long, and it had closed like a curtain. She went back to her newspaper and the next time he glanced at her she had fallen asleep on the sofa. He didn't wake her until it came time to leave for the airport. There was little conversation between them as the Heathrow Express skimmed through London, the sleeping, grey suburbs, the dormitory towns. At one point she grinned in an amiable way. 'This is where the audience lives.'

He was torn between the hope that she would ask if she could come to his place and the dread that she would tell him she was going to the hotel in Bray; and he knew, if the latter turned out to be what she wanted, that he wouldn't have the courage for a fight. In the event, she told him she was tired, had an early meeting in the morning, would take her own taxi, would call him in a few days. What he felt on arriving back to the musty apartment by himself was that he would never see her again.

VI

Encounter on Duke Street

A week became a fortnight. Catherine did not call him. He went back to attending the hospital on a fortnightly basis as an outpatient. His medication was adjusted – 'tweaked', the psychiatrist said. She was new, American; more or less his own age. There was a form of Cognitive Behaviour Therapy he might find useful, she advised. It would involve family discussion sessions, conducted here at the hospital. His brother and father would attend and contribute. She seemed interested in the vehemence of his refusal.

'You can be a little obsessive,' she told him. 'It's something you need to watch. That controlling thing is often a cover for what we actually need.'

'If there's one thing I need like a hole in the head,' he countered, 'it's my father and my brother and their views.'

'You're making light,' she insisted placidly. 'You're displacing. Try not to. I'd like you to think about it. I believe it could help. There's stuff from the journals I can give you to read. All these strategies of avoidance and denial you have – I mean, everyone has them, you're far from alone – but it's like you get fixational. It's wood-from-the-trees. There's nothing very original in what I'm saying.'

'When I was Dr Madison's patient before, he suggested it too. The family thing. But I just couldn't buy it. More out of embarrassment than anything else. It isn't how Irish families are wired; probably families anywhere. We don't wash the dirty linen, in public or private, we just sprinkle it with deodorant and call it clean.'

'That's a clever way of putting it but it comes out the same. And a lot of the time, being honest, it mightn't matter that much. But with certain kinds of depression, particularly when there's sleeplessness, stuff starts spilling over. Like, delusional feelings, over-identifications. People sensing they're someone else, or becoming disembodied – seeing themselves in the third person, like someone in a story. I want to be really careful about labelling anything, I'm just letting you know where things can go. We can medicate – we will – and you're going to be feeling better – but psychiatry is looking through water at the stones on the riverbed. I'm saying let's clarify options that might give us a new path.'

'Not with my brother and father. Won't be happening.'

As his preparations continued for returning to the university, it became his habit to walk from his apartment into the city in the late afternoons. Stephen's Green was a sort of destination but often he would continue beyond it, to the bookshops on Nassau Street, the National Gallery, Trinity College. Autumn was coming. Darkness descended earlier. Children gathered around the college cricket field to fell conkers.

It had always been the season when he saw most beauty in the city. One afternoon he walked to the National Library to see an exhibition on Yeats. It was one of those Dublin days that smells of fresh linen; pale golden light was spilling into the streets and it made the shop windows seem magical. There were couples strolling around. A girl with a ukulele was singing ballads to a bus queue. Delighted-looking tourists taking snaps of Georgian doorways. You could fall for Dublin on an evening like that.

He had paused to look at the window display of an antiquarian bookshop when he felt a presence behind him on Duke Street.

'Cian?'

He turned.

She smiled at him with defensive hope.

'Aifric. Christ. How's tricks?'

'I'm well. What a surprise. I was literally only thinking of you.'

His impulse was to hurry away. He felt doors opening inside him and he didn't want to enter them. 'What has you back in town?'

'Just a weekend with the folks. It's Mum's seventieth on Saturday. They're having a party up at the house. You can imagine the stress. You'd swear they were organising an opera.'

The crowd moved around them. A fire-juggler began performing.

'You look good, Cian.'

'No I don't.' He tried to laugh. 'I've put on a few pounds.'

'Could we maybe get a drink or something? You've probably no time, do you?'

'I've been off the drink a while.'

'A coffee, then? Are you pushed?'

He didn't want to go with her and yet found it impossible to decline. They passed through the street and to

Bewley's café, which was too crowded to find a table at first, so they stood together on the stairway that leads to the mezzanine. He was hot, shocked, badly fumbling his sentences; he had never been good at getting taken unawares. He could smell the musk of her moisturiser, the one she had always used. He wondered if there was some way to leave without making a scene he'd no heart for. All the time they waited for the waitress to beckon them to a place he kept up his side of the conversation while trying to get his thoughts into line. Desperately, he wished he could smoke.

'It's been too long, Cian. I meant to write or call.'

'You're busy, I know. You look well on it anyhow.'

A silence descended. He could see she was anxious. A hubbub of shouts and whistles arose suddenly from the street below where some kind of public event was beginning. There were press photographers and cameramen milling around a trio of leather-clad young women, one of whom was brandishing an electric guitar.

'I think about you often, Cian. Every single day. There's so much I've wanted to say to you. About what happened, I mean.'

He hadn't a reply. She looked younger than he remembered. Strangely painful, to hear her speak his name. She'd had her hair done differently, was wearing a thumb ring he had bought her in Galway, and expensive-looking clothes of the type he wouldn't have imagined she'd like. It was too hot in the café; his glasses were misting. A bell tolled from the church in the alley.

'So you're a mum,' he managed to say. 'How are the nights treating you?'

'They're not so bad really. He's a fairly okay sleeper.'

'That's good.'

'I've a photo on my phone here if you'd like to see it?'

'Do you mind if I don't?' He spoke it too abruptly.

'Sorry. Of course.' She glanced around herself at the tables.

'So how's your dad?' he asked. 'Still bashing away at the golf?'

'Grand. You know Dad. Getting older and crankier. And yours?'

'Same as ever, really. Nothing strange or startling. I'm trying to think of something I can tell you. There must be hundreds of things. Seeing you so suddenly has me a bit fingers and thumbs, to be honest.'

'I heard you left the bank? Major decision. Or was it?'

'Just got browned off with it, I suppose. I was kind of treading water, to be honest. I'm heading back to college in October – at my age, would you believe.'

'To UCD?'

'Back to Belfield, yeah. I'm half thinking of teaching. That's if I don't fuck off out of the place – maybe Australia or Canada. I've been looking into Montreal a bit.'

'And I hear whispers there's someone floating around for you. You know how it is.'

'That's Dublin. You can't piss crooked. Nothing ever changes.'

'A Londoner, I believe? She's in television, right?'

'Yeah, I'm sleeping with the enemy.' The stupid line fell flat. 'She's great. I met her a while ago. We'll probably move in together soon. She'd like to have a child. We've talked about it a lot.'

The lies came spilling. He almost believed them himself.

'She's very lucky.'

'Course she is. I tell her that every day.'

'The cow. I'm jealous. Am I allowed to say that? I suppose I've no right. Is she beautiful?'

'She's nice-looking, right enough. I don't know how serious it is sometimes. I mean I *know*; it isn't that. It's just something that happened. She's a sort of anchoring thing about her. I didn't think about it much. There's times I don't know how she puts up with me at all.'

'You're such an actor, Cian. It's why I fell in love with you.'

He looked at her. 'Love? Is that what you fell in?'

'Come on,' she said placatingly. 'Don't be giving me a hard time.'

'I don't think we should go there. There's no veins to be opened. Let's just say I kind of got my bubble burst when you walked out the door.'

'I hurt you. I know. It isn't something I'd have wanted.'

'Just came naturally, did it? Congratulations.'

'Don't hate me. For five minutes? I couldn't bear it, Cian. If you have to, I understand, but give me the ghost of a chance? Because I never had anything like I had with you, Cian. And I'm asking you for mercy if there has to be a word. I'm not even asking for forgiveness.'

What could you say to it? There was still the option of leaving, and it wasn't that he didn't want to, more that he couldn't. He seemed to see himself flailing away from her in a thunderstorm of gritted rage, through the noisy throngs of Grafton Street, the crowds on the Green, her staying behind, finishing her coffee alone, the taxi that would hurry him through the rush hour and the bus lanes, away from the small thing being asked. You couldn't do it without cruelty, and she didn't deserve it. He wasn't sure what she deserved, but not that. He knew she wouldn't follow him. She had never done pursuit. And he was afraid of what would happen when his rage met the nightfall in the emptiness of the silent apartment.

'There's things we should have talked about,' she said. 'With a counsellor or someone.'

'There's nothing I want to talk about. You went. That's that.'

'I let you down. I know it.'

'Is this where I'm supposed to say you didn't?'

'It wasn't easy for me when you'd get so down. It was frightening sometimes. You'd say shocking things when we were fighting. Annihilating things.'

She blinked away tears. He wanted to take her hand. Waitresses were laughing together.

'Aifric,' he said quietly. 'I'm sorry.'

'It's me that's sorry, Cian. I should have looked for help. My parents still don't know. Not the full story anyhow. I couldn't deal with their sympathy. I don't know why.'

She was interrupted by ugly music from the street, an explosion of drumming and discordant blasts of synthesiser. The leather-girls were miming a rap to a firestorm of flash-bulbs. Diners stared out the windows impassively.

'We should maybe drop the subject,' he said. 'Do you want to?'

'Yeah.'

'Are you okay?'

She nodded. 'If you'll wait for me a minute, I'll just go to the loo. Unless you've to head? Go on if you have to.'

'No, you're grand. Where are you staying, with the folks?'

'No at Blooms, down in Temple Bar.'

'Can I walk you there?'

'If you've time.'

There was a whomp in his chest as they moved together through the crowded streets. Silently she linked his arm as they crossed College Green. In front of Trinity gate, young people were waiting for their dates and a Traveller woman with a baby in a blanket drifted between them holding out a paper cup. It was five o'clock now and the offices were closing. He was walking through Dublin with the woman he had married. She was talking about the weather, the life she had in England; or aspects of it anyway; the ones that didn't matter. How good a teacher he would make; she was encouraging, careful. A living-statue performer gave a judder and swivelled his hips obscenely, raising screams from a party of passing schoolgirls. He was made up as a bronze Oscar Wilde turned greenish by verdigris. His mouth formed an 'O' as he winked. Too quickly they were standing by the steps of the hotel. A cat tripped the automatic door, which opened and slowly closed. Wind overturned a rubbish bin, blew newspapers along the street.

'Could I come in for a while, Aifric?'

She looked at him.

'Do you think that's a good idea?'

'I'm sort of past caring whether anything is a good idea.'

'If you came up, we both know what would happen.'

'Would that be so bad?'

'Babe – please, don't.'

'It wouldn't have to do with anything. Other situations, I mean. It's being in a room. Nothing more.'

'There's rooms I can't be in. People would be hurt. We're not kids any more. I wish we were.'

'So I'm supposed to shake your hand and stroll away into the sunset?'

'Come on, don't be like that.'

He tried to laugh. 'You're gas.'

'Please don't cry, Cian. I'm so sorry I hurt you.'

'No, I'm sorry too. I better head.'

VII

Advent at Ardmore

Catherine phoned a couple of times, leaving brief, equivocal messages. He found he was returning her calls at times when he knew she wouldn't be available. Twice they ended up speaking, and it was jocular enough, there was never a boiling over, but something had been broken, the old easiness was gone. In a way, the jocularity itself came to seem a form of disingenuous camouflage. The summer became a thing that would have to be let go. He sensed the messages from her were either a duty she felt she had to keep faith with or a sort of weaning-off he felt he needed too. They were unmooring one another. Perhaps nobody would be hurt. He met his brother one night for a drink and told him a little of Catherine Dwyer, realising – it was his brother who pointed it out – that he was speaking of her in the past tense now. His brother said it would be foolish not to declare how he felt. What was holding him back? He owed himself to try. The worst that could happen was rejection, but so what? Could he continue in a lie she must surely be able to recognise for what it was?

October came in, and traffic worsened. Students returned to college. The weather was unpredictable. Shooting began on her film. The Sunday newspapers had little colour-pieces and gossip-mentions about the actors; photographs of local people who had been taken on as extras, delighted with themselves in period costume. One evening when he wanted to walk near the Sally Gap, the road had been closed for night-filming and he was forced to turn back. It had occurred to him to tell the security guards he knew someone involved in the production, that she might even be on the set he could see arc-lit in the distance. Instead he asked their help with the three-point turn, for the boreen was so narrow and the ditches so deep and the overgrown hedgerows so high.

He dreamt about her that night, they were walking Russell Square in London, and there was such freedom and lightness in whatever they were saying that to wake in the dark of morning was hard. He began what soon became a love letter; it was honest, too lengthy. He wrote that he had come to think of her as the source of whatever happiness and courage he knew; that the thought of a future without her was unbearable. He considered a long time before writing the word 'unbearable', sensing that declarations of such heatedness would frighten or anger her – they would certainly have this effect on him. And then he simply let go, writing anything he felt, for he knew he would never send it, lacked the mettle to be revealed. Foolish phrases came crowding. It didn't matter now. Quotations from love poems and from a film they had seen together, from songs that had come to mean something in the course of the summer. As he pressed the delete button, he felt he had wasted an hour. Perhaps he had been writing to himself.

A brief email would arrive from her occasionally, explaining that things were manically busy, and then the periods between mails began to lengthen. He did not hear from her at all in the month of November, was busier at the university by then, not quite certain of what he was doing there. The corridors of the campus. The Perspex tunnel that led to the library. Teaching was like politics, a sardonic lecturer told them. The goal was to make the audience want you to say the things you intended saying anyway; to convince them what you were saying was in fact what they thought. It wasn't a fashionable or politically correct view, he would smile. But it might be useful in the classroom situation.

He continued at writing, working long into the evenings after his essays and assignments had been completed. From the ruins of his play, he had salvaged seven or eight sequences which might make short stories, he felt. A Dublin newspaper published a regular page of new prose by beginners. Perhaps he might try his luck.

He would pour himself a vodka, a finger's width, rarely more, and settle with a pack of cigarettes and a pint-glass of water. Women sang quietly from his iPod in the corner, or instrumental music played low. Many paragraphs felt gruesomely obvious, any sort of subtlety had eluded him, but to have found a shape for some of the stories appeased him. There was one piece in particular he felt might take its chances. It placated the mathematician in him, the sense that it was what it was, that it didn't contain any lie. And if most of the others had sentences that made him squirm with shame, there was an integrity, a cleanness, in having done one's midnight best, in arriving at the end of the expedition or at least at a new point of departure. Sixty pages of text, imperfect certainly, but it was work that had required purpose, a seeing down roads, and the doing of it came to seem its own reward. One rejection letter asserted that his writing was not utterly devoid of merit; that with a hardness of approach and a more nuanced sense of craft, something might be chipped from the stone. 'The scene where the boy steals the shilling in the church works well,' the editor remarked. 'Maybe you should strip the whole thing down and start again with that sequence? The paragraphs about the Docks, your father's childhood, are great. You should *read* a lot more. You need to think about the audience. Leave certain scenes out and a story acquires dimension. What they want is an experience of empathy, not an account of what you think.' *Get a life and murder your darlings*: this was the counsel. There were inventive ways of dressing it up.

He thought of her often and let the thoughts go. Possibilities arose with a fellow mature-student at the university, a beautiful Galwaywoman who had a teenage daughter and had been separated for some time. He allowed it to settle into a chumminess, a collegiate agreement over daily coffee that young people, with notable exceptions, were a pain in the hole. 'Some teachers we'll make,' she often said.

It was early in December when an envelope arrived at the apartment, containing a heavy-stock, gilt-edged invitation. The Awards Night Ball of the Irish Film Board was to be held at Ardmore Studios in a fortnight. He had been invited 'as a guest of *Wuthering Heights*'. It was important to RSVP ASAP – Catherine had scribbled a joke about the abbreviations on the back of the card. 'We won't be talking in actual sentences, just in acronyms and glances. It's always like that in television. LOL.'

They spoke on the telephone. It would be marvellous if

he could make it. The event would be 'bloody ghastly', one of her favourite terms for anything she didn't want to admit might be enjoyable. She kept saying he was probably busy and should feel no obligation, as though wanting to be reassured of her casual unimportance to him. Mixed signals were better than none – this is what he had come to feel. He lied that he would be happy to attend.

'I know you won't,' she chided. 'Be happy, I mean.'

'I wouldn't miss it for the world,' he said.

It had been a long time – years – since he had last donned a tuxedo. In the rental shop, a soon-to-be groom and his slightly pissed companions were trying on kilts and sporrans. The usual jokes were being bantered. He found it heart-warming to hear them. The manager, a man for whom laughing had become a professional necessity, told him he was a well-built fellow, 'a prop forward'. He might consider a waistcoat or even a cummerbund. Such a look tended to flatter the fuller man.

Artificial snow had been pumped on to the car park at Ardmore. Tapers burned along the pathways leading to the hangar-like soundstage in which the event was taking place. He found her very quickly; she was drinking with friends of hers from the production, a personable young electrician and a couple of older Americans who didn't seem to want to say what their jobs were. He had always thought her beautiful and magnetic and strong, but to see her arrayed in the dress she told him had cost her a remortgage was to realise there were facets of her he had never apprehended were there, and his thoughts tumbled over one another like waves out at sea as she air-kissed him so as to preserve her make-up. She had washed her hair in something expensive.

People told her she looked 'fantastic'. He could feel his planned cautiousness evaporating around him, settling in the form of sweat.

Anjelica Huston and the Taoiseach and Liam Neeson were in the room. The President was coming, someone said. A forties-style jazz band played swing tunes and beguines, and from time to time a girl with a lily corsage and long white gloves belted out a good Billie Holiday. There were speeches. He found the actors endearing and intelligent, possessed of a subtlety that was easy to write off as superciliousness. The mode at his table was to chuckle at their vanity. But it seemed to him not so much a matter to be mocked as a way of survival, of meeting a set of expectations. To be seated next to her felt good. It began to flower in him again that there must be many men she could have invited. 'Sorry to have subjected you to such a palaver,' she smiled at one point. 'But it seemed the only way I could get together of actually seeing you again.'

'So you've been well?' he asked her.

'Just up to my tits. And you? How's college? I bet it's strange.'

'You look amazingly beautiful.'

'You clean up well yourself.'

'How's the production going?'

'On schedule. Just constantly stressful. The weather's been so changeable and there's a lot of the show to be shot at night. You'll be pleased to know I've invested in long johns.'

'Can I get you another drink? Or would you like to have a dance?'

'Oh Christ, are you serious? Let's wait till a slow one.

I've been arrested for my dancing. There's a few people I want you to meet.'

He was older than almost all her colleagues, who were fashionably dressed-down and who clearly adored her companionship. They were ironic in their small talk, faultlessly solicitous to him, in the way that a member of the British royal family would welcome a Rastafarian community worker to a garden party. There were jokes about cocaine. He didn't join in. His psychiatrist had advised him not to converse socially about drugs. It was important for a former user not to make light. He had told her he'd never thought of himself as 'a user'. It hadn't been a habit, hadn't interfered with his life. 'You need to watch your evasions,' she had quietly countered. 'We shouldn't confuse the symptoms with the sickness.'

'Is this himself?' a girl asked, eyeing him with mock curiosity, as she stepped out of the crowd and approached.

'This is Cian, yes. This is Angela Carthy. Angela's designed the costumes for the show.'

'I've all the gen on you, Cian.' Her tone was playfully flirtatious, a bit drunken. 'I believe you're going teaching. God, I wish I'd had a teacher the like of yourself.' She spoke with a beautiful Kerry accent, all vowels and lugubrious music, and was adorable looking and wide-eyed and slightly too thin. She looked as though her make-up had been applied by a professional who had appealed to her in vain not to mess with it. The glass in her hand was empty except for its cluster of ice cubes but she appeared not to notice and kept sipping it. She had a blowsy way about her conversation that made him think of a cockney. Men approached her often; she touched them comfortably and mock-enticingly, brushing dust from their lapels, occasionally ruffling their hair, unfastening one suitor's bow tie.

When Catherine went to find the bathroom her friend remained with him. There was that particular silence that can arise between two recently introduced people when the introducer has left them alone. They spoke briefly of Kerry – she had heard of his childhood visits there. He explained that he would be spending part of next summer in the Dingle Peninsula, had been hired as a kind of tour guide for visiting American students. The money would be fairly desperate but it would be a good place to spend August. It became clear there was something on her mind.

'You won't freak if I ask you something, Cian?'

'Sure. What's up?'

'I knew Aifric a bit at college – Catherine probably mentioned. How's she doing these days? I hope everything's okay.'

'She's living in England now. I believe she's fine.'

'It's nice that you're still in touch. I was very sorry to hear what happened. I didn't know her well. But it must have been tough.'

He was apprehensive now. Chasms were opening in their talk. 'We're not in contact, really. Whatever way it worked out.'

'I understand. Do you smoke, Cian?'

'I'm trying to pack them in.'

'Shite. I'd love a drag. My daughter's forever nagging me to give them up. When she isn't around I'm always feeling I should take advantage.'

'I'll ask someone, if you like. Or Catherine usually has some.'

'Ah, *ná bac leis*,' she said. 'Don't trouble yourself. I swear to Jesus, I'm after smoking so much on this fecking beast of a production, it'll probably do me in before the close.'

'Catherine says the same. I've been trying to get her to quit.'

'Listen – this is none of my business, Cian – but that's a girl has it bad for you. You probably haven't twigged it. Fantastic girl, really. Best in the world if you want my opinion, not that there's any reason you would, like. Only she's after getting it into her head you're seeing someone else on the quiet or not interested or whatever. I think that's what she thinks. As I say, it's none of my business. I'm just playing Cupid for a minute.'

'I understood there was someone on the scene for her. Someone fairly serious.'

'Shite happens,' she said. 'We've all had our scenes back the road. I just noticed whenever she talks about you, she starts looking a bit gooey. And she wouldn't be the type, like. Anyway, now you know.'

'She's a great person,' he said evasively. 'She's one in a million.'

'She told me you're a fucking hand grenade in bed. You don't look like you are. *Are* you?'

'Yeah. First World War.'

When Catherine came back from the bathroom she was pale, a bit uneasy. She wasn't feeling the best, she said. He offered to drive her to the hotel if she wanted to leave, and he was surprised when she accepted without hesitation.

A snap frost had whitened the windscreen of his car and they had to wait while one of the security guards produced a scraper. He gave her his coat. She appeared a little better.

As they eased down the driveway and on to the back road for Bray, she drank from a bottle of water he'd brought.

'It's honestly nothing. I had a heavy nap this afternoon,' she said. 'I've been feeling a bit blood-sugary all day since waking up. I really need to catch up on my sleep.'

'We'll have you home in a few minutes.'

'It's very good of you.'

'Don't be silly.'

'You looked incredibly dapper. Angela clearly fancies you.'

'Not at all. She was just being friendly.'

'You should have a drink with her some time. She's single, I think.'

He said nothing to that. The car moved through the darkness.

'Oh, I got you a Christmas present,' she said, as though suddenly remembering.

'There was no need. But thanks.'

'Is there somewhere we could go for coffee?' The question surprised him. 'Or if you felt like a walk on the seafront?'

'There might be a chipper or a kebab place. You're sure you're not too tired?'

'Oh, maybe you're right. We can catch up another time.'

Drizzle speckled the windscreen. He flicked on the wipers. Past an abandoned thatched cottage, its walls beaten in. Whatever street lights existed became less frequent. She had pulled out a hairclip and was slowly untwisting it with her teeth.

'I've offended you, Catherine? You seem down. Is there something on your mind?'

'No, no. It's just work. And probably – I don't know. Parties make me nervous, I always feel I'm missing something. I mean I *like* them, it isn't that. But I sometimes think I like having been at them more than actually being at them. If that's makes any sense. Which I'm sure it probably doesn't.'

'Have you Christmas plans made? I suppose it'll be London?'

'I'm not sure just yet. And you?'

'I've an arseload of study, there's a mini thesis I have to get going on. I suppose I'll be with my dad for the day itself. He sends his regards, by the way. "That tall girl from England."'

'He's a darling, your dad. Do give him all my love. Tell him I said *"The live-line is open"*.'

'Oh, I think he knows. He'd fucking shoot himself if it ever closed.'

'You'll spend the whole break with him? Will you go away somewhere?'

'He likes to be home for the big day and then he goes to my brother's. I was half planning on heading to Donegal. Just over New Year. I'm not the world's biggest fan of New Year's Eve.'

'I never trust anyone who is.'

'Listen, I was thinking. Probably mad. But would you like to come with me? If you've nothing else lined up, I mean.'

'Where?'

'Well, to Donegal. My dad used to buy tweed there, back when we were kids. He'd sometimes bring us in the summers. We still know some of the locals. They're interesting people.

You'd get a kick out of them, I'd say. Some of the oldsters are amazing.'

'Cian – I'm not your girlfriend.'

'I know you're not. I didn't say—'

'Then stop acting as though I am. Because you're scaring me. Okay?'

'For fuck sake' – he laughed – 'I was only thinking you'd like it. I'd the impression you needed a break. I probably read it wrong.'

'Don't get hostile, okay?'

'I'm not. I'm very sorry. Forget I mentioned it at all.' They were halted at lights, the indicators were clicking. He opened his window a couple of inches. Wind rattled the flagpole in the grounds of a church.

'I'd hoped I'd made it clear what was possible between us,' she said. 'I'm not free. I told you. I was straight with you from the go. I'd feel strange meeting people from your childhood – you can understand that, surely.'

'All I had in mind was a break. Like when we went to London that time.'

'London didn't really work, if I'm absolutely honest.'

The remark didn't surprise him. He concentrated on the road.

'You spent the whole weekend being preoccupied, Cian. I didn't know what was wrong with you.'

'There was nothing *wrong* with me, Catherine. You were the one acting strangely.'

'Hardly very surprising, given the way you were going on. One night you were talking in your sleep. About Aifric.'

'I didn't realise you were listening. You must send me your notes.'

'Don't come the fucking smartarse. It's about time you got over yourself. Someone ought to tell you you'd want to cop on.'

'I've no doubt you're right. Thanks a million for the advice.'

'Let's not end things like this.'

'Is that what we're doing, Catherine?'

'I thought we could have a nice night. As friends. That's all.'

'Remarkably considerate.'

'Don't you want to be my friend?'

'I suppose I sometimes thought something more might be happening between us.'

'Like what?'

'Like nothing. Let's leave it. I'm sorry I spoke.'

'I don't want it. I told you. I have it already. Look I'm practically fucking *married*, Cian. I told you. Be fair.'

'You didn't tell me that.'

'I told you it was serious.'

'You said you were on a break.'

'We were. We are. Look – he's coming over on Thursday.'

'From New York?'

'For a week. I should have told you earlier. I wanted to. I should have.'

'So does he know?'

'About what?'

'About us, what else?'

'There you go *again*. There isn't any *us*.'

'That isn't fair, Catherine. But if that's what you want.'

'I didn't say it was fair. It's the way it is, that's all.' She lit a cigarette he didn't know she had and peered ahead of herself at the street. 'Look – if I were free, it would be different. If that matters at this stage. I'm not saying I have no feelings for you. You know I do. Don't you?'

'It's fine. I understand. Well, I don't, not really.'

'He's been five years in my life. What's so hard to understand?'

'Five years in your life and you're so wonderfully contented you're sleeping with someone else in a hotel room in Bray?'

'We had a fling. I didn't deceive you. You're moving the goalposts.'

'Then forget I ever mentioned it. It really doesn't matter. If you think I'm going to beg for you, you can think again.'

'I'm not doing this, Cian. It's too much and you know it.'

'I said we'll drop the subject. Let's talk about the weather.'

'You can let me out at the garage. I need to get fags.'

He pulled the car over so abruptly that it grumbled and cut out. 'Tell you what. You can walk. It's the chauffeur's night off.'

She didn't leave and he didn't make her, and the wind blustered up, and the street lights of Little Bray glinted yellow and white. He had never seen her weep and she wasn't doing so now, but she had the look of a person reminding herself she wasn't the crying type and finding the reminder hard. A police car snouted out of an alleyway and headed slowly towards the town. She took her keys from her bag and unbuckled her belt.

'You're a fucker. You know that, Cian?'

'I'm glad I was good for something.'

'I don't deserve your shit. You're thinking of someone else. I only hope you know that. I'm someone's fucking stand-in. Half the things you've ever said to me were aimed elsewhere. You just didn't have the cop to see it.'

'If that makes you feel better.'

'Yes. It makes me feel better.'

'Sound. Have a nice life. Goodbye.'

'So that's that, is it, Cian?'

'Seems to be, yeah.'

'All right.' She got out and walked away.

Three mornings afterwards a package was delivered to the apartment.

You had no pictures. Think of me sometimes. I'm sorry. Take care.

It was a framed sketch of a rural landscape with many fallen trees, a black roiling sky, stone-filled fields. It had been titled by the Dublin dealer from whom she had bought it. 'Partial Draft of *Scenes from a Hurricane*. Lost work by Seán Keating. Charcoal on paper. 1950s.'

It sat in the ruins of its gift paper for a couple of weeks. On Christmas Eve, realising he had forgotten to get something for his sister-in-law, he re-wrapped it and brought it to his brother's house with the presents for his nephews. His sister-in-law said it was beautiful and hung it over the fireplace. His brother kept looking at him strangely.

When their father arrived, he appeared frail, a little shaky. Christmas was hard for him. Both his sons knew it. They sat with him, playing poker, listening to his stories, and they watched as late in the night he went down on his knees and placed a glass of wine by the tree 'for Santa Claus'. He was silent as he knelt. It was a small, vivid image. The kind you'd want to remember.

On New Year's Day, he was taken to hospital. At Easter, he was admitted again.

VIII

Requiem, September 2012

My name is Cian Hanahoe. Colm was my father.

It would have meant a great deal to him, seeing so many of you here this morning.

He was baptised in this church, seventy years ago this month. It was here that he made his Communion, and later his Confirmation. It was here that he once robbed a shilling from the collection plate on Palm Sunday, to his parents' mortification, and to some extent – but only some – his own. 'Didn't I spend it taking a nice blonde on a date,' he used to laugh. 'She was worth the few weeks in Purgatory.'

The occasion of sin was Anne-Teresa O'Brien, the beauty of Prussia Street flats. It was here before this altar that she and my father were married, in the April of 1963. He was fond of telling people that the ceremony took place on April the first. As you know, he had a sense of humour. Allegedly.

But there were other sides to Colm. It's those I want to remember this morning. He was a very private man, like many of his generation. A man who didn't care for a fuss. In saying goodbye to him now, my brother Paul and I want to put aside for a few moments his modesty and grace, or to say where he learned those gifts. Dad was an old-school guy. He didn't like displays. I'll try not to cry when I read these recollections. If I fail, I ask his forgiveness for the embarrassment.

Dad was born in Hanover Street in the South Dock of Dublin, maybe the city's oldest neighbourhood, a place of fierce autonomies. The Liffey flowed adjacently, a dirty, eddying river serenaded by the seagulls through its mizzle and stench. Only twenty years before his birth it had borne into history the last British garrison ever to guard Ireland's capital. The river that once brought them had taken them away, under the conquering gaze of Michael Collins.

The South Dock was a district that had its own rules. Nationalism's pieties, if often acknowledged, were complicated by other, more pressing realities into which your patriotism, if you possessed any, had to be resolved. 'Pray and Save' was the motto of Ireland at the time, slogan of a regime that favoured obedience above all other modes – but Hanover Street said more than its prayers. It was a place of river-traders of one kind and another: boatwrights, caulkers, hoopers, stevedores, professional tide-watchers, survivors, adapters, with as many sceptics as true believers. The ruins of the warehouses built by Huguenot merchants were the tenements of my father's childhood. Jonathan Swift's ghost was said to walk the old, abandoned wharves, with Robert Emmet's and James Clarence Mangan's. Colm's mother, as a girl, had seen the black bunting strung along the quayside in commemoration of the hundreds of her neighbours who had died in Britain's armies. From Bloemfontein and Spion Kop and Gallipoli and Ypres, from countless unpronounceable battlegrounds of empire, many sons of that waterfront had never returned. Their absence from those streets was itself a kind of presence. It suggested allegiance was more complicated than you'd been told.

The breeze brought a heavy oaten aroma down from the brewery, wrapping itself around Colm's childhood, an intimation of large things being done, and the barges plied the river bringing barrels of Guinness to the world many Dublin children of his class would never see. The grid through which he moved had its landmarks and lighthouses – this church, the Christian Brothers' School, Sir John Rogerson's Quay, the lanes and the markets, Pearse Street library – and wider latitudes might be glimpsed in the neighbourhood's picture house, and in the stories, or the silences, of relatives living close to him: a separated uncle, a grandmother who had been a scrubwoman in Kilmainham Jail, an elderly cousin whose single room near Beggars Bush barracks had among its long-undisturbed clutter of ships-in-bottles and socialist pamphlets a bible that once belonged to James Larkin. But the map of Colm's childhood had limits not only geographical, and beyond those he rarely strayed.

My father was born in the autumn of 1942, to Evelyn Moore and James Hanahoe, Dubliners. In the early years of their marriage they had tried their luck in Brooklyn but come quietly back to Dublin when their bravery had not been blessed. My grandfather, a dock-worker, suffered an accident in New York. Money and options were scarce. Kindly neighbours assisted them homeward to Ireland with their children. Thus my father was born in the quarter of his ancestors, who had been living there before the empire ever began counting its subjects in censuses. A child of returned emigrants, in the district of ships, he would never be an emigrant himself.

He grew up a bright-hearted, resourceful, tough-minded boy, qualities respected by his mother, who I remember as a personification of them. The class of people who inherit nothing but their genes and their mettle are always the most courageous. She had managed a family business, a little chandler's shop on Britain Street, which provided no opulence but at least imparted a talent for survival, a sense of your possibilities in the world. His father, a man who believed in God and Éamon de Valera, was stringent in authority, in the way of fathers then. He had a vein of melancholia and fixed sometimes on his disappointments, as perhaps who would not, given the realities he had faced. Paul and I remember him as a kindly and mischievous grandfather, a boxing fan, a chuckler, a man who kept greyhounds, and who told me, in an era before Irishmen were much given to such avowals, that he loved my grandmother and his children. But his fathering, in its time, had esteemed the straight and narrow, encouraged, when he felt it necessary, by physical punishment. He had been a rifleman, a sharpshooter, at some point in his life, in the South Dublin brigade of the old IRA. You didn't want to find yourself in the cross-hairs of his glance.

The South Dock, nowadays, has restaurants and offices. Immigrants came during the boom. Many have now left. But there are stores offering foodstuffs from Eastern Europe and Asia, there are Polish internet cafés and African hairdressers'. You wouldn't recognise it as the district of my father's boyhood. There were barefoot children, parents utterly beyond coping, whole families, usually large ones, in one-room flats, and there was a sense of the celestial irrelevance of the poor to the fantasies of the Republic they lived in. In my father's class at the school there were forty-nine boys, of widely mixed ability, some of hardly any, all taught by an arts student in her very early twenties, Alice Harding, a Presentation nun born in Liverpool. His lifelong loyalty to his Church had much to do with Alice Harding, who died in Siérra Leone at the age of twenty-nine, the woman who had taught him to read.

Colm, as a restless, questioning boy, had a facility in Drawing and English. These were abilities fostered carefully by his three older sisters, beautiful girls all, darkly Hispanic in their looks. Such avidly hungry readers were those gorgeous young Dubliners that they would tear out the pages from whatever paperbacks could be afforded and share them around the kitchen in turn. A magazine, *Our Boys*, containing short stories and verse, was 'my Disneyland', Colm once told me. He fished mackerel on Graver's Wharf. He won medals for Gaelic football. Aged seven, he'd earn an odd penny from an old sailmaker on Grand Canal Quay who taught him to stitch pennants and jacks. He was the sort of child who enters contests, learns definitions, tells stories, gets often into fights, never forgives a broken promise, believes the answer to almost anything can be found in a book and is sometimes impatient as a wasp. I see him in his sisters, in my own beloved brother, the finest man I have ever known. I see him in the older Ireland that is passing away. And I see him, as have others, in myself. But he was not to receive the chances Paul and I would know. A scholarship was offered him so that he could continue schooling into his early teens, an unheard-of notion for a boy of his place and time. His parents did their best, but they could not afford the loss of his wages. So my father's childhood ended.

He started work at the age of twelve, in a Dublin cloth-importer's office, located in the cellars of one of those crumbling Georgian town houses that still stand about the city looking mournful. Once inhabited by the well-to-do, many were sold when independence came, as their proprietors removed to more amenable locations. Some were simply abandoned to the weather. I find it haunting to think of him, a boy not old enough to shave, on his walk through the pre-dawn streets of his town, perhaps cold, certainly alone, past the chapels and the pawnshops, to that house of lost prosperities and cracked old plaster, where he would let himself in, the first to arrive, and build and light a fire against the damp. That is my picture of my father in childhood. A boy greatly loved, but alone in that house. His hand on its banisters, his footfall on its floorboards, his body moving slowly through its spiderwebs and spectres, as he waited for his life to begin. The smell of old dust, in the passageways, on the staircase, and the stucco discoloured by time. The knife-grey light of the Dublin dawn, glimpsed through the bones of the fanlight over the door. Were there moments, I have wondered, when he imagined a future: a home without want, a family of his own? If what the poet Eliot says is correct, and we all feel what he means, that time past and time future are contained in time present, is it possible, in some sense, that I was already with my father as the coals fizzed and smouldered in the grate? Perhaps other ghosts were there, too, of the past and the future. Perhaps all of us gathered to say goodbye to him this morning were there.

What might be gleaned from books – this was always his interest, as he worked to help support his family. It was a curiosity he shared with the girl he would marry, who was complicated, eloquent, mercurial, gifted, a trainee librarian, a reader. She looked like Grace Kelly, heartbreakingly beautiful. In a photograph I have of the two of them, clad as for an interview, you might mistake them for kids dressing up, scrubbed and innocent as apples, though by the time that photograph was taken they had been working ten years.

Somehow they scrimped enough to place a deposit on a one-bedroom flat. 'A hundred pounds,' Colm told me, 'It cost us a thousand hours of work.' It was a little way around the coast, in the fishing village of Irishtown. My mother had an inner-city girl's love of the seafront. Over many nights of courtship, he had promised her a beach. Sandymount Strand was the one he delivered, a place where I always think of them fondly. The flat was on a street called Ballylee Row, which had been named by some genius of suburban development after the rural retreat of Yeats. The street is gone now. A Tesco stands on the site. A terrible beauty is born.

I believe there were happy years. He made the drapery trade his study, did exams, worked by day, learned book-keeping and pattern-cutting. In this he received help from his employer, Basil Eliot, who sent my father to night college, paying his fees, insisting on accepting no recompense. He took a boy of the Dublin tenements under his wing, became a mentor, a friend, a protector. I mention that he was an Irish Presbyterian for no other reason than to record that the filthy bigotries of Ireland, long clung to by some, have long been despised by others. A gentle tweedy soul, renowned for his dry Ulster wit, he lived with his widower father among their mannequins and looms, and would frown with biblical gravitas as he imparted the eleventh commandment: 'Good curtains last longer than a promise.' I was born in County Wicklow, to a mother I never knew and whose story is too painful to tell here. When my parents adopted me, they gave me the second name Basil. It wasn't a name you mentioned too often in the playground, since it tended to raise references to Barcelona and mocking cries of '*Que?*' But I find, as I age, that I feel honoured to have it. It marked, for my parents, an extraordinary kindness, and I think, in the early years of their brave life together, that they saw it as an offering of all they had, an acknowledgement, and an act of faith.

With his employer's help they moved to a house, near the suburb of Goatstown, six miles south of the city. It was a network of modern estates, a place that had recently enough been countryside. Many of the houses and roads were unfinished; there were footpaths without paving, walls without capstones, knolls of splattered pebble-dash in the driveways and the gardens, where once had been cowpats and rushes. In time Colm opened his own business, consisting of him and one seamstress, his sister, who did the filing, such as it was, and made tea and bought stationery and answered the telephone if it rang. It can't have rung often in the early months of the business, but before too long he was busy.

Often, at the weekends, he would visit a prospect some-where in the new suburbs, taking me with him for company on the road. What I remember is the way Ireland was hardly built at the time. Shopping centres barely finished. Some were only building sites. We would wander those hopeful hives of concrete and steel, Colm taking measurements and talking the beauty of Italian silk drapes. I remember doodling on his order books in his ancient van while he drove, a comradely, companionable silence between us. Jobs were coming faster. The country was changing. Its younger politicians were easing out the old revolutionaries who had gunned the state into being. They were ambitious, tough; they believed in power. My father, a political sceptic, joined the Fianna Fáil party, thinking the contacts would be good for his business. He worked longer, harder, in every county in Ireland, in the towns surrounding Dublin, in the Republic and in the North. This was the early seventies. There was trouble beyond the border. In certain parts of the North, a southern registration plate could get you killed. He went there anyway, though my mother begged him not to. He went where the work was, as he had since his childhood. It's what South Dock people did.

Often, when I went to bed, he would be sewing at the kitchen table, in shirtsleeves and tie, his eyes raw with tiredness. And often in the mornings, as I readied for school, he would be there again – measuring patterns, stitching curtains – so that it seemed to me, as it may have seemed to him, as though he had sat there working all night. He sang as he shaved, little nonsenses or bits of arias, or the skipping chants learned in his Hanover Street childhood. By the middle 1970s he was father to two children, both of us adopted in circumstances I don't wish to detail here. Everything was about to change.

Some years into the Troubles, there was a night when he was driving home from the North and he stopped, exhausted, by the side of the road, near the border town of Newry. He fell asleep in the van, slumped over the steering wheel, and was awakened by the shouts of a patrol of British soldiers who were probably younger than my father. He was searched, pushed around a bit. It got out of hand. They pointed their rifles; there were roars and confusions. There had been a riot earlier. Newry was burning. One of the soldiers, a corporal, struck my father in the face. My father punched him back. He wasn't a man you struck. Colm was born in a time and a place where a man learned to put you in hospital if you struck him. What happened subsequent to the fight is a matter of who you talk to. All I know for certain is that my father was badly beaten that night. I cannot imagine his thoughts as he was finally permitted to drive on, with the flames in his rear-view mirror.

And still he worked, up and down the roads of Ireland, through its vast new estates and its factories in the hinterlands, often driving many hours at the end of the day so that a ritual we had could be honoured. Of such tender observances is fatherhood made. He would read to me a while before I slept.

His taste was for the English Victorian sagas, those well-sprung poems and epics to which he had been introduced by a young teacher, Alice Harding, in Hanover Street School, South Dock. And I can never read any poem without hearing Colm's beautiful Dublin voice, its inflections and subtleties, its colour and hesitance, its peakings and fallings away. Calming as the purr of a cello on a rainy night, it was a voice that loved the miracles and mercies of language, and my counterpane saw empires rise and slowly fall by the power of a father's solidarity. It was how I had learned to read, or certainly why I wanted to; his finger tracing capitals on a yellowed old page, by the light of a lamp that was shaped like a toy soldier, bought by my parents on a holiday in Scarborough. When Mam became ill, I was aged eleven. They were painful days for all of us, for Paul and for me, and they were painful for her and Dad too. 'In sickness and health' is easy to promise, on a sunny April morning, in the church of your childhood, where people who love you are happy for your hope and the confetti is waiting to rain. Those words were said by Colm, twenty years old, on the spot where I am standing now. He wasn't a saint. But he meant what he said. A morality he inherited from his mother and his sisters. A value he believed in, hardly noticing it was there, as the sailor believes in the lighthouse. He was stubborn. He was tough. He didn't do maybe. He believed you should mean what you said.

Anne-Teresa was our mother. When nobody wanted us, she gave us the best she had. It wasn't enough. But I believe it was her best. And even when her illness worsened, when knowing her grew hard, when her behaviour could be frightening, when she said things she didn't mean, I never heard Colm utter a word about Anne-Teresa O'Brien that was cruel or lacking in mercy. Whatever care was available in the Ireland of those years, he took pains that Mam would receive it. He spent nights by her hospital bed, ensured she was never alone, arranged for someone who loved her to be always in our home and clung to the insistence that a human being in pain was more than someone else's diagnosis. If there was comment or gossip, Dad reminded you we were a family. It's how he was raised. He'd never lie down. 'Tell the others to brush the dirt on their own side of the street,' he'd say. 'We're South Dock people. We don't beg from beggars. Mam is your mother. Don't forget it.'

'The Passing of Arthur', from Tennyson's *Idylls of the King*, tells of the death of the patriarch and the fate of Excalibur in a version so strange that only a child would understand it. Arthur, fatally wounded, is dying near the lake and wishes to be rid of his sword. But the false knight, Bedivere, can't fling it away, despite his orders and the honour of his code. The poem circles around his reluctance, the humanity of his weakness, his lies, disobediences, evasions, justifications, before finally permitting him to walk into myth as the hero who murdered his doubts. It says the world is full of troubles, incomprehensible evils, wolves in sheep's clothing, lost battles, dead hopes, and all we have to counteract them is one another in the moment, and everything else is illusion. Our beautiful trinkets – even those will be thrown from us, to be grasped by the brandishing hand that awaits all vanities and drawn back to the depths they belong to. There is no destiny waiting, no preordained path to safety. What happens is that those we love become that destiny; it is simply a matter of recognising them. It was Colm's favourite poem. He knew that portion of it by heart. He recited it on the night of Paul's graduation with tears of pride in his eyes. And Dad wasn't a guy who wept. He told me on the morning he died that my mother felt close, that he believed with every fibre he would see her again. That all the pain she knew in life would be taken away. That his Anne-Teresa O'Brien would be lovely as the first day he ever saw her, in Prussia Street flats, as a boy. He wanted a sentence from Tennyson placed on his gravestone. 'Lightly went the other to the King.'

He would have been seventy next Sunday. I picture him reading. He was fond of poetry when it rhymed, horse-racing novels, yarns of the American West, detective stories. In recent months, a schoolfriend of mine and Paul's, a lawyer with an office on Rogerson's Quay, told me he'd often see Dad in a café near the Grand Canal Theatre, sitting alone with a book, sometimes gazing out through the windows at the waterfront that was once his childhood.

Some time ago a child came into my own life, the daughter of my beloved partner, Angela Carthy. Dad adored Angela. He adored Sarah, her little one. When I met them, I was afraid. He advised me to be brave. The path that brought me to Angela was strange and unexpected. In other ways, it was so ordinary that you'd hardly notice your life was changing. We were introduced at a Christmas party by someone we knew, a London girl only passing through Ireland for work. Where she is now, I wouldn't even know. Dad said so what? He was a great believer in providence.

Sarah, aged seven, saw in Dad a kindred spirit. She has something of what I imagine to have been his outlook as a child, and something of her Kerry mother's courage. The other week she was in a school production of Dickens's *Oliver Twist*, playing one of the hungry urchins so detested by the powerful ('Are there no *prisons*? Are there no *workhouses*?'), a role that required a costume of photogenic raggedness, as well as a suspension of parental disbelief. 'It's great fun being poor!' she chirped to me after the final rehearsal, dancing in her tatters, pointing gleefully to her patches. The perfect incognisance of a seven-year-old's laughter. 'I wish we could be poor all the time, Cian.'

I thought about my father, at the same age as my stepdaughter, standing in Britain Street, perhaps with his mother, the ghosts of the past and the future all around them, with the gull-song and the reek of the river. And I thought of the frightened boy, whose name I do not know, who had one day sat beside him, in Hanover Street School, begging his classmates for food. And other pictures, too, formed themselves in my mind – but some of them I pushed away. The performance was about to begin and Sarah was nervous I would miss the start. A father has to do what he can.

Announcements were made. The lights went down. The orphans came and went, fluffing lines, missing cues, and the cameras clicked dutifully and the videos rolled, and the teacher wrung her hands and chivvied and beckoned, as the children appeared from backstage. A couple of months previously, we had learned that Angela was carrying our baby, a child who will be born in my grandparents' city, my daughter, a sister to Sarah. I was thinking of the first time I saw that face, the image of that face on an obstetrician's monitor, the shock of that moment, and the fierceness of that heartbeat as it filled that room in Dublin. It sounded like joy, only wilder, more ardent. The moons of those eyes as our child turned and rolled; a space-girl, a traveller unimaginable. A couple of nights after the scan, Colm came to us for a family dinner. He was enthralled into silence by the X-ray we showed him. Angela, with great gentleness, gave him a copy, and it never left his possession again. It wasn't long afterwards that he was readmitted to hospital. He knew what was coming. He was brave. He was asked by the priest in the hospice, as the end came close, if he wished to hold a bible or a set of rosary beads or a holy picture. He held the photograph of my daughter as he slipped from the world. The last thing he ever did was touch it to his lips.

* * *

There were many times in my life when I was certain I would never be a father, and indeed did not wish to be, for the role was so frightening. Now that I am to be one, all the dreads have not disappeared, but there isn't the time to consider them any more, and anyway it wouldn't be useful. It's to Colm I owe the inheritance that we only have hope. We need to be brave. Always brave. There are no guarantees. To say so is a lie. The cloth is unrolled and you cut it.

Dickens, the sentimentalist, believed in the possibility of redemption, even to the most twisted and crippled of men. His story of a motherless child who is saved by a sacrifice is far more complex than it seems. Its resonances sounded quietly through Dun Laoghaire Parish Hall, as Sarah and the other children masqueraded their hunger with the innocently fervent faces of those who will never know it. The audience was very small; there were rows of empty seats. But as she shuffled and grinned and spoke her few lines, the darkness around me seemed inhabited, watchful; closer than any of us imagines.

Acknowledgements

Sections, drafts or different versions of some of these stories first appeared in *New Dubliners*, edited by Oona Frawley, *Ireland in Exile* and *Finbar's Hotel*, both edited by Dermot Bolger, *Best New Irish Short Stories*, edited by David Marcus, *What Might Have Been*, the catalogue for an exhibition at the Lower East Side Tenement Museum, New York, and *The Comedian*, part of the Open Door series, edited by Patricia Scanlan. The family in 'Orchard Street, Dawn' existed. The story is a work of fiction based on the known facts of their lives, researched by the Tenement Museum's archivists. It's important to state that the letter from Bridget Meehan to her mother was written by me. 'Two Little Clouds' is a response to James Joyce's short story 'A Little Cloud', in which a London Irish émigré returns briefly to Dublin. A handful of sentences from my novel *Ghost Light* appear again in the present collection. 'A Nation Once Again', slightly misquoted in 'Boyhood's Fire', was written by Thomas Osborne Davis (1814–1845). The quotation at the start of 'Figure in a Photograph' is from 'Patti Smith: Can You Hear Me Ethiopia?' by Scott Cohen, *Circus Magazine*, 14th December 1976. The ballad Cian

Hanahoe sings in 'Wintertime in Wicklow' is a variant of a nineteenth-century Irish song sometimes called 'The Cuckoo' or 'The Maid of Bunclody'. I heard these lyrics sung by a street musician in Astor Place subway station, New York, in the winter of 2010. The fact that County Wexford contains no River Claudy doesn't necessarily detract from the song. It may add to it.

I thank my editor, Geoff Mulligan, and his colleagues at Harvill Secker and Vintage. Also my agents Carole Blake and Conrad Williams at the Blake Friedmann Literary Agency, London. I thank Anne-Marie Casey and our sons James and Marcus, my father Seán and stepmother Viola, my brothers and sisters, and the Casey family; also Daniel Arsand, Hans-Juergen Balmes, Luigi Brioschi, Sarah Bannan, Ciaran and Julia Carty, Frances Coady, Michael Colgan, Tony Glavin and Adrienne Fleming, Lolies van Grunsven, Beth Humphries, Madeleine Keane, Declan Kiberd, Philip King, Dominique Lachelle, Sarah Moore, Marian Richardson, Mariachiara Rusca, Ellie Steel, Mary Wilson, and my former students at Baruch College, City University, New York, where I was Harman Visiting Professor of Creative Writing in 2009, and at the School of English, Drama and Film, University College Dublin, where I was Writer in Residence in 2010. The writer Claire Keegan made me a gift of a notebook in 2007. Many stories were born in those pages. Seán Keating created no painting called *Scenes from a Hurricane*, as his biographer, Dr Eimear O'Connor, my sister, can confirm. Every character in this collection of stories is fictional.

J O'C, Dublin, 2012